THE

BOLSHEVIK'S

REVENGE

A SAM KLEIN MYSTERY

THE BOLSHEVIK'S REVENGE

A SAM KLEIN MYSTERY

ALLAN LEVINE

GREAT PLAINS
PUBLICATIONS

Great Plains Publications
420 – 70 Arthur Street
Winnipeg, MB R3B 1G7
www.greatplains.mb.ca

Great Plains Publications gratefully acknowledges the financial support
provided for its publishing program by the Government of Canada
through the Book Publishing Industry Development Program
(BPIDP); the Canada Council for the Arts; the Manitoba Department
of Culture, Heritage and Citizenship; and the Manitoba Arts Council.

Design & Typography by Gallant Design Ltd.
Printed in Canada by Kromar Printing

CANADIAN CATALOGUING IN PUBLICATION DATA

Main entry under title:
Levine, Allan, 1956 -

The Bolshevik's revenge

ISBN 1-894283-33-3

Title.

PS8573.E96448B64 2002   C813'.54   C2002-910619-2

PR9199.3.L4674B64 2002

In memory of Kerry Kluner (1956-2001)
A good friend who liked to laugh

Author's Note

THE WINNIPEG GENERAL STRIKE was one of the most significant events in the city's history and shaped relations between labour and management in twentieth century Canada. It thus is fitting to use the strike and the many issues, fears and concerns it raised as a background for *The Bolshevik's Revenge*, the third Sam Klein mystery. It needs to be stressed, however, that this is a work of fiction. And although many of the events connected to the strike did occur, I have taken a fair amount of literary license with the chronology of these events and with some of the key personalities. As in the previous Sam Klein novels, several of the secondary characters—including the strike leaders, Bob Russell, William Ivens, William Pritchard, George and Helen Armstrong and Roger Bray—were real people, but they did not speak all of the words I have put in to their mouths. As I have done in the past, I have tried to keep their attitudes and actions as historically accurate as possible.

In reconstructing life in 1919 Winnipeg, I utilized a variety of primary and secondary sources. The books I found especially useful included: Alan Artibise, *Winnipeg: An Illustrated History* (Toronto: James Lorimer, 1977); Paul Avrich, *Anarchist Portraits* (Princeton, N.J.: Princeton University Press, 1988); David J. Bercuson, *Confrontation at Winnipeg* (Montreal: McGill-Queen's University Press, 1974); J.M. Bumsted, *The Winnipeg General Strike of 1919: An Illustrated History* (Winnipeg: Watson & Dwyer, 1994); Harry Gutkin and Mildred Gutkin, *Profiles in Dissent* (Edmonton: NeWest Publishers, 1997); Norman Penner, ed., *The Strikers' Own History* (Toronto: James Lorimer, 1975); Steven Selden, *The Story of Eugenics and Racism in America* (New York: Teachers College, Columbia University, 1999); Alix Kates Shulman, ed., *Red Emma Speaks* (New York: Random House, 1972).

Acknowledgements

THANKS FIRST and foremost to Great Plains publisher Gregg Shilliday for his continuing support of my fiction writing and for his suggestions in transforming the manuscript. This is our third Sam Klein novel together and Gregg continues to be as enthusiastic as he was when I delivered *The Blood Libel* to him back in 1996. The success of the series, including its popularity in Germany, owes a great deal to his efforts. Thanks, too, to his staff—office manager Jewls Dengl, copy editor Douglas Allen and marketing director Cheryl Miki. I am most appreciative as well for the hard work Hilary McMahon, my talented literary agent, does on my behalf—not the least of which is dealing with my numerous e-mails. Besides her business acumen, she is always a source of encouragement and a font of sage advice. My mother Bernice Levine-Rissin has turned out to be a fine proofer. I thank her for, among many other things, her eagle eye and, most importantly, for ensuring that my book launches are always well-attended.

And last but certainly not least, I am once again grateful to my family: my wife Angie, and our children Alexander and Mia, for their love, support and inspiration. They make my writing work all the more meaningful.

One final personal note: You don't have a lot of good friends in your life and I lost a close one at the end of August 2001. Kerry enjoyed the first two Sam Klein mysteries and I know that he would have liked this one as well. He left his family and many friends far too early. It's for this reason as well as a hundred others that I dedicate this book to his memory.

A.L.
Winnipeg, August 2002

Also by Allan Levine

NON-FICTION

The Exchange: 100 Years of Trading Grain in Winnipeg

Your Worship: The Lives of Eight of Canada's
Most Unforgettable Mayors (editor)

Scrum Wars: The Prime Ministers and the Media

Fugitives of the Forest: The Heroic Story of Jewish Resistance
and Survival During the Second World War

Scattered Among the Peoples:
The Jewish Diaspora in Ten Portraits

FICTION

SAM KLEIN MYSTERIES:

The Blood Libel

Sins of the Suffragette

"To be a good animal is the first requisite to success in life, and to be a Nation of good animals is the first condition of national prosperity."
Herbert Spencer, 1914

"The revolutionary is a dedicated man. He has no personal feelings, no private affairs, no emotions, no attachments, no property and no name. Everything in him is subordinated towards a single exclusive attachment, a single thought and a single passion—the revolution."
Sergei Nechaev, Revolutionary Catechism, 1869

Prologue

Pontiac, Michigan
June 4, 1916

THE AUTOMOBILE, a red 1914 Studebaker, was parked a block from the Pontiac Railway Station, as he had arranged. He placed a small black leather bag on the passenger seat, cranked the engine and slowly sputtered north. By the time he reached the dirt road leading to the gates, it was dark. He pulled over and stopped in a clump of weeds under a cluster of tall pine trees, not far from the river.

He got out, lit a cigar and gazed upwards. There wasn't a cloud in the sky and he could see the stars for miles in every direction. Any other evening, he might have enjoyed such a sight, but not tonight. He pulled out his watch from his vest pocket. Half past eleven. He knew that he had to wait until at least 1:30 a.m. before he could begin. By then most of those nosy nurses would be asleep and things would go easier.

He ground his cigar into the dirt and undid his jacket. "Damn heat," he muttered as he wiped his brow with a white handkerchief, a present from her, supposedly, last Christmas. Probably didn't even know she had given it to him, he thought. The night air was hot and humid, though—had he stopped to think about it—he would have been sweating no matter what the thermometer registered.

He had almost told Caddie what he was planning, but at the last moment he had changed his mind. He realized that she would never understand, never share his concerns or fears about the future. From Vancouver to New York—especially New York—it was the same.

Wretched cities swamped with immigrants who couldn't speak English. Slums, opium, crime, corruption and decay. The continent was being transformed into a cesspool of foreigners and degenerates. God help us all when they started marrying each other.

He was not about to add to humanity's problems. He'd known that twelve years ago, just as he knew it today. Nothing, in his mind, had changed. He only wished he had had the courage to act sooner. That would have saved him and Caddie a lot of aggravation and money. After listening to Paul Popenoe last year at the conference in Battle Creek, he was convinced more than ever of his duty to the human race. Popenoe's eloquent words still echoed in his head.

"Science knows no way to make good breeding stock out of bad, and the future of the race is determined by the kind of children which are born and survive to become parents in each generation." Bold words from a great man. And there were others. Roswell Johnson, Charles Davenport and Robert DeCourcy Ward had all left a positive impression on him.

This situation was Caddie's family's fault. He knew that much. It was that senile old grandmother of hers. He could barely stand to be in the same room as that woman. She had the defective genes and now he was stuck with the problem.

It was time. He left the automobile where it was parked, grabbed hold of his bag, and walked the half-mile to the metal gates. Fifteen minutes later, he could see the towering spires shimmering against the night sky. He reached the gates, and gently pushed. Good, they were unlocked. Is there anything that money can't buy, he wondered. He continued walking towards the main building, a massive red-brick structure. The place always reminded him of the Houses of Parliament in London. So regal and proud. Yet they were profoundly different. One institution was about extending and preserving the power of humanity, the other about weakening it.

He knew the front door would be open, just as the gates had been. He had only to dangle fifty dollars in front of Chelsey to get the job done, and he would have paid as much as was necessary. He turned the gold handle and pushed. The door gave way and a antiseptic odour filled his nostrils. It was a sickening smell that always nauseated him.

Chelsey had assured him that the night duty nurse did her rounds and then had a cup of tea at 1:30 a.m. each night. He checked his watch. It was 1:40 a.m. and not a soul was around.

To reach her room in the south wing, he had to proceed down the stairs to the tunnel that would take him through to the other side of the building. He tread softly through the archways, and with each step he took any lingering doubts he had were dismissed. Love was not the issue, he reasoned, survival was.

Five minutes later, he stepped up the stairs leading into the south wing, walked down the hall and stopped in front of room 206S. He gently turned the handle and entered. She was asleep, a small clump under the thin blanket. He had fought Caddie when she had insisted on sending her across the United States. "They have the most progressive treatment there," his wife had lectured him. "Dr. Singleton is doing wonders. Real wonders." He had eventually relented and Caddie had brought her here herself. He did not visit the hospital for about a month. That was a year ago. Since then, he had been here three times and did not notice any improvement, no matter how much Caddie or the doctors insisted otherwise.

He stared at her for a moment, hesitating. But there was no turning back now. He opened the black bag, took out the bottle and the rag. As silently as he could, he opened it and poured a sufficient amount of liquid on the cloth, careful not to spill any. His discussions with a physician he trusted back in Canada had convinced him that, given her various health ailments, the chloroform would be both painless and efficient. Once the cloth was wet, he walked closer to her and swiftly placed it hard over her mouth and nose. She awoke suddenly, her large blue eyes looking up at him in the dim light. There was a sign of recognition, or at least that is what he later remembered. She thrashed about for only a moment and then began to heave. It was her heart. The chloroform had trigged another attack. She gasped again, and then fell silent. Slowly, he released his grip. He stared down at her limp body and felt nothing but relief. He placed the top on the bottle and returned it to his bag along with the soaked rag.

He covered her with the blanket, stared at her one final time and left. He quickly made his way through the tunnel and towards the front entrance. The nurse was returning from her rounds as he reached for the door. Outside, he stopped for a moment, but heard nothing. Good, he thought, she had not seen him. He walked down the dirt path in the direction of the main gates. It was 2:35 a.m. The entire exercise had taken less than a hour. He reached the gates, opened them and began to walk faster and faster until he was running. He glanced behind him. That would be the last time he would ever have to set foot in the Eastern Michigan Asylum. She was dead. Caddie would have to accept it. Maybe, someday, they could try again.

1

"UP, DADDY, UP!" Little Bernice pulled herself up on the bed next to her sleeping father. "Daddy, wake up!" When she did not get the desired response the two-year-old jumped with all the power she could muster from her thirty-pound body. This time she hit her intended target on the head.

"Oh, what is it, Neicee?" grunted Sam Klein. "What time is it?" He rolled over and nudged his wife. "Sarah, what's the time?"

"Daddy, up!" shouted Bernice.

Klein rubbed his eyes and grinned as his daughter planted a kiss on his cheek. "What am I going to do with you?" he asked. Then without warning, he grabbed her and tossed her in the air, catching her in his arms. Bernice giggled with delight.

"More." And with that, Klein hoisted her up with his right arm.

"Why do you get her all worked up like this, Shailek," groaned Sarah, using her husband's Yiddish name as she usually did at home. "You'll wake up Freda." Sarah gently eased herself up from the bed. She was six months pregnant and, like her other two pregnancies, she had not had an easy time. A few weeks ago, Dr. Raitter ordered her to stay in a bed for four days. But since then, she had been feeling better and the pains in her abdomen had vanished. Nonetheless, she was forced to let Janice run the shop without her and that concerned her. Janice was charming and few women in the city knew more about cosmetics than she did, but as for business, that was another matter.

"Come here you," said Sarah, taking Bernice from Klein's arms. "Let your father get dressed and I'll give you something to eat before you wake up the whole block."

"What's going on?" demanded a voice from the next room.

"Freda, honey, go back to sleep for a few minutes. It's only seven."

"It's okay Mommy. I'm not tired anyway." Freda walked up to the bed rubbing her eyes.

"You're becoming more beautiful every day young lady," said Klein, giving his elder daughter a peck on her forehead. "As beautiful as your mother."

And it was true. Freda, born on the 3rd of August 1914 as the Great War was beginning, was the spitting image of her mother. She already had Sarah's slender nose and high cheekbones. "I don't want to think what will be when she's seventeen," Klein liked to joke.

Bernice, on the other hand, born three years to the day in August 1917, looked like her father. So much so in fact that most people thought she belonged to Klein's sister Rivka. "No, she's really my daughter," Sarah would say, somewhat annoyed by the whole issue.

Freda, at five years old, truly loved her little sister, yet still remembered how her sibling's birth had utterly ruined her birthday festivities. Last August, it sunk in that she would never again have her own birthday. It would always be "Freda and Bernice's birthday."

Looking at his family, Klein sometimes thought his heart would burst with pride.

"Do you think they'll do it?" asked Sarah, placing the kettle on top of the large stove that dominated the far corner of the kitchen.

"What's that, dear?" Klein replied, searching for a cigarette amongst several empty tins on the kitchen table.

Sarah sighed. Her husband only read the paper for the latest news from the racetrack. "The strike. Is it going to happen?"

Klein nodded as he pulled a lengthy butt from the ashtray. "Coffee ready yet?"

"You don't seem too concerned, Shailek. No streetcars, no milk and bread delivery. What about the shop? No one will be downtown. They won't have any money to buy anything. I'll be out of business in a month."

"You worry too much. Have I ever told you that?"

"Yeah, well someone has to." Sarah smiled at her husband. "You want a piece of bread and jam?"

Klein shrugged. Sarah took that to mean yes. She placed a hot mug of coffee, a slice of fresh rye and a spoonful of Rivka's homemade jam in front of him.

Klein lit his cigarette as he rubbed his sore knee. Thank God his sister Rivka had paid attention to their mother's endless cooking instructions. Sarah was still as beautiful as the first day he had set eyes on her in Madam Melinda's brothel, but in the kitchen her talents left much to be desired.

"Your knee acting up again, Shailek? Did you take that new pill the doctor gave you?"

"It doesn't do any good, that pill. A waste of time. I'll just have to live with the pain. It's Marv's revenge."

Three years ago, not long after dealing with a notorious case involving the murder of Emily Powers—who had been found dead with her Italian lover behind the Walker Theatre on the night of Nellie McClung's famous mock Parliament—Klein had been hired by Seema Shaffsky to spy on her husband Marvin. Seema believed that Marvin, a pleasant enough guy, was cheating on her. Klein hated cases like that, but Seema was persistent and, like always, he needed the work. It didn't take him long to track Marvin to a hotel room in St. James where he found him in bed with his 25-year-old *shiksa* secretary, a voluptuous brunette by the name of Mildred. That would have been the end of it, except Marvin, an accountant and an excitable one at that, mistook Klein for Mildred's husband Walter. Before any explanations could be offered, Marvin had reached for a pistol and fired a shot. The bullet grazed Klein's left knee, tearing the cartilage—or at least that's how Doc Raitter explained it to him. All he knew was that it hurt like hell.

In the end, Marvin and Seema reconciled, as did Mildred and Walter. Klein, however, spent a few weeks in the hospital recovering and the injury left some permanent damage. Enough damage that when he contemplated enlisting in the Royal Winnipeg Rifles to fight overseas—a momentary lapse in judgement, he later decided—he never got past the medical examination. That was the end of any patriotic thoughts about fighting—or rather dying for his country. Since then, he had to endure the stares and whispers of strangers who wondered why he was not doing his duty for King and country.

"You have to take those pills. Sometimes you're a very foolish man, have I ever told you that?"

"Several times, in fact."

Klein took a last deep drag on his cigarette and butted it in a metal dish beside him. He broke off a piece of sugar and slipped it between his teeth while he sipped on the coffee. "It'll be fine," he said as his two daughters bounded into the kitchen for their breakfasts. "My knee and the shop."

"*Er hot nit zorg,*" Sarah said shaking her head. "My husband hasn't got a worry." She turned to her daughters. "Here's some porridge for both of you."

"No porridge," Bernice complained.

"That's what you're having and not another word," Sarah admonished her.

"Daddy, bread?" asked Bernice.

"Listen to your mother," said Klein. At that Bernice began to pout.

"Oh for God sakes, here's some bread."

"You'll spoil her rotten, if you keep that up," said Sarah.

Klein wasn't listening. He knew that his wife was right. Not about his knee, he could live with the pain. The city's economic troubles were another matter and well beyond his control. Rivka had assured him only yesterday, after she returned from a noisy gathering at the Labour Temple on James Street, that strike action was imminent.

The financial consequences were going to be worse than Premier Norris's foolish and ineffective prohibition act of 1916. Despite Mayor Gray's contention that public drunkenness in the streets had declined during the past few years, the provincial legislation, which closed the bars on Main Street, merely drove the liquor trade behind closed doors. Almost everyone Klein knew had constructed a still in their basement; the sale of home-made beer was popular, and druggists, who could provide liquor to their clients as long as they had a doctor's prescription, were making a killing. It was also possible, as the inventive Bronfmans had discovered, to circumvent the legislation by setting up a liquor mail order business in Kenora, Ontario—since federal law regulated the importation of booze between provinces. Nonetheless, most Winnipeg hotels, so-called temperance hotels, were suffering badly. And though he hated to admit it, alcohol helped fuel the passions that provided work for a private detective.

Now things were going to get even worse. The massive strike the labour leaders were planning for today would undoubtedly have a dire effect on the city and its commercial future. It also just might drive Sarah's cosmetics shop out of business.

The shop, a small store located two blocks west of Eaton's in the first floor of the Boyd Block, had recently started paying for itself and leaving a little extra for the family each month. Sarah's partner, and Klein's old boss Madam Melinda, had kindly deferred her share for at least another year. At first, the business had been doing very well and competed with Eaton's, the Hudson's Bay store, and even Hollinsworth where the wives of Winnipeg's finest families purchased the latest in cosmetics. Thanks to a friend in New York, Sarah and Melinda's store was the first in the city to carry Elizabeth Arden hand creams, soaps and lavender water. Whether these products were worth the extra dollar or two was another matter, but for a Winnipeg woman who desired to look just right the cost hardly seemed to matter.

Despite early optimism, the war had dragged on into 1915 and then 1916. Prices started going up, but wages did not follow. A story in the *Western Labour News* that Rivka had showed Klein summed it up: since 1914, wages had risen by eighteen per cent so that a bricklayer was making 80 cents per hour, a janitor who cleaned the floor of the factory much less. But prices had risen nearly eighty per cent. Bacon, bread, shoes, and clothing had all jumped in price. According to the paper, the average family of five with three children was bringing home about $136 a month when they actually needed $196 just to survive. It was a bad situation for everyone, even the rich. Sales at the store, which had been fairly steady, slowed down. Who had money for expensive face powders and lipsticks when there was not enough money to feed their children?

When the war finally ended this past November, Klein thought business would improve, but, in fact, things had gotten worse. The soldiers coming home from Europe wanted their jobs back, yet there were none to be had. On top of that, the unions, especially those in the metal trades, were demanding higher wages and recognition for collective bargaining. Management and business wanted none of that, comparing the union leaders to Bolshevists and revolutionaries. Klein was no Red-lover—he was too much of a street-level capitalist to embrace the theories of Marx or Lenin. "If you work hard, you ought to keep what you earn," was his motto.

Of late, this had led to endless debates with his sister. Still, no matter how much Rivka berated him about "social justice," the "rights of workers," the "proletariat," and a "living wage," he also knew deep down that she was no revolutionary. A socialist, perhaps, yet certainly not as violent or as radical as newspaper editor John Wesley Dafoe and the *Free Press* had portrayed workers like her. The only negative thing anyone could say about Rivka was that—with her short bobbed hair and her wire glasses—she resembled the New York "Queen of the Anarchists" Emma Goldman. Rivka ignored the comments, but sometimes Klein felt that she was more than a little flattered by the comparison.

Last month, Sarah brought home $125—about the same as what a clerk made at the F.W. Woolworth Company's stores, but a good fifteen dollars less than what a 'Hello Girl' was paid by the Manitoba Telephone System. The money had just covered the Kleins' rent, and allowed them to stock up on some much-needed groceries from Manitoba Stores.

Klein, on the other hand, had not had a good month. Ever since officials in Ottawa had conscripted prominent Winnipeg lawyer Graham Powers at the beginning of 1915 for a wartime administrative job supervising supplies, Klein's work as a detective had been slow and erratic. The older lawyers in the city were not interested in using his services and Alfred Powers, Graham's father and Klein's old friend, was semi-retired from the legal profession. He had never been the same since the tragic death of his wife Emily in 1914. There were, of course, jobs here and there following husbands and wives, and Klein had picked up a couple months of work from Great West Life watching one of their clients whom the company was certain had committed fraud. But if he took home $15 most weeks, he was doing well. That was not going to get his family out of the crowded Lady Angela Apartments and into their own house in the North End. Who knows what they were going to do once the new baby arrived? Where was he going to get $500 for a down payment, let alone find a banker who would give him a mortgage? Two weeks earlier, Sarah had dragged him to look at a house on St. John's Street. It had four rooms, a kitchen with a new gas stove, a small stable in the back—all for only $3,200. For the moment, that was way out of his league.

Klein did have one other option. Last year during the labour troubles Klein had received a telephone call from Tom Deacon, the head of Manitoba Bridge and Iron Works. Deacon, a former mayor of the city, was a civil engineer by profession. He put himself through university by working in lumber camps in northern Ontario and later tried his hand at gold mining before he came west. When he finally made some real money in the Winnipeg iron works business, he was not shy or embarrassed about letting everyone know that he was a man of means. He was one of the city's leading citizens, a member of the Board of Trade and an executive member of the Canadian Manufacturers' Association.

Last May he had called Klein with a proposition. Some of his men had gone out on strike and he aimed to put a stop to it. "I'm bringing in strike-breakers from Montreal and I want you to supervise them. Keep them in line. I need someone I can trust and I've heard good things about you, especially the way you handle yourself on the street. Hell, I was mighty impressed by the work you did back in '14 when Powers got himself in all of that trouble."

At first Klein had hesitated. He was an independent sort of fellow and he didn't like the idea of being one of Deacon's lackeys. On the other hand, Deacon had always struck him as a tough-talking but honest man. "The job'll pay $75 a week. Where are you going to make that kind of money as a detective, Klein? What do you say?"

What could he say? Deacon was right; Klein could not turn down $75 a week. Besides, he appreciated the fact that Canada had offered a home to his family and he wasn't sure the majority of the strikers felt the same way about his adopted country.

He finally agreed, but the job turned out to be a disaster. Three days into it, Klein ended up getting into a brawl. Not with one of the workers on the picket line, but with one of the burly strike-breakers, a real son-of-a-bitch by the name of Ferrier. This ex-cop split open the skull of a young striker, barely more than a boy, who had stepped in front of a truck attempting to push through the picket line. When Deacon refused to fire Ferrier, Klein quit.

Then, three days ago, just after a promising job for a prominent divorce lawyer fell through, Klein picked up the telephone and it was Deacon again offering him a job. "This next strike is going to be the big one. I need someone I can trust. It'll be $90 a week and you're the boss. You can hire the men you want. I aim to keep this plant running and no one is going to close me down," he told him before Klein could get a word in. "I already had to get rid of that troublemaker Lizowski, bloody Red. He came right into my shop and started rousing up the men. Said he was going to Bill Simon's place next."

"That ought to be interesting," Klein had remarked in a neutral voice.

As everyone in the city knew, Bill Simon, the powerful and wealthy owner of the Stafford Iron Works Company, hated the Reds even more than Deacon did. And the fact that Metro Lizowski was a Galician—an enemy alien as Simon put it—would have made a confrontation between them ugly. Simon's latest obsession was writing letters to the *Free Press* about the threat of the "One Big Union" ever since the labour convention was held in Calgary in early March. Simon was certain that revolution was on the horizon.

"I'll have to think about it," Klein had told Deacon.

"Well, don't wait too long. I figure the city will be shut down by the morning of the fifteenth. And if you don't want to help me, I have to find someone else who will. Remember Klein, this is war. I know some of your people have Red sympathies. It would look good if you could help balance the scales. Whose side are you going to be on?"

It was now the morning of May 15th and Klein had still not telephoned Deacon with an answer. He finished his coffee and stared across the kitchen table at his two daughters. What choice did he have? Sarah was soon going to have a son. He could feel it in his bones.

A man had to provide for his family, that much was clear to him. And no client he knew was going to pay him $90 a week. Just yesterday, he had had a discussion with Fred Black at the P and B Store about his ever-increasing grocery bill. He had promised to pay him at least $15 within the week and he was not quite sure where he was going to find the cash.

"Shailek, you want more coffee?" asked Sarah.

"No, I have to make a call."

He walked over to the wall and picked up the receiver.

"Operator? Operator, hello."

There was no answer.

"Hello, girls, anyone there?" he repeated.

The line was dead. The Manitoba Telephone operators, the Hello Girls, all six hundred of them, had walked off their jobs.

The Winnipeg General Strike had begun.

2

"YOU SURE YOU KNOW WHAT you're doing?" asked George Runciman. He leaned back in the black leather chair opposite Bill Simon's king-size mahogany desk. The first thing you saw when you entered Simon's inner sanctum was the mounted head of a buck with a full rack of antlers. Simon had shot the deer on one of his hunting trips up north of the Shoal Lakes. He did not eat anything he killed; for him it was the challenge of matching wits with the beast. That was the real mystery of life, according to Simon.

Behind the desk was a tall bookshelf containing volumes of all shapes and sizes and all variety of topics. Science and history were among Simon's favourites, especially works by Herbert Spencer, Francis Galton, Benjamin Kidd, and Houston Stewart Chamberlain. To the right were two large arched windows that looked out on Sutherland Avenue and the rest of Point Douglas, a working-class neighbourhood of industrial enterprises, small side-by-side wood bungalows and the city's infamous red light district. The ladies of the evening were more discreet than they had been a decade earlier, but on most weekend nights the parade of men were still boisterous and rowdy.

It was here in Point Douglas and in the rest of the North End immigrant quarter that Winnipeg's labourers first started thinking of themselves as part of a separate class. They toiled each day at places like Simon's Stafford Iron Works from eight in the morning until six at night, six days a week and were lucky to bring home $130 a month. Their union leaders promised to improve their wages and working conditions, providing they did as they were told.

"That's why I'm the boss and you're an underling, Runciman," said Simon. "Some men were born to rule, others to follow, sheep to be herded. Yes, I know exactly what I'm doing. For God's sakes, look around here. Look what I've built. With nothing but my own two hands..."

"And a bit of help from the bank," interjected Runciman.

Simon ignored the remark. "When I came to this city I had twenty dollars in my pocket. But I knew something about business, something about the building business. Now look at what I've accomplished. It's in my blood. That's the only answer. My father was a smart man and my grandfather smarter than him and so on. You know I can trace the family tree back five generations, right back to my namesake, William Simon of Penkridge in Stafford County. Started out as a farmer and ended up as an agent for the King's army."

No one could ever accuse Simon of being a modest individual. Like the majority of Winnipeg's elite, he, his wife Carolyn and their two sons, lived in a grand mansion on tree-lined Wellington Crescent. He played golf at the St. Charles Country Club and dined regularly at the Manitoba Club. His summer home was at Victoria Beach, where the foreign riff-raff was thankfully not welcome.

"I still think it's a gamble that won't work. Face facts, this city is headed for a bout of serious trouble."

"That's what's wrong with you, Runciman. You never see the big picture. What is happening here is not just about Winnipeg. There's been trouble in Seattle, there's plans for the One Big Union in Calgary. We are on the brink of a Socialist upheaval that is going to make what happened in Russia seem small by comparison."

"And you aim to stop it?"

"I'm going to try, yes."

"You want to tell me how you're going to achieve this miracle?"

Simon laughed. "For the moment, no. But don't you worry, no Bolshie like Lizowski is going to outwit me. For one thing, he doesn't have it in him. Who were his ancestors? Peasants from Galicia or some other God-forsaken place, living a hand-to-mouth existence on some tiny plot of land. He doesn't have a chance. Besides, you should worry about your own problems, Runciman, and let me save the city on my own." He made an attempt at a self-deprecating grin but his face muscles weren't used to it and it came out like a frown.

"Now, you do know what you have to do? We've been through this over and over again."

Runciman stared at his boss for a moment. He never should have taken this job. He was 33, had a civil engineering degree from the University of Toronto where he graduated at the top of his class. He had been featured in the *Telegram* recently after his election to the Board of Trade. He had Katie and the children to come home to each evening and a nice home on Spence Street just off Broadway Avenue. Why did he need to put up with Bill Simon's boorish and arrogant behaviour? Sure the money was good, probably $200 more a month than Deacon or the Barrett brothers would have paid him. Still, Simon had this bad habit of meddling into his personal affairs and he didn't appreciate it.

"These are my own problems," he said with some bitterness. "Why don't you go save the city and keep out of my life."

"Don't use that kind of tone with me, Runciman. You have no idea—" A knock at the door interrupted him. "Gertie, I said I didn't want to be bothered," he bellowed.

A slender woman with brown hair pulled back into a bun and pug nose peeked inside the office. "Apologies, Mr. Simon, but Mr. Franklin's here."

"Well, let him in."

Gertie opened the door and a tall bulky man, wearing a black suit, bowler hat and crisp white shirt strolled into the office.

"John, good to see you," said Simon. "You remember George Runciman, my manager."

"Sure," said Franklin.

Runciman was not certain what to make of John Franklin. One day, maybe three months ago, Franklin had appeared in Simon's office. All Runciman was told was that Franklin was a contractor from Vancouver and was interested in doing business with the company. But on the few occasions that Runciman had chatted with Franklin, he had an uneasy feeling about him. He doubted that he was a contractor. The man could not tell him the difference between a blast furnace and an iron railing, never mind knowing how to build anything. When he had asked Simon about it, he was told to mind his own business and that Franklin should be given due respect.

"What's it like out on the streets, John?" asked Simon.

"It's quiet, but there are signs of life."

"The operators have walked off already," added Runciman. "I hear the rest will join them at eleven this morning. It should be…"

"Runciman, I have to speak with John privately," said Simon, cutting him off.

"Yeah, George," said Franklin, "Why don't you run along."

Runciman rose to his feet, his face red, and left the room.

Ever so softly, he caressed her face and ran his fingers through her long dark hair, as he knew she enjoyed. Her naked body shivered as his hands wandered down her breasts, slowly across her stomach and abdomen.

"You are so beautiful," he said. "My little *tovarishch*." There was a gentleness in his voice that was genuine. At least, that was what she wanted to believe. They lay silently in each other's arms, holding each other tight, almost afraid to let go. Finally, he reached across her to the small table beside the bed and grabbed his pocket watch.

"Christ, it's nearly ten, I have to leave, I'm sorry. I told you I have this meeting."

"You don't have to apologize, Metro. As long as you come back later."

"I…I don't think I can. Not tonight. Who knows what's going to happen with the strike. Anyway, don't you have a union meeting yourself?"

"You're never going to leave her? Are you? This has nothing to do with the strike."

"Rivka, please. Not now," he said standing up. "Not today. I have to see that bastard Simon. Says he has a deal to offer that will make the labour problems disappear. Can you believe that pompous fool? If there was ever a capitalist that was meant to burn in hell, it's Bill Simon. "

"You better not say that so loudly, it might just happen."

"You've read Maxim's last letter?"

"I did. My God, the world has turned upside down there. Lynching in the street and a group of young children, no older than my nieces took part."

"Revolution can be cruel, you know that more than most people."

"Cruel? Metro, open your eyes. All that Lenin has brought so far is corruption and martial law. They shoot unarmed civilians in Petrograd. They steal church property and kill priests. And the Cheka sounds as bad or worse than any secret police force the Czar ever had."

"It'll get better there, trust me."

"Metro, I love you, but you're wrong. Did you read about the new slogan?"

"Looting the looters, sounds clever to me."

"Yeah, they steal from the rich. Throw them out of their homes, widows, children, it doesn't matter."

"I thought you believed in the revolution, about what we are trying to accomplish here?"

"I do. You know that. But what's happening in Russia makes you stop and think. Lenin and Trotsky are no better than any other masters that country has had."

"Listen to yourself," he said shaking his head. "It'll improve. Lenin's way is the right way. After all, Emma approves, how come you don't?"

"Emma…Emma is wrong."

"Is she? So why don't you tell her?"

"As a matter of fact I've tried. I've written to her in prison, but all my letters have been returned."

"She'd tell you that you were wrong."

"I thought the revolution was about equality and social justice."

"It is."

"No. They've given the country nothing but bitterness and hatred."

"Even if that's true, who's to say it won't be different here? You think people are going to march down Wellington Crescent invading the homes of Ashdown, Powers, Patterson, and the rest? Rivka be sensible. Now, I really have to go."

Metro Lizowski buttoned up his trousers and shirt, fastened his suspenders, and laced up his boots. He was rugged and darkly handsome, despite his broken nose. And his hands, so large and rough, made Rivka Klein tremble when he touched her.

"I have a meeting at Helen Armstrong's at five o'clock," said Rivka. "We plan to organize a food centre. I think Helen has already spoken to a few downtown hotels. I heard Rosenthal at the Strathcona is sympathetic."

"I'm certain everyone'll be well looked after. Besides, how long do you think the rich in this city will tolerate no telephone, no mail, no streetcar. Not long, I think. They'll meet our demands. I guarantee it."

Rivka laughed. "I love you, Metro, but you're far too optimistic. If I've learned anything in the factory it's that the owners won't budge an inch if they don't have to and even then they'd fire their own mothers before they'd give up some of their profits. If I were you, I'd be careful with Simon. The man is dangerous."

"I can take care of myself," he said kissing her. "I'll try to drop by later, maybe around eleven this evening. But I can't promise anything."

"She's going to find out one way or the other, you know that?"

"Let me handle this, Rivka, please." He gave her another kiss and left the apartment.

Rivka made herself a cup of tea, admired her new straw hat that she had picked up at the Hudson's Bay store, straightened the green ribbon, and wondered how she had gotten herself into such a situation. If her mother were alive, well, she didn't even want to think about that. Sam didn't know about Metro. She knew he'd never approve. And who could blame him? Lizowski was a 34-year-old Socialist party leader, a key member of the Ukrainian Labour Temple Association, and a former head of the banned pro-Marxist Ukrainian Social Democratic Party. He also had a wife and child.

Rivka and Metro had first met about six months earlier at a massive labour rally at the Walker Theatre, where the impetus for the strike had been born. At first, it was all business. They shared their passions about the need for something more radical than the Trades and Labour

Council executive was advocating. Neither of them entirely trusted the brain trust—Fred Dixon, John Queen, George Armstrong, Bob Russell, Bill Ivens and the rest of them. As far as Lizowski and Rivka were concerned, these men were all talk and no action. Sure, Russell proclaimed that "capitalism must eventually disappear," but Rivka suspected that's not quite what he meant. A general strike was as far as he and the others were prepared to go. At that time, she thought it wasn't enough. They didn't want a real revolution; they wanted to work within the capitalist system, despite its inherent weaknesses.

That night, she and Metro had shared a cup of coffee and the attraction was instant. She even found his habit of quoting Lenin in conversation endearing. "The substitution of the proletarian for the bourgeois state is impossible without a violent revolution," he would say out of the blue. Sitting in a smoky café on a freezing Prairie night, he was Vladimir Ilyich and she was Red Emma.

Ever since Rivka had attended a lecture delivered by Emma Goldman back in 1907 at the Labour Hall on Higgins, she had been a loyal follower. She had heard Goldman talk passionately about education, and the plight of Jews in Czarist Russia. Emma had style, wit, confidence and courage. Rivka remembered that some men in the audience commented that Goldman looked dowdy and unattractive, but not to Rivka. After that, she devoured anything and everything that Goldman produced—pamphlets on birth control, Russian literature, European theatre, the eight-hour work day and the evils of capitalism.

It was Goldman who had made Rivka really question religion as an institution. And then a few years ago, when Rivka had tried to emulate New York revolutionaries by organizing a 'Yom Kippur Ball' Rabbi Aaron Davidovitch and the city's other rabbis publicly castigated her for blasphemy. No matter, she took solace in the opening words from Goldman's book, *Anarchism: What It Really Stands For.* The passage never left her head: "The history of human growth and development is at the same time the history of the terrible struggle of every new idea heralding the approach of a brighter dawn."

Rivka had initially believed in that spirit, but that was before she had read Metro's letters from his cousin Maxim in Petrograd. They had been smuggled out of Russia to Paris and then sent to Winnipeg by one of Maxim's friends. The stories of brutality and dictatorship had shocked her. It was as if the revolution in Russia had unleashed dark and savage forces. Overnight, people who had worked as servants, tailors, dressmakers, and street cleaners had tasted power and enjoyed it so much that they now wanted their former masters to suffer. And suffer they did. Maybe Metro was right. Maybe life would settle down once the Bolshevik rule was more firmly established, and once the current civil war with the Whites was won. In many ways, she needed to believe that; she needed to believe in Metro.

Rivka was 35 years old and had no real prospects for a husband. She had accepted that. She had her work at the garment factory, had an honoured place on the executive of the local International Ladies Garment Workers' Union or the ILGWU—the only woman to hold such a position—and she had her two beautiful nieces, Freda and Bernice. While her mother was still alive, she had dated Saul Schwartz and then in 1915 had been engaged to Solomon Volkon. She and Solomon had nearly married, but a week before the wedding she had called it off. Poor Solomon, he was a good and decent man. She knew that she had hurt him, but the marriage would have been a disaster. She had not loved him and she had been fooling herself to believe she did. With Metro, it was different.

To be fair, he had not lied to her. He had told her he was married, and that his wife Sylvia was a fine woman, although after four years of marriage their relationship had become routine and uneventful. They had a three-year-old son, Frederick, who was named, Metro had proudly told her, after Frederich Engels.

Three nights after they had first met, he had appeared unannounced at her apartment. When he first kissed her, the intensity of her feelings had astonished and frightened her. She had not pressured him, but recently she could not help herself and the future of their liaison started to matter to her. Here they were about to participate in the greatest moment of labour history and all she could think about was Metro Lizowski in her bed. She sipped her tea, fiddled more with the ribbon on her hat and contemplated the days, and nights, ahead.

Metro Lizowski was fortunate to get a seat on the Main Street streetcar. A rally was planned for shortly after eleven at the corner of

Portage and Main. Later, all of those people could tell their children where they were the day the Winnipeg General Strike began.

He had not told anyone on the labour council that he had arranged a meeting with Simon. They would have thought that he was mad. Among the city's leading capitalists, Simon was the least open to new ideas. So why was he wasting his time? Lizowski was not certain, only that his gut feeling told him to hear Simon out. Perhaps he did have something tangible to offer. If Lizowski could deliver a way out of the strike, it might just get him the leverage he needed in the party. Then, and only then, could he make the real changes that he believed were necessary for the working-class to survive into the new century. This was war—Marx's "class struggle," was no theory—and anyone who thought differently was ignorant, naïve or plain stupid. Besides, if things did not work out the way he wanted them to, he had other more extreme options.

He avoided eye contact with any of the other passengers. Staring out the window as the car passed Pritchard Avenue, his thoughts turned to Rivka. He knew he would return to her apartment later that evening, even if he had to lie to Sylvia—again. There was no easy solution to this dilemma. He knew that. His father and brother and the rest of his family would never understand. He and Sylvia had known each other since they were twelve years old. Nor would the members of his family open their homes and hearts for a Hebrew woman. Lizowski had heard his father curse many times about the damn kikes doing this and that. And what about Frederick? How could he abandon his only child? He had no answers for the moment, but Rivka was right about one thing, this sneaking around could not last forever. He would have to speak with Sylvia and tell her the truth.

Twenty minutes later, Lizowski sat uncomfortably across from Gertie's desk in Bill Simon's outer office. There were two black couches, a chair and a few non-descript paintings hanging on the wall. A pile of *Maclean's* magazines sat on a table in front of him. He flipped through the most current issue with a photograph of Major-General Morrison on the cover. With his cap pulled low over his forehead, Morrison had the look of a military man pre-occupied with the affairs of war and peace. Lizowski also glanced at a story about life in the Arctic hinterland written by the scientist Vilhajlmur Stefasson. When he came upon an article by John Dafoe of the *Free Press* about the peace talks at Versailles he slammed the magazine down. He detested Dafoe as much as the great editor hated the Bolsheviks. Another ten minutes passed in silence—that is, other than the clicking of Gertie's Underwood typewriter. Finally, the door to Simon's office opened.

"Gertie, please show Mr. Lizowski in."

Gertie waved her right hand in the direction of the door.

"Thanks," said Lizowski, "I'll let myself in."

Simon was seated behind his desk smoking a cigar, reading the *Telegram*. A pile of files and papers were strewn about in front of him. There was no one else in the office.

"Lizowski, glad you could make it. Should be quite a day today. What do you think?"

"You won't find what you're looking for in that rag of a paper."

"The *Telegram*? Best of the three I'd wager. Says here that all the trouble is being stirred up by 'a handful of English and Scotch agitators who are openly and even proudly Red.' What do you think about that?"

"Let's wait another ten minutes and we'll see what will be."

"They'll follow the labour council's directions?"

"They'll follow them, even your men, Simon. The plant should be dead quiet this afternoon. Unless you got other plans, that is?"

Simon laughed. "I always have other plans. You should know that."

"Look, I'd love to stay here and chat all day with you. But you asked me to come here for a reason. You want to tell me what the hell it is?"

Simon took a deep drag of his cigar and blew a puff of white smoke into the air above him. "Fifty thousand dollars."

"What's that?"

"You heard what I said. I'm prepared to pay the labour council and you fifty thousand dollars. And I'll toss in another five for your personal troubles."

"And what do I have to do for this generosity?"

"Simple. First, call off the strike by six this evening. Second, the labour council has to disband. And third, you and every other member of the Socialist Party executive, as well as the Reds at the Ukrainian Labour Temple have to leave the city within forty-eight hours."

Lizowski leaned back in his chair. "Maybe you want to cancel Christmas as well. Have you lost your mind? No one will accept terms like that. You think you and your filthy money can buy anything. These are men of principle I work with." He shook his head. "What's the use? You have no idea what I'm talking about." He stood up.

"Seventy-five thousand," said Simon. "And ten for yourself. What's your price Lizowski? How much do your Bolshevik principles cost?"

"I hate to tell you this, you son-of-a-bitch, but some things aren't for sale. I doubt you'd understand that."

"Don't you understand," said Simon, his voice rising. "This strike is only the start. My God, man, we've begun plunging into an abyss from which there is no return. Already, crime statistics are rising, mixed marriages have started a degenerative cycle…"

"What the hell are you talking about? Simon, I'm leaving."

"I said I'm not finished with you yet. Sit down you Galician imbecile. I'm trying to help you."

Lizowski moved toward the door.

"If you don't listen to what I have to say and don't accept the deal I'm proposing, tomorrow's newspapers will feature a headline story about your love affair with that Hebrew whore."

Lizowski lunged toward Simon. As he did so, the door to the office flung open and John Franklin lumbered forward. He grabbed the collar of Lizowski's coat and twisted hard. Lizowski immediately swung his fist at Franklin's face. The larger man ducked and connected with his right fist on Lizowski's nose. Blood flowed from his nostrils, down his face and onto his shirt. The two men faced each other, hesitating for a moment.

"Enough," shouted Simon.

Lizowski wiped his face and nose with the sleeve of his coat. "You come near me again, Simon, or if you print anything about my personal life. So help me…"

"Are you threatening me?" Simon asked. "You Red piece of trash. Get out of my office or I'll call the police."

Lizowski took out a handkerchief and covered his nose. He walked past Franklin, shouldering him, and left the office.

"You okay, Mr. Simon?" asked Franklin.

"Me? That Bolshie couldn't hurt me. Well, I tried to stop it. Let it rest on their heads."

"What about that other problem we talked about? You want me to take care of it?"

Simon lit another cigar and stared out his office window. "Yeah, deal with it tonight."

3

KLEIN HAD AGREED TO MEET Tom Deacon at the Royal Alexandra Hotel for breakfast at eight o'clock. There was no streetcar service so he turned right at Burrows and Main and started walking. Although sunny and warm, the streets were eerily silent. The usual morning crowds of pedestrians, shoppers and delivery wagons were absent. By noon the previous day, nearly all commercial and industrial activity of any type had stopped. More than twenty thousand workers had walked off their jobs, and the stereotypers and pressmen had promised to join the strike today. That would make it impossible for the city's three daily newspapers to continue regular operations. While firemen answered the strike call, the police union heeded Mayor Charles Gray's urgent plea and remained on the streets for the time being.

As Klein walked by the corner of Selkirk and Main, he noticed that garbage was already piling up. A few stores were open on Selkirk Avenue, but it was hardly the normal hubbub of daily trading and bartering that characterized the North End's famous bazaar and marketplace.

Food was not yet a problem. Like other Winnipeggers, he and Sarah had stocked up on bread and milk, but their few bottles of milk could not last much past the next day or two, especially if there was no ice delivery. Did the strike leaders bother to think what would happen? If there was no milk delivery, how were the workers' own children supposed to manage? They had shut down the city and did not really comprehend the consequences of their actions. So narrowly focussed were they on winning the battle with their employers that they did not stop to think about how they themselves would be affected by the shutdown. What would the workers do for money? They had no big savings accounts like their managers and bosses. Who would supply them with food?

Near Euclid Avenue, Klein saw two girls he recognized from Melinda's. They were out searching for cigarettes and a newspaper. "The strike could be good for business. Right, Sam?" one of them said. Her name was Maggie. She had bobbed blonde hair and was wearing a velvet skirt with a fine white lace blouse that was much too small for her. It hugged her body, leaving little to the imagination, hardly the way most women in Winnipeg dressed. "All of these men with nothing to do. We could keep them busy," she said with a smile.

"I'm sure you could," grinned Klein. "If they had any money. Be sure to say hello to Melinda for me."

Maggie lightly ran her right hand over Klein's cheek. "You don't visit us much any more, Sam."

"Ladies, I have an appointment."

"Suit yourself, Sam. You know where to find me."

Klein tipped his hat and continued. His life as a minder at Madam Melinda's brothel in the years before the Great War seemed far away now. And who even remembered that Sarah had once been Melinda's star attraction? Even then, Sarah had a lot of class. He often wondered what she would tell Freda and Bernice about her past, once they were old enough to understand. Maybe some things were best left buried.

Klein walked under the subway. This was the dividing line of the city: the CPR rail line and yards demarked the affluent south from the immigrant north. As he grew more successful, Sam Klein felt more at home crossing into the downtown. But it had taken a long time. He turned left on Higgins Avenue towards the majestic Royal Alexandra Hotel.

"G'morning, Johnson," said Klein to the hotel's blue-uniformed doorman.

"Mr. Klein, quite a day. Glad I don't belong to any union. The Missus would kill me if I didn't bring home the pay."

Klein kept moving into the lobby, lushly adorned with a rich red carpet and fine wood furniture. He saw Tom Deacon waiting for him in the hotel's magnificent rotunda, a favourite spot for afternoon tea, conversation and music.

Deacon waved Klein to a chair. "I don't have much time for small talk. I have to be at the Board of Trade within an hour. There's an emergency meeting at two o'clock and I think General Ketchen is going to be there. So is Graham Powers, Bill Simon, and some men from the Grain Exchange."

The burly industrialist leaned forward. "Listen Klein, the Citizens Committee of 1000, that's what we're calling our association. We are not about to allow a Soviet-style revolutionary band of Reds take over this city. Not when I'm around. You remember what I told anyone who couldn't hold a job a few years back?"

"Yeah, I remember. Who could forget it?" said Klein with more than a hint of sarcasm.

"Hit the trail, that's what I told them and that's what we aim to tell those revolutionaries on the Trade Council—hit the trail. This strike isn't about whether or not unions are right or wrong or whether collective bargaining is acceptable. No, there is only one question to consider: are we going to permit a collection of workers to destroy this city?"

Klein had heard Deacon's bravado before and it didn't impress him. On the other hand, he knew that Brigadier-General Herbert D.B. Ketchen, a former member of the North West Mounted Police and the current commander of Military District 10 was all business. He already had his men drilling at the Fort Osborne barracks across from the Legislative Building on Broadway. If there was trouble, and Klein was certain there would be sooner or later, then Ketchen had vowed to do what he had to in order to keep the peace. The general did not bluff.

"Now, do we have a deal?" asked Deacon.

Klein hesitated. Then he remembered his two little daughters. "I hire my own men and…"

"No, not exactly."

"Well, then what? I don't like you changing the rules."

"Sorry, Klein. It's my company. I built it from nothing. I have to do what I think is best. I've arranged to bring in thirty men from Toronto, Sudbury, and Dryden. They'll be in the city in three days. I want you to make sure they get to work on time and that there's no trouble. I've already arranged for them to sleep at a boarding house on Meade Street. Any problems with this?"

"Yeah, I do. I'm not going to work with homicidal maniacs like the last time."

"Don't worry. Boy scouts, every one of them."

"And it's still ninety a week? You haven't decided to change that, have you?"

Deacon smiled. "Yeah, Klein. Ninety a week, as long as you give me results. I figure it might take two weeks to get this mess sorted out. You'll have to be at my disposal all day, every day."

Klein nodded and lit a cigarette. He threw the match into a silver spittoon close to the table. He hardly relished being Deacon's strong arm, even for two weeks, but Sarah would kill him if he turned down a sure $180.

"How about you come by the office tomorrow at nine and I'll give you more details. Plus a week's wages as an act of good faith."

At that moment, Johnson the hotel's doorman walked forward. "Mr. Deacon, sir, a boy just delivered this letter for you. Said that it was urgent you see it."

"Let's have it," said Deacon. He tore it open, took out a single piece of paper and glanced at the note. "My God," he whispered.

"What happened, Deacon? You look a little pale."

"It's from Chief MacPherson."

"And?"

"Bill Simon's dead. Murdered. They found him in his automobile. They think that he was strangled. Damn it. It's started, Klein, don't you see that?"

"What are you talking about?"

"The class war. I can guarantee that if Simon was murdered, then some rotten son-of-a-bitch Bolshie did it. Who was more outspoken against the workers and socialists than Bill? No one."

"Aren't you jumping to conclusions a little here? Why don't you wait—"

"There's no doubt in my mind, Klein," said Deacon raising his voice, "that a Red must have done this. C'mon. Let's go."

"Go where?"

"You're coming with me to the station."

For a moment, Klein thought about arguing, but he was curious. Bill Simon was a well-connected businessman with lots of friends and, probably, lots of enemies too. Maybe Deacon was right. Maybe Simon had been in an altercation with a strike leader. He hoped not. The city could never handle that. Besides, he was a detective. Maybe Deacon would open his pockets to guarantee the murderer was caught. Before it was too late.

4

A SMALL CROWD OF police officers in dark blue double-breasted uniforms and British-style bobby helmets greeted Klein and Deacon at the main doors to the Rupert Avenue station. The men were gathered around a fellow officer. Klein immediately recognized the man as John O'Shea, a veteran constable. He was tall, broad-shouldered and had a nasty Irish temper. He and Klein had had their differences in the past, but they now shared a grudging respect for each other.

"And I say to you," O'Shea proclaimed to the gaggle of police, "We owe our fellow workers support. Without a walkout, city council will never deal properly with the union."

"Yeah, John, then who'll watch our homes and neighbourhoods?" shouted one officer.

"That's exactly the point, isn't it? The Commission, Gray and the aldermen will have to listen to our demands and give us what we want. We can be in control of this situation, as long as we stand united. Tell me, can any of you live on $100 a month? With prices going up everyday?"

"They promised us a raise soon," another constable remarked.

"Next week, I hear," said another.

"Exactly," said O'Shea. "They promised us a raise. Well, I'm tired of waiting. And so are my wife and kids."

"O'Shea," bellowed a voice from an open second floor window, "Don't you have rounds to make?"

O'Shea looked up into the scowling face of Chief Donald MacPherson. "I got ten more minutes until my shift starts—"

"We had this discussion already. You men have a job to do. You understand that?"

O'Shea's face darkened. Then with a scowl, he shrugged and put on his helmet. There seemed little point in arguing.

"The rest of you men. Go about your duties."

At that, the small gathering quickly broke up. "Deacon," MacPherson said seeing the former mayor with Klein. "Wait there, I'll be right down."

A moment later, MacPherson opened the large metal gates guarding the station. The gates had been installed in 1916 following what became known in the city as the "Army Riot." When a few drunken soldiers were taken into custody, a rowdy group of their friends from the Fort Osborne Barracks attempted to force their release. The men took out their anger on the civilian police, but the original arrests, in fact, had been made by the military police. Nevertheless, in the ensuing melee, almost every window at the station had been broken. The metal gates were installed two weeks later.

"What the hell are you doing here, Klein?" demanded the Chief.

Ever since Klein had successfully intervened in the murder investigation of Emily Powers and Antonio Rossi back in 1914, MacPherson regarded him as a "Hebrew troublemaker."

"I asked Klein to be here, Donald. I think he can help."

"My detectives will solve this case in a day or two."

Klein smiled.

"You have a problem with that, Klein? I've told you before, leave this kind of work to professionals."

"Just trying to make a living, Chief."

"Yeah, well do it somewhere else. I hear San Francisco is a nice place to live."

"Enough bickering. What happened to Simon?" asked Deacon."

"Let's go inside and I'll give you the details."

MacPherson led the two men through the gates, up the stairs to the second floor, then down a narrow and dark corridor into his office. Two people were waiting for them.

"I think you both know Detective McCreary."

"Yeah, we've met before," said Klein. Bill McCreary and Klein had been associates for nearly a decade, although the detective had never been open about the relationship. Each had assisted the other and McCreary had come to respect Klein's resourcefulness, intelligence and guile—even if he would never admit it. Klein, too, thought McCreary was a boor, but a talented and quick thinking detective. When he was in trouble or stumped on a case, McCreary was the first person he sought out for help.

"McCreary, I heard you retired," said Klein, goading him.

"Not quite yet," said McCreary lighting a small, foul-smelling cigar. "I'll be still investigating murder cases when they put you in the old folks home."

Klein laughed. "I don't know, Bill, what's all that grey hair under your hat?"

"You two finished?" asked MacPherson, not waiting for a reply. He motioned for the woman standing beside McCreary to come forward. "This is Mrs. Hannah Nash, our new policewoman. Been on the job about six months now. She's been mainly helping Franks in the Morality Department and working with the women in Point Douglas. She'll be assisting Detective McCreary on this case. Made a real difference, I'd say, don't you think McCreary?"

The detective rolled his eyes. "Yeah, a real difference."

Hannah extended her hand towards Deacon and then Klein. She had short brown curly hair, dark large eyes and a slender figure under her white blouse and ankle-length navy blue dress. Like the handful of other women in the department, Hannah did not wear a uniform and, in fact, until today had rarely left the station on official business. Klein figured she was in her early thirties. "Nice to meet you Mr. Klein, I've heard some interesting tales about you."

"All good, I hope."

"Depends who you speak to."

She seemed pleasant enough, even somewhat attractive, Klein thought, but he had some serious reservations about women doing police work. MacPherson must have been smoking opium when he decided to pair Mrs. Nash with Bill McCreary. Ever since Alex Taber had returned to New York two years ago, the detective had not found another partner to his liking. Not that he seemed to like anybody.

"We going to stand here all day yapping or get moving on this investigation," muttered McCreary.

"I agree," said Deacon. "Can we talk about Bill Simon? There's going to be questions at my meeting."

"You sure you want Klein here, Tom?" the Chief asked again.

"I want him here," said Deacon. "Now what happened to Bill?"

Without another word, MacPherson shut the door of his office and beckoned Deacon to sit down.

"This is what we know so far," said MacPherson. "Yesterday morning, Simon met with Metro Lizowski."

"That goddamn Bolshevik? What the hell was he doing with him?"

"Tom, your language, please."

"Sorry, Ma'am," said Deacon, glancing at Hannah.

"No offence taken. I've been with McCreary all day, don't forget."

McCreary walked over to the open window and flung his cigar out into the street. He had little patience for MacPherson at the best of times, but now that he had been ordered to spend a few days with Hannah Nash, he was downright ornery. As far as he was concerned, it had been a mistake to hire women on the force. They could not be trusted and the thought of one day going into a dangerous situation with a woman like Mrs. Nash guarding his back made his stomach churn. In McCreary's view, women were meant to be at home, tending to children and making their husbands happy in the bedroom. Giving women the vote three years ago was about the most imprudent decision the Manitoba government had ever made. Everyone knew that Nellie McClung and her gang of cackling suffragettes had pressured the premier into passing the legislation. But as far as McCreary was concerned, this new-found freedom could only lead to serious trouble in the future.

He suspected that this business with Mrs. Nash was really about MacPherson's desire to show up the Edmonton police force. It disturbed MacPherson to no end when the papers reported on the success of the country's first policewoman, Annie Jackson, who had been hired back in 1912. As soon as MacPherson had taken over from

Chief McRae, he had been campaigning for the Commission to hire a group of women. He said he wanted to make the Winnipeg force "more progressive." It took until December 1916 before Mrs. Mary Dunn became the city's first woman constable.

"According to Simon's secretary, he and Lizowski had a loud argument," continued MacPherson. "Lizowski left the office angry."

"That's it?" asked Klein. "Doesn't sound like much of a case to me."

"No, that's not it, Klein. Simon left his office about four yesterday afternoon. He told Gertie, that's his secretary, that he was leaving early. Something about plans he had to finalize concerning the strike. He asked Gertie to help him carry a stack of files to his auto. She says that when they got to the barn, Lizowski was waiting for them. Simon told her to go back to the office. That was the last time she saw him alive. Seems an open and shut case to me."

"It would," said Klein.

"I don't care what you think, Klein. McCreary's done the preliminary investigation and he's satisfied."

"That right, detective?" asked Deacon. "You think Lizowski did this?"

"Looks that way. I got a dozen men out looking for him. When we bring him in, then I guess we'll all know. But ask Mrs. Nash, she's the one who questioned the woman."

Everyone stared at the policewoman.

"The Chief's quite right," said Hannah. "Looks like there was some kind of struggle and Lizowski killed Mr. Simon. But before I jump to any conclusions I'd like to hear what Lizowski has to say."

"Glad we agree," said McCreary.

"Where's the secretary now?" asked Klein.

"She's down the hall, why?"

"I'd like to speak with her."

"That's out of the question, Klein," said MacPherson.

Tom Deacon held up his hand. "You think it would help, Sam?"

"Maybe."

Deacon turned to the chief. "There's going to be a lot of questions about this, Donald. You know that if Lizowski is charged with murdering Simon, any labour problems you're dealing with today are going to seem very small. The strikers are going to think Lizowski's been arrested for a different reason, because of who he is and what he stands for. Let Klein speak with her. Let's be certain about this."

MacPherson looked over in McCreary's direction. "What do you think, Bill?"

McCreary shrugged. "Klein won't find out anything we don't already know. But, hey, this is politics. That's your area."

The Chief was silent for a moment. "As long as Mrs. Nash is in the room with Klein at all times."

Klein followed Hannah into the room. He couldn't help noticing her graceful walk and, just below the hem of her skirt, two well-turned ankles. He was about to make a pleasantly innocuous comment when he saw Simon's secretary Gertie standing by the window. She looked exhausted.

"Can I please go home? I've answered all of your questions. What more do you want from me?"

"This is Mr. Klein. He's a friend of Mr. Deacon."

"Is Mr. Deacon here?" asked Gertie. "I'd like to speak with him."

"Yes, of course," said Hannah. "But first Mr. Klein would like to ask you a few more questions."

Gertie's shoulders sagged. "Is this really necessary?"

"It'll just take a few minutes, Miss Viola. We'd appreciate it. You do want us to find the person who did this to Mr. Simon, don't you?"

"Yes, yes. I do. It's just been a long day, that's all."

Klein was impressed by the way Hannah handled the situation. He could see that she was not only a striking woman, but an intelligent one as well. While Klein would not have necessarily admitted this to the boys at the bar, he preferred the company of women to men. It was not merely the obvious physical attractions he may have felt. He genuinely liked their style and demeanour. Most of the women he came into contact with, whether it was at Melinda's house or at Sarah's cosmetic shop, were clever and could laugh at themselves and the world more than the men he knew. And, as Sarah usually pointed out to him, they in turn reacted positively to Klein's natural charm.

"All right, Mr. Klein. What would you like to know?" asked Gertie.

Klein pulled out his silver cigarette case, took one out and offered one to Gertie. She looked at Hannah.

"Go ahead, it'll calm your nerves."

More surprises, thought Klein. He'd figured Hannah for a rigid tee-totaller—no alcohol and no tobacco. He struck a match and lit Gertie's cigarette and then his own. She then related to him the same story she had told MacPherson and McCreary: how she had seen Lizowski in the back alley behind the factory and how she had left Simon with him. When she returned two hours later, her boss was sitting in his auto slumped over the steering wheel.

"How about this argument that Lizowski and Simon had earlier in the day? What was it about?"

"I don't know for sure. The door of the office was shut. I think it had something to do with the strike."

"And they were alone?"

"What do you mean?" asked Gertie, fidgeting in her chair.

Klein looked at Hannah. "I mean, was there anyone else in the office besides Lizowski and Simon?"

"I…I don't think so. No, they were alone."

"You don't sound sure of yourself. Were they or weren't they alone?"

"They were alone, yes. No one else came into the office that day. Now can I please see Mr. Deacon and then go home?"

"Any more questions, Mr. Klein?" asked Hannah.

He stared at Gertie for a moment. "No, I'm done. For now."

Klein was mulling over his interview with Gertie, when a shout came from down the hall. "They have Lizowski," yelled a constable. The young cop was out of breath. "Take it easy, Kennedy," said the Chief, emerging from his office. "What happened?"

"The call just came in on the box. Michaelson and King found Lizowski in a rooming house on Agnes Street. There was some kind of scuffle and Lizowski was shot."

"Is it serious?"

"I don't think so. Just wounded him in the arm. They're at the hospital with him now and said they'll be here in about two hours."

"You go down to the hospital and join them, Kennedy. It's your responsibility to make sure they get here on time and with the prisoner in one piece. That understood?"

"Yes, Sir."

Deacon joined Klein and Chief MacPherson by the front door. "Good work, Chief," said Deacon. "You hear that Klein? They got Lizowski. But we have to do this by the books. I don't want McCreary beating a confession out of him."

"No one's going to hurt a hair on his head. Isn't that right, Bill?"

McCreary respected the law, but intimidation was part of the job. He was not above being a little rough if it expedited a case.

"Let Mrs. Nash do the interrogation. I'll just watch."

"I don't know about that," said MacPherson, struggling between politeness and prejudice.

"Why not?" asked McCreary. "You wanted me to teach her about being a detective. This could be a good lesson."

"What do you think, Mrs. Nash, are you ready to handle something like this?"

There was no hesitation. "As long as McCreary is in the room with me."

"I'd like to be there too," said Klein.

"Never. I draw the line there," said the Chief. "This a police investigation."

"What about after?"

"We'll see what Lizowski has to say."

Deacon excused himself and the Chief and Mrs. Nash walked with him to the front entrance. Once they were gone, Klein turned to McCreary. "Mrs. Nash seems like she can get the job done."

"Yeah, you don't have to work with her. I wish Taber were here to see this."

"Well, he was a *schmuck* on any day of the week. Who cares what he would've thought. But Mrs. Nash seems different, more capable. Where does she come from?"

"Don't know and don't much care."

"And her husband?"

"Don't know that either. Ask MacPherson."

Klein nodded his head slowly. "You think Lizowski is guilty?"

"It looks that way to me, Klein. Why, you have other ideas?"

"No. It's just that…"

"What?"

"There's something about the secretary's story."

"What about it?"

"She's not telling us everything she knows."

"Why? What did she say to you?"

"Same story she told you. It's a feeling I have, that's all. There's something else."

"And I think you've been working too hard. Listen, come back in a few hours. I'll let you know what Lizowski has to say. By the way, you must be having a bad month to go to work for Deacon again."

"Just trying to pay the bills, that's all," said Klein. He stared out the window towards Main Street. Gertie Viola was not telling them everything about what had gone on in that office.

5

"YOU NEED ANYTHING ELSE, Ma'am?" asked the constable. He was standing on the walkway leading to the entrance of Gertie's River Avenue apartment. Like so many of the city's new apartment blocks, it was an impressive and finely crafted stone structure, exuding a European charm.

"I'm fine now," said Gertie. "Thanks very much for your help." She waved to the police officer and made her way inside. She was about to check her mailbox, but then reminded herself that no mail was delivered today and probably would not be until the strike was settled. What an inconvenience, she thought. She was tired and scared. What would happen now? Who would run the company? Poor Bill. The image of Simon, slumped over in his automobile raced through her mind.

Her apartment was on the third floor. The hallway had electric lights, but the landlord, a frugal-minded businessman named McGee, insisted that they not be turned on until after six p.m. in the winter and after nine in the spring and summer. Gertie adjusted her eyes to the darkness and trudged up the stairs. As she opened the door to the third floor, she heard something behind her.

"Gertie. You're back," said the voice.

"Who's there?" said Gertie. "Step out of the shadow or I'll scream."

"Why would you want to do that?"

A large man moved towards her.

"Mr. Franklin, what… do you want?"

"I want to hear what you told the police."

"Just what you said I should say. You know you can trust me."

"You didn't tell them I was in the office?" He moved closer to her and grabbed hold of her right arm.

"I…I didn't say a word," pleaded Gertie. "You're hurting me. Let go."

Franklin twisted her arm a little tighter. It wasn't enough to break it, but there was no doubt in his mind that she knew he was serious.

"That's real good, Gertie. You just forget about anything you heard or saw that day, except about that scum Lizowski, that is. And if they should ever ask about me…"

"I don't know you, that's what I'll tell them. I promise. My arm."

Franklin relaxed his grip slightly and ran his other hand across her cheek. She could smell chewing tobacco on his breath. It sickened her.

"I know you won't disappoint me, Gertie. Otherwise I'll have to pay you another visit."

"I didn't kill anyone. I don't know what you're talking about," repeated Metro Lizowski. His hair was dishevelled and he had a perfectly round bruise just below his eye where he had been struck by a police billy club. "Resisting arrest," was all one of the constables involved had told MacPherson.

Lizowski sat on a small wooden stool in the middle of the room, while Hannah Nash strolled around him asking questions. McCreary sat in a chair on the far side of the room, smoking a cigar and growing impatient. Still, she was starting to make some headway—even McCreary had to concede that.

"Once more, Mr. Lizowski," she spoke softly but firmly. "Tell me about the meeting with Mr. Simon. You went to his office."

"I went to his office. He tried to bribe me and the other members of the council. Said he'd give us fifty thousand dollars to leave the city."

"Fifty thousand?" McCreary snorted.

Lizowski nodded. "I know it sounds crazy, but that's what he said."

"And you refused the offer?" asked Hannah.

"Yeah, I turned him down. But like I keep saying, there was someone else there. Find him. He'll know what happened to Simon."

"Who was he?"

"Don't have a clue. He was tough as a mule. Tall, had a black moustache. Never seen him before. I think Simon called him John."

Nash sighed. "What if I told you that Gertie Viola, Mr. Simon's secretary claims you were the only one in the office at that time."

"I'd say she was a liar."

"I have to tell you Mr. Lizowski, this does not look good for you. You were the last person to see Mr. Simon alive and the two of you had an argument. A jury is liable to think…"

"Damn it, I'm telling you I didn't do it." Lizowski started to stand, then took a look at a smiling McCreary and sat back down.

"So where were you yesterday evening? We already spoke to your wife, she says you were not at home."

"I was out doing strike work."

"By yourself? No one was with you?"

"That's right."

"I think we've heard enough," said McCreary. "Why not let Lizowski think about things in a cozy cell down the hall?"

Lizowski sneered. "Go ahead. But I didn't kill anyone."

"I've been at this job a long time," added McCreary, "and I can usually tell when someone is lying about something."

"Why not arrest the mayor then, and the premier."

At that moment, the sound of breaking glass echoed from an adjoining office. McCreary opened the door of the interrogation room. One of the hall windows had been shattered into a dozen pieces.

"Someone threw a rock," said McCreary. He peered outside. "Christ, there's a mob ten deep outside."

"Some of my friends, I'd wager," said Lizowski.

"Mrs. Nash…"

"You don't have to tell me McCreary. I'll get him to a cell right now." She checked that Lizowski's handcuffs were secure and took him by the arm. A constable took charge of the prisoner at the end of the hallway leading into the cellblock. She returned to join McCreary.

"This doesn't look good," he said.

Nash looked out the window and could see a group of about a hundred people, maybe more. They were standing on the street directly in front of the station, milling about and shouting. "Let our man go! Let our man go." They repeated it again and again. A small contingent of constables, billy clubs at the ready, their revolvers still in their holsters, stood on the steps a few feet from the steel gates.

"Now there's the real trouble," said McCreary. "You see that group on the other side of the street?" He pointed to about a dozen young men. "They're soldiers, just back from Europe. That's Jack Scott leading them. I know his father, Mike. They don't look friendly and I can tell you they hate the Reds more than anyone in this city. We'd better get some reinforcements down there."

For more than six months a small war had been playing out in Winnipeg, one that pitted labour against a contingent of war veterans. As a group, the former soldiers were extremely disillusioned. They had marched off to war full of idealism, believing in the cause of freedom and having faith in those who led them. But the bloody battles at places like the Somme, Verdun and Vimy Ridge, had showed them another side of war—its futility, waste and destruction. They had watched their friends die in vain as foolish British generals insisted on sending the men "over the top" into a no man's land where they were met by tangled barbed wire and relentless machine gun fire. Their Russian allies had deserted them when the Bolsheviks finally took power in October 1917, convincing the majority of them that Reds and revolutionaries were not to be trusted—not ever. Then, they had returned to Canada where foreigners and women had taken their jobs. They were frustrated, anxious and angry about the future.

During the past few months, there had been several confrontations between the soldiers' groups and anyone they felt was being disloyal. That included most unions, Socialist Party members and certainly anyone connected to Ukrainian, Jewish or "alien" organizations no matter what their political affiliation. "We'll enforce democracy here the same way we did in France," one soldier told a *Free Press* reporter. And they did. There were scuffles at Market Square when labour leaders attempted to speak in public and in one especially nasty incident a group of soldiers invaded the Socialist Party headquarters on

Smith Street, ransacked the second floor office and threw files and papers on to the street along with a piano. The men paid unannounced visits to factories or companies employing "alien" workers and threatened to destroy the places if the foreigners were not fired.

By the time McCreary and Hannah reached the front door of the station a full-scale riot had erupted on Rupert Avenue. One of the soldiers had thrown a bottle that hit a woman in the labour group on the side of the head. She fell senseless to the ground. A few of the Socialist Party men charged the soldiers. The veterans responded with their fists and swung wooden batons that several of them had brought. At least two workers were cut open.

"Get more men out there," MacPherson ordered.

Within ten minutes or so, twenty constables had separated the groups but not before they too had used their billy clubs on more than a few of the participants.

"Arrest him," said MacPherson, pointing to the soldiers' leader, Jack Scott. "And him too."

"What did I do?" asked the man. He wore navy blue overalls, scuffed black boots and a tweed flat cap on his head. His hands were so dirty that the skin had a permanent blackish tone.

"What's your name?" asked MacPherson.

"Joseph Zalusky," he replied. His accent wasn't thick, but it was noticeable.

"I saw you charge the men on the other side of the street. You started this fight."

"He threw that bottle at my friend," Zalusky protested, pointing his finger at Scott.

"You're a bloody liar," shouted Scott.

"Get him out of here," MacPherson told one of his constables

"You protecting them over us now, Chief?" asked Scott. "Where's your loyalty? What kind of man are you?"

"Lock him up," MacPherson repeated.

With some help from her friends, the injured woman got to her feet. She held a white cloth to the side of her head. "Joseph was just trying to help me. He didn't mean any harm."

"You look familiar, Ma'am. What's your name?" asked MacPherson.

At that moment, McCreary and Hannah arrived. "Rivka," McCreary said to the woman, "You okay?" he asked. "This is Klein's sister, Rivka."

"I should've known," said the Chief. "This is no place for a woman, Miss Klein."

"Metro Lizowski's a friend of mine. He couldn't have done anything wrong. Certainly not kill someone."

"How did you know about that?" MacPherson asked. "We just brought him in for questioning."

"Bad news travels fast in the North End."

"Well, Miss Klein, you go get your wound tended to and leave the police business to us."

"What about Joseph?"

"He might've had a good reason to go charging across the street, but that's up to a judge to decide." At that, the constable holding Zalusky took him into the station.

Rivka marched up to the chief. "This is only the beginning. The working people of this city have rights and sooner or later the bourgeoisie will understand that we mean business."

MacPherson glanced at McCreary and Hannah. "Either of you know what she's talking about?"

"I'd say, Chief," Hannah said slowly, "that we'd better prepare ourselves for more trouble. This strike is a long way from being over."

"Rivka, what happened to you?" asked Sarah opening the door to the apartment. She gave Rivka a hug. "The bandage? My God?"

"It's nothing. Don't worry. I had an accident at the police station earlier."

"You were there, this afternoon, during the fight with the soldiers?"

"What's all the shouting about? You'll wake up the girls," said Klein. "Rivka, what are you doing here?"

"Shailek, I have to talk to you."

Sarah took Rivka's jacket and they moved into the kitchen.

"We'll have to speak softly. I think Bernice is still awake and if she hears your voice, she'll never get to sleep. Now sit down, and I'll make some tea."

Klein lit a cigarette and planted himself on a chair by the open window.

"Shailek, is it true what I hear?"

"And that is?"

"That you're working for Deacon at Manitoba Bridge. Helping strike-breakers? How could you do that? Protecting scabs?"

Klein was silent for a moment. He had been dreading this conversation. Now, seeing his sister with a bloody bandage made things even worse. "I have to feed my family. It's as simple as that."

"Nothing is as simple as that and you know it. Selling yourself to the Devil. What would Mama, *ala-vashulem*, say if she was alive?"

"She'd say that a man has to do whatever he can to provide for his family."

"And work for the rich like a servant? I don't think so. Not today, not ever."

Klein sighed. "And what do you think this strike is going to accomplish, Rivka? You think men like Deacon, Lyall, Godfrey, Botterell and all the others are simply going to allow the unions to take over the city? Have you any idea who you're up against? You and your comrades. Christ, Rivka, they've called in the bloody army. This isn't Moscow, you know."

"Enough, Shailek," said Sarah, placing a cup of tea before him. "Can't you see she's had a terrible day."

"I doubt you'll help that Red Lizowski by protesting outside of the station. From what I hear, he's in a lot of trouble."

"That…that's really what I wanted to speak with you about, Shailek. About Metro Lizowski."

Sarah stared at Rivka for a moment. "Oh Rivka, go on, it'll be fine."

Klein stared first at his wife, then his sister. "What'll be fine? What's she talking about? Is there something I don't know?"

"There's lots you don't know," said Sarah. "That's your problem."

"Mama, mama." The cry was from the girl's bedroom down the hall.

"A minute, Neicee," yelled Sarah.

"Let me go to her," said Rivka.

"No, I'll do it. You had better tell him, Rivka."

Klein broke off a piece of sugar from the bowl on the table, slipped it between his teeth and sipped his tea.

"I need your help," said Rivka, after a moment's hesitation.

"Why? They didn't arrest you, did they? I asked McCreary…"

"No nothing like that. If you'll let me finish. I want you to help Metro Lizowski. Or rather, the party wants you to. They can pay you fifteen dollars a day."

"I see. I don't know if there's much I can do, Rivka. Simon's secretary says that Lizowski was in the office and had an argument with Simon. Then she saw him later that afternoon outside near Simon's car. You and your friends will be wasting your money."

"He didn't do it. I know he didn't. He wasn't there."

"How do you know? And why do you care so much?"

"I care, isn't that enough. We're comrades."

"Comrades?" Klein shook his head. "What *narishkeit.*"

"It's not nonsense. We believe that people were not meant to be exploited by the wealthy."

"Stop, Rivka. When you start with that Marxist drek my stomach hurts."

"I didn't come here to argue with you. I know you'll never see things my way. All I know is that Metro's innocent."

"And I ask you again. How do you know?"

"Because….because he was with me at my apartment at five o'clock. He couldn't have killed Simon."

"At your apartment?" Klein stared at his sister for a moment. "You and Lizowski? Jesus, Rivka, the man's married. He's got a family. And he's a *shaigetz.*"

"Save the lecture, Shailek. Remember, I never worked in a whorehouse."

Klein nodded slowly. "How long?"

"How long have we been seeing each other? A few months. What difference does it make? Two days ago at five o'clock he was with me. He was fine. His clothes were not messed up. There wasn't a mark on him. I'm telling you, Shailek, he didn't kill anyone. Not then, not ever."

Klein sipped his tea and lit another cigarette as Sarah walked back into the kitchen.

"You knew and didn't tell me," said Klein to his wife.

"Rivka just told me two weeks ago and she asked me to keep it a secret."

"From me?"

"From everyone," Rivka interrupted. "Now will you help?" She looked at her brother. Tears were swelling in her eyes.

Klein blew smoke to the ceiling. "You care about the man that much? What do you think? He'll leave his wife for you?"

"That doesn't matter."

"Even if he was with you at five that day, it doesn't mean he couldn't have done it. You know that don't you?"

"He didn't do it, Shailek. Just go ask some questions. You'll see what I'm saying is true."

Klein stubbed his cigarette into the ashtray. "I suppose the Socialists can't pay more money for this?"

"Shailek, honest to God," said Sarah.

"A joke," said Klein. "Okay, Rivka. I'll speak with McCreary tomorrow about the case. And I'll tell Deacon that I can't start for him yet. Not that I want to join the revolutionaries, but if you say the man was with you, then probably he's innocent." He nodded to himself. "And I guess I'll have to find the real murderer before this whole city explodes."

6

MAY 20, 1919, WINNIPEG

To: A.B. Perry, Commissioner
Royal North-West Mounted Police Headquarters
Regina

From: Agent No. 12

Sir:

The recent sight of milk and bread delivery wagons on city streets marked with a large sign: "PERMITTED BY AUTHORITY OF STRIKE COMMITTEE" has confirmed my view that the Trades and Labour Council has transformed itself into a Bolshevki style Soviet with the aim of establishing the dictatorship of the proletariat. They have even issued their own newspaper of late under the editorship of William Ivens, a pacifist and social gospeller. The Council has also "permitted" the following to remain open or on the job: Hospitals, theatres, pictures shows, and police. Although the police may walk off yet. The recent altercation at the Rupert Avenue Station between the revolutionaries and soldiers left a bad taste in the mouths of many policemen, I have been told. The general consensus among the constables is that the city owes them better wages and they aim to take advantage of the current labour situation to make their demands.

The RNWMP contingent on its way from Ottawa is very much needed. I suspect that more trouble on the streets will be forthcoming.

My conversations with General Ketchen have been amicable and we seem to agree that peace and order must be maintained at all costs. Both of us agreed that the provincial and civic authorities are incapable of dealing adequately with the possible consequences of this strike. They are unprepared for the armed revolution that may follow. And the dispatch of the Lewis guns you mentioned in your last memorandum should be expedited. I suspect we will need them sooner than later.

As for the Citizens Committee of 1000, they have shown a remarkable display of civic responsibility. Volunteers are manning fire stations and working at gas stations—this includes several women. The leadership of the committee is in the hands of some prominent businessmen, including Tom Deacon and J.E. Botterell of the Grain Exchange. Bill Simon would have been, of course, a source of great strength and his murder is deeply regretted by all. George Runciman has taken his place on the committee.

SIMON INVESTIGATION: The police have the murderer in custody, a Red named Metro Lizowski, a Galician. Certainly he could be tried for murder as well as sedition. Graham Powers, a well-known lawyer whom I believe you know, has been directed by the committee to oversee any legal issues. He has had daily discussions with Chief MacPherson and the Attorney-General. I believe that his trial may be delayed until the labour difficulties have ended. The Socialists have hired a private detective, a Hebrew by the name of Klein, to undertake their own investigation of the case. He will find nothing of substance, as there is nothing to find. But I am watching this development personally.

KLEIN HAD TO ADMIT he was getting nowhere with his investigation. Maybe Lizowski was guilty, as the police had charged. He had been digging around the city for nearly a week and had turned up nothing that could help his client. What he had learned about Lizowski did not impress him. The man was mixed up in every labour dispute and agitation in Winnipeg going back to the Street Railway strike of '06. He had been thrown in jail for disrupting the peace at least a dozen times. From what Klein could gather, this Galician was narrow-minded, convinced that socialism was a panacea for all the world's evils and would argue with anyone who thought otherwise. Even more problematic was that Lizowski was famous for his nasty temper. "That man would blow up at the drop of a pin," one former vice-president of the Socialist Party had told him. And he wasn't the only one. What Rivka saw in him, Klein had no idea. Still, his sister was as loyal and as resourceful as he was—which is why he was standing at this hour of the morning at the entrance to a grand house on Wellington Crescent.

Two days ago, Rivka had paid a visit to the same residence on the tree-lined boulevard, home to the city's elite. This was Committee of 1000 territory and no place for a socialist. Yet Rivka had been desperate. No lawyer in the city was willing to take Lizowski's case. He had been declared 'untouchable' by the Committee and every lawyer she or the party executive had approached—whether they were members of the Committee or not—had turned them down. Word on the street was that the authorities were soon going to charge Lizowski with treason and sedition as well as murder. Running out of time and options, Rivka had no one else to turn to but Alfred Powers.

Once a leading light of the Winnipeg establishment, Powers had more or less retired as a practising lawyer several years ago, about the time the war started. He still oversaw some property arrangements and occasionally sat in on complicated financial negotiations, but for all intents and purposes he left everything else to his son Graham. It had taken the elder Powers a long time to recover from the tragic events of 1914 when he had lost his second wife Emily. Eventually he had forgiven her for betraying him, yet the pain had never entirely disappeared. Then just last October another tragedy: his daughter Elizabeth had died, a victim like so many others of the influenza epidemic that had torn the heart out of the city and country. There was not a family in Winnipeg who did not lose someone from the flu of 1918.

Klein walked up the wide pathway and past a white McLaughlin-Buick with leather seats and turquoise spoked wheels. Klein stopped for a moment to admire the workmanship.

"She's a beauty, isn't she Sam?"

"Alfred," said Klein extending his right hand. "It's been too long."

Alfred Powers still had a firm handshake to go along with his soldier-like bearing and full head of hair. But the hair was completely gray now and his eyes had a permanent sadness lurking behind their bright intelligence.

"I just got her a month ago," said Powers, rubbing the silver headlamp. "The factory in Oshawa built it on a special order."

"Must have cost a pretty penny, Alfred."

"Can't take it to the grave, Sam. By the way, I saw Rivka the other day, but I'm sure you know that. In fact, I'd wager that's what this unexpected visit is all about."

Klein looked around. "Can we talk for a moment? Privately?"

"Let's go in the back yard on the patio. I'll have Ethel bring us some iced tea, unless you want something stronger."

"I thought that was illegal."

Powers laughed. "Damn nonsense is what it is. The Americans will learn that soon enough. They have no idea what they've gotten themselves into with that Eighteenth Amendment. My doctor prescribes a quart of good Scotch whiskey a week for this ache in my back. You sure you don't want a taste?"

"No thanks, Alfred. Too early in the day for me."

Powers led Klein through a thatched walkway to the back of the house that looked out on to the Assiniboine River. Several neighbourhood children were swimming. The Powers yard was abloom with daffodils, tulips and lilacs.

"Tell me, how's Sarah and those beautiful daughters of yours?"

"Sarah's fine. She's expecting, probably around middle of November. And the girls are growing every day. Bernice is a real handful and Freda's more like her mother everyday."

"Maybe it'll be a son this time, Sam. Nothing better, you know."

The two men settled into wicker chairs under a sprawling cottonwood. Powers's expression turned sombre. "I hear there's a big rally this afternoon in Victoria Park. Are you going?"

"Not sure yet. Depends on the rest of the day. What do you think, Alfred? Is there a way to solve this mess?"

Powers shook his head. "I don't know. Graham tried to recruit me for the Committee but I refused. I can't stomach some of those men and between you and me Bill Simon was the worst of them. An arrogant bastard. He had some strange ideas about right and wrong, spouting all of this nonsense about 'survival of the fittest'. God knows what the hell he was talking about half the time."

"Is that why you agreed to represent Lizowski? I'm guessing Graham wasn't too happy to hear about it."

Powers laughed. "That, my Hebrew friend, is putting it mildly. If he could, I suspect he'd disown me right now. Says I am a traitor to the 'cause'. Defending a Red for murder. Poppycock! Everyone deserves a fair defence. They'll railroad Lizowski if they can. He's headed right to the gallows unless I can prove some reasonable doubt. He still might hang, but at least he'll go down fighting. Besides, your sister is awfully hard to refuse."

"You're telling me. You think I wanted this case?"

Powers's maid set down a tray with two glasses of ice-tea. "Here Sam, drink up and try one of these," he said, holding out a box of cigars.

"Egyptians?"

"The only kind I smoke, you know that."

"Alfred, did Rivka tell you, um...?"

"That she and Lizowski were more than friends? Yes she did. But so far Lizowski refuses to use her as an alibi and won't let her come forward. Says it'll hurt Rivka's reputation and probably kill his wife."

"It'll kill his wife more to see him hanging from a rope."

"Quite. I think he'll eventually come to see that he has no choice. Look, I know the Party has you on a retainer. But we need to work together on this. You don't need to report everything back to them. I'm not at all sure who we can trust these days."

Klein nodded his head in agreement.

"Good. There's two people I think you should investigate and one should be easier than the other. First, the secretary, Gertie Viola. She says Lizowski was at the car and he says he wasn't."

Klein was glad to see Powers shared his suspicions about Gertie. "And the second thing?"

"This could be more difficult. Lizowski claims that when he and Simon had their argument earlier in the day, there was another man in the office. He and Lizowski got into a scuffle."

"Who was he?"

"I don't know. All Lizowski says is that he was big, more than six feet tall, had big hands, a moustache, and Simon called him John. Have a word with a few of the managers at Simon's factory. Maybe, they can tell you who he was. So far the only person who's actually mentioned this guy is Lizowski. McCreary says it's a good story but that's it. You might want to speak with George Runciman, Simon's foreman. He's a decent person. Or the secretary, she'll know—if there's anything to know, that is."

"And if she talks."

"I thought you had charm with the ladies. That's what Emily used to say."

Klein grinned. Most of the women he had known in his life had been whores. As long as he had money in his pocket, whores had been easy enough to charm. "I'd like to talk to Lizowski. You think you can arrange that?"

"May be difficult, especially during the strike. All this nonsense about the city being taken over by the Reds. Preposterous! If those bone-headed executives like Deacon and the Barretts would only offer their employees some incentive to work, recognize their right to form unions and improve their working conditions, the strike would be over by this afternoon. I guarantee it. Instead, they've called in the army and the Mounties. Just what we need here, the federal government telling us how to run the city."

"You sound kind of ornery, Alfred."

"Old age, I'm afraid. It'll happen to you one day soon, Sam."

Klein butted his cigar in a glass ashtray on the table and gulped his ice-tea.

"Check back with me later this evening," said Powers standing up, "and I'll let you know when you can speak to Lizowski."

By the time Klein arrived at Victoria Park, a crowd of several thousand had assembled. It was an impressive display of labour solidarity. Many of the people held signs. "Down With The Profiteers—Up With The People," was printed on one. "Britons Never Shall Be Slaves," declared another. Everyone was dressed in their Sunday best—the men in suits, ties, and fedoras and the women in tasteful embroidered blue, rose, green and white dresses and bonnets or wearing the latest fashion, narrow-brimmed summer hats. At least a dozen constables were also present, no doubt, Klein thought, to stop any trouble with the Loyalists, as the anti-strike veterans were now calling themselves. Klein looked out on to the mass of people, searching for Rivka.

On the platform at the front of the gathering stood a short, stout man. Despite his suit and tie, he appeared uncomfortable and dishevelled. Klein recognized him at once as Roger Bray, one of the war veterans who supported the strike. Holding the Union Jack hoisted high on a pole, he was shouting loud enough for Klein to hear.

"The Norris government has spoken," said Bray. "They're not with the people. They've chosen to take the side of the Citizen's Committee. Will we stand for that?"

"No," yelled the crowd.

"That's right," continued Bray. "I stand for veterans of the Great War who believe in this righteous cause. We will never concede victory. Never."

Again the crowd cheered.

The next speaker was George Armstrong, a big man and a better speaker than Bray. Armstrong, a carpenter, had been living in Winnipeg since 1905 with his wife Helen, a labour organizer, and their three young daughters. He quickly moved up the ranks of his union, the United Brotherhood of Carpenters and Joiners Local 343 and was eventually elected to the Trades and Labour Council. Armstrong was also a loyal member of the Socialist Party and no one could ever accuse of him beating around the bush.

"There is only one solution," he told the workers in the audience.

"Tell us George," they cried, knowing exactly what he was going to say. They had heard it many times at Armstrong's regular lectures at Market Square.

"The end of the capitalist system, that's what it is," Armstrong said, his voice rising. "What we're out for is the downfall of capitalism and the institution of a new order of society: socialism. Most of the members of the Committee make more in a day than you and I will make in a year. Is that justice? Is that fair?"

"No, no," the crowd shouted.

"The greater the wealth in capitalist society, the larger is the percentage of its population in absolute poverty. By our actions this week we have declared to the world that we will no longer be wage slaves to the wealthy of this country. We must stand together against the interests of property and money!"

Cheers echoed throughout the park. Many of those in attendance may not have shared Armstrong's Marxist views, yet in the excitement of the gathering, they were swept away by his passion and his principles.

Finally Klein spotted his sister on the other side of the park. She was standing with a group of Jewish women from the garment trade. He tried waving to her, but it was pointless. He would have to make his way through the massed crowd. He started to move, pushing against the sweating bodies, when he felt something hard and sharp poking into his back.

"Don't move, Klein," said the voice, "Don't even think of turning around or I'll drive this knife right through your back and into your gut."

Klein stopped. No one in his vicinity paid much attention to him as Bob Russell mounted the platform to rolling cheers. There was no room for him to spin around and disarm his assailant, let alone run.

"All right," Klein said quietly. "It's a little warm out here. Let's make this quick."

"Forget about Lizowski. Let things be. I wouldn't want to hurt one of those little girls of yours."

Klein started, but the man jabbed the knife with more force. Klein spoke through clenched teeth. "If you so much as come near my family, I'll…"

The man laughed. "You'll do nothing, Jew. Now have I made myself clear?"

Klein flinched at the pain. "Yeah, very clear."

At that moment, a bald man with a wide smile, moved through the crowd towards Klein. "Sam, is that you? I knew I'd find you here."

Klein didn't always look forward to seeing John Maloney, a sensationalist reporter. But on this occasion, his timing was perfect. Klein felt the man behind him shift away. With that, Klein deftly spun around and elbowed his assailant hard in the face. The man fell back into a group of men standing nearby.

"Maloney, grab him quick." Maloney did as he was told but was met by a punch to the jaw. His legs buckled and he fell to his knees. Klein tried to grab the man again, but he stood up and started pushing people aside. Klein was trapped, but he got a good look at his attacker. He was a large man with a thick neck and an even thicker moustache. Klein would remember that face. Three constables were converging on the scene of the commotion and Klein was in no mood for a chat with the police. Besides, he was certain they'd never believe him. He pulled Maloney up to his feet.

"Come on, we're leaving now."

"Hey, Sam. I got a job to do. What's going on?"

"Now, Maloney. Hurry up."

Just as the constables were nearly on top of them, a great roar erupted from the crowd as Bob Russell finished his speech with the words, "Workers of the world unite!" People started cheering and throwing their hats in the air, blocking the police from reaching Klein. He and Maloney soon reached the far side of the park and the constables were nowhere in sight.

"Christ on a stick, will you tell me what's going on, Klein?" demanded Maloney, out of breath. "That guy could've killed me."

"Maloney, you saved me again. It's getting to be a bad habit. Here sit down," said Klein, leading his friend to a park bench. "You okay?"

"I'll survive," he said, rubbing his jaw. "It's not broken. You're trouble, anyone ever tell you that?"

"Yeah. Part of the job, I guess. Now what are you doing in Winnipeg? The last I heard you got a job with the *Star* in Toronto."

"I'm still writing for them. They sent me back here to cover the strike. What a story."

Klein nodded. "And Leila and the kids?"

"She's fine. She's managed to keep her job in the theatre and look after Charlie and Paul at the same time."

"Still as beautiful as ever?"

"Of course. And Sarah?"

"Expecting our third."

"Klein, you never cease to amaze me. Give her my regards. Now," he said, pulling out a notepad, "are you going to tell me what that was about?"

"Maloney, put that damned thing away and we'll talk."

Klein proceeded to relate the story of Simon's murder, Lizowski's arrest—omitting Rivka's involvement—the testimony of Gertie Viola and the alleged man in the office.

"You think that lout was the guy you're after?" asked Maloney.

"Don't know. But if you're interested, you can snoop around the station to see what you can find out."

"Oh, I'll bet MacPherson will be glad to see me. I have to wire a story about this rally. I hear the Loyalists are planning a parade for tomorrow and the Premier is supposed to be making some kind of announcement. Today's leader in the *Star* came out in favour of the strikers. My boss doesn't think there's a Bolshevik revolution going on here. Mind you, what I just heard…"

"They're just getting the crowd excited. Norris has no idea what he's doing and Charlie Gray will go along with whatever the Citizens Committee tells him."

"Can I quote you on that, Klein?"

"No, but you watch how this situation will get worse, a lot worse, before it gets better. You remember that riot back in '11 on Selkirk Avenue?"

Maloney grimaced. "Are you ever going to let me forget that?"

"Maybe when you turn sixty-five, Maloney, but not before. Hell, if it wasn't for you, I'd probably be still minding the store at Melinda's."

"The store?" Maloney laughed. "Hey, that's my kind of shopping. Say hello to the girls next time."

"They'll really be thrilled to see you."

"I'm glad you haven't lost your sense of humour, Klein. How about if we talk tomorrow evening and I'll ask around about this guy who jumped you. I got a hunch about him. But let me look into it."

7

"SEEMS TO ME," declared Hiram Maxwells, chewing on a cigar, "and mind you this is only my opinion, that the government may have chosen the wrong man to represent us."

Several men around the large table nodded their heads. The smoke in the room of the Winnipeg Board of Trade building, the headquarters of the Committee of 1000, was already thick and the executive meeting had only started thirty minutes earlier.

"What do you mean by that?" demanded Tom Deacon. "Why don't you just tell us what's on your mind?"

Deacon had known Hiram Maxwells, the president of the Real Estate Exchange for many years. And while they had done business together—Deacon himself had invested in several parcels of property on the outskirts of the eastern part of the city—he had always found him boorishly irritating.

"All right, Tom. Have it your way. There's no need to be coy in this room," Maxwells said, glancing at the dozen other men seated around the table. "I want to know how any of us can have faith in Graham Powers to represent our interests with the government in Ottawa when his father has decided to defend the Red who killed Bill Simon."

Everyone in the room began talking loudly all at once. Sitting to Maxwells's right, Graham Powers shook his head in disbelief. "Will someone pass that decanter, please," he said. "I need a bloody drink."

"I think I'll join you," said George Runciman, who was seated across the table from him.

"Enough, gentlemen," Deacon finally said after a few moments. "Hiram, you're point is taken, but I think I speak for a majority on this committee when I say that you're a fool."

"There's no need to be insulting, after all…"

"Yes I think there is," continued Deacon. "Everyone in this room knows and respects Graham Powers and if Prime Minister Meighen and Robertson have decided that Graham should be reporting to them, that's good enough for me."

"Hear, hear," a few men said.

"Can I say something?" asked Graham Powers.

"By all means," said Deacon.

"Hiram," Powers said, looking in Maxwells's direction. "I assure you my interests in this matter are the same as yours. I want nothing but to see the end of these cursed labour difficulties. And to be perfectly honest, I'm not happy with my father's decision to involve himself with Lizowski, but as those of you who know my father…well, there's not much I can do about it once he has made up his mind. I'm afraid we'll have to make the best of this."

"That satisfy you, Hiram?" asked Deacon.

"Of course. Graham, I was only thinking of the Committee."

Powers nodded. As an experienced lawyer, he knew when to get mad and when to stay calm. "No offence taken." He turned to Deacon. "Tom, if there are no further objections, I'd like to continue with my report."

"By all means, unless anyone else has something to add?"

The room remained silent, as Deacon motioned to Powers.

"I've been appointed a special deputy of the Justice Department and have been instructed to investigate whether or not the activities of the strike leaders are of a seditious or treasonous character. And then to recommend appropriate action."

"Excellent," remarked John Botterell. "If you need any assistance, I know at least four managers at the Exchange who would be willing to help you."

"I quite agree," said Hugh Lyall. "Put the bastards on trial and send them to Stony Mountain for the rest of their lives. Traitors are what they are, living in this country and starting all of this trouble. I mean look at those signs on the milk wagon—'Permitted by authority of the strike committee'. Who do they think they are? The bloody government? It's just more proof that their real aim is to establish a Bolsheviki regime in this country. Anyone could see that…"

"That's not what today's *Toronto Star* says," interrupted Maxwells. He pulled out a long telegram. "Listen to this editorial, wired to me by brother. 'It is becoming more and more clear that the issue is not Bolshevism or any attempt to usurp the government of Canada, but a dispute between employers and employed on the question of wages, hours, recognition of unions…'"

"Stop Hiram, please," said Graham. "I don't care what that Liberal rag has to say. I assure you that if the socialists were marching down Yonge Street, that paper would be writing something a little different."

"Agreed. Now, Graham is there anything more in your report?" asked Deacon.

Graham shuffled his papers for a moment. There was something else he might relate to the Committee executive, but he had been asked by Prime Minister Arthur Meighen as well as the RNWMP Commissioner to keep the actions and activities of Mountie operatives private for the time being. "No. I'm done. I'm meeting with Meighen in a few days in Fort William and will have more to report at that time."

"Fine," said Deacon. "Hugh, do you have the new edition of the *Citizen* ready for us to have a look at?"

"I do indeed," said Lyall, a long-time member of the Winnipeg Board of Trade. He opened his black leather briefcase and pulled out a four-sided broadsheet. Ever since the strike committee had launched its own newspaper, the *Strike Bulletin of the Western Labor News*, the Committee of 1000 had been pressured to release its own sheet. "I decided to focus the main story on the issue of collective bargaining as we discussed at the last meeting."

"Why not just read us the beginning of the story?" suggested Deacon.

Lyall stood up. "Nothing like the *Star*, I promise. Here is it is, then. 'The one big issue is NOT shall trades form union. It is NOT collective bargaining. BUT—is every individual dispute between employer and employee to continue to disrupt the life of the whole community.' And it goes on in much the same vein."

A few men around the table clapped. "I think," said Deacon, "that we should distribute as many copies of the paper as possible. Let's raise some money for ads in the *Free Press* and the *Telegram* too."

"And the *Trib*," said Lyall, "It's good to see that all three of the papers have managed to get their editions out again. We should keep advertising as much as we can. Keep our message before the people. In any event, I have a long list of volunteers, starting with my niece Susan and several of her friends to ensure the *Citizen* is on the streets by noon tomorrow."

"I don't know about you, gentlemen," said Deacon, "but the way in which the young women of this city have conducted themselves during the past week, working the gas pumps, distributing newspapers, helping with fire patrol...most impressive, I'd say. And as you all know, I didn't vote for the Norris government or their women's suffrage platform."

Several of the men laughed. "Times change," added John Botterell. "You can't be left behind."

A knock on the door interrupted the conversation. Deacon walked over to the door and opened it. "General, glad you could join us. Come right in." Brigadier-General Herbert Ketchen, in full uniform, his thick black moustache drooping, marched into the room.

"Gentlemen, if I could have your attention," announced Deacon. "I have invited Brigadier Ketchen here today to brief us on what we might expect from the military during the next few days until the strike has ended. Brigadier, please."

Ketchen stood tall and erect at the front of the table, his hands clasped behind his back. "Good afternoon. As you may know, my plans for the security of the city have been proceeding, and, thanks to your assistance, I have now assembled approximately six thousand able bodied men who have volunteered for service. Each group of two or three thousand have trained for approximately a week thus far. The men are aware they might be called up on a moment's notice, depending on the circumstances in the city. I have also spoken to Mayor Gray about the need for more policemen and he has taken my suggestions under advisement. I believe that if the problems at the police department are not resolved satisfactorily in the next forty-eight hours, veteran volunteers will be asked to join a special police squad."

"Are you anticipating more violence, General?" asked Hugh Lyall.

"I hope not, Mr. Lyall, but as an officer in his Majesty's service, preparation is essential." He paused to check his pocket watch. "I can now report to you gentlemen that within the hour, several crates will arrive by railway containing a total of twenty Lewis machine guns."

There was a murmur around the table. "Is that necessary?" asked Botterell.

"Of course it is, John," said Deacon. "This is war, my friends. Don't forget it."

"I agree with Mr. Deacon," added Ketchen. "The trouble in the city is far from over. As you well know, any efforts at mediating the strike have thus far failed. It is unfortunate that Bill Simon was not successful…"

"Successful with what?" asked Lyall.

"Yes, please tell us," added Botterell. "Tom, do you know what he is speaking of."

The General shifted uncomfortably. "My apologies, Mr. Deacon, I assumed everyone knew."

"Knew what?" repeated Lyall.

George Runciman got to his feet. "Please allow me to explain. As you all know, Bill was a man who liked to do things his own way. Shortly before the strike began he offered Metro Lizowski a fair amount of money to call it off, I think about fifty thousand dollars, is that right, Graham?"

"That's what he wired me, while I was still in Ottawa," said Powers. "To be honest, I told him that I thought he had lost his mind."

"In any event," continued Runciman, "Lizowski turned him down, but they did have an argument. And well, you all know the result of that."

"Here I thought that damned Red was just getting even," said Lyall, "and all along there's more to this story. Maybe Lizowski wanted more money."

"Yeah, right," said Botterell, "a Bosheviki who wants to be a capitalist."

A few of the men chuckled.

"I should've figured Bill would try to be the hero," said Lyall.

"I believe that was his intention," said Runciman. "No one loved this city more."

"Or himself," added Lyall.

"No reason to talk ill of the departed," said Deacon. "Bill Simon was a strong personality, I'll grant you that. He had some strange ideas about the future. But he did mean well. And who's to say that his approach with the strikers was wrong. Isn't that right, George?"

Runciman smiled and nodded. If they only knew the truth about his former boss, he thought, they might not be so complimentary with their comments. Still, there was no point worrying about that now. Simon was gone and the world was better off for it, even if the men of the Committee of 1000 did not truly appreciate that fact. Lizowski would pay for his crimes and everything would unfold, as it should.

What Klein really felt like was a pint of beer. Two days after the knife incident at the park, he was no closer to proving Lizowski's innocence. The more he learned about the man, the less sure he was that the damned fool hadn't killed Simon.

He had had a long day. He had walked up and down Main Street, but all anyone wanted to talk about was the strike. No one cared much about Bill Simon and Metro Lizowski. A few of Klein's regular sources—One-armed Eddie at the Brunswick Hotel, the doorman at the Royal Alex, a street whore by the name of Lizzie—had much the same thing to tell him: that he was probably wasting his time; Lizowski was guilty of the murder and he was in trouble. According to Eddie, Lizowski had more enemies on the Trades and Labour Council than he did on the Committee of 1000.

"The way I heard it," he told Klein over coffee at one of the few restaurants open on Main Street, "was that half the Brits on Council hate him for being too radical and the rest just hate him cause he's a Galician."

Later in the day, Klein had found Tom Deacon at the Board of Trade Building. He had put that meeting off as long as he could. Needless to say, when he finally informed Deacon that he would be unavailable since he was working on the Lizowski case, the former mayor was furious. "Go ahead, waste your time, Klein," he had told him. "That Red will hang and you'll be ruined. Who's going to hire you from the business community after this?"

Klein had dismissed the threat, but he had to admit it was not an angle he had given much thought to. He had never been overly concerned about politics, certainly not to the same extent as Rivka. In Klein's view, the world was as it was. If the price of freedom in Canada was poverty for some and enormous wealth for others, he could live with that. Besides, what he most liked about this country was that anyone could make a buck if he tried hard enough. Look at Israel Abrahamovitch who grew up three doors down on Flora Avenue. Now he calls himself Izzy Brahms and the last Klein heard was that he was the proprietor of a dozen Maritime newspapers. They were now calling him a "tycoon." There was hope for himself yet, Klein thought, although the only tycoon detective he had ever heard of was Pinkerton.

Still, maybe Rivka had a point. There wasn't much doubt that all of those factory workers who toiled for the big bosses were entitled to a better wage and decent working conditions. He doubted, however, that unions were the answer. He figured that one day, given the right opportunity, they would become as domineering as the greedy capitalists they were challenging. In his opinion, Rivka was foolish for thinking otherwise, but she would have to learn that for herself. She was even more stubborn than their mother had been.

As for his losing work or being unpopular with the wealthy, he was confident that once the strike was over and things got back to normal his services would again be required. A woman trying to find out about her cheating husband or a man who wants to know if his partner is crooked, does not much care whom their detective voted for in the last election. It was results they were after, and Klein had a reputation for getting results. Which was the main reason Klein felt like a beer. He wasn't used to being stymied. He decided that after his last interview, he would go home, have a few drinks and just think about the case. Maybe he was doing too much running around and not enough thinking.

Klein had told Sarah that he would be home for dinner by eight o'clock and she should go ahead and feed the children first. Sarah had promised to make his mother's roast chicken recipe, one of Klein's favourite dishes. And maybe this time, she would be successful. Burned meals, along with sexless nights, were becoming more and more common as Sarah's pregnancy continued.

As he walked past Broadway Avenue and headed for the Osborne Street Bridge, he could see a large group of men on horseback conducting training exercises in the barracks field. Some had their batons out, while others were holding rifles. Klein knew that Mayor Gray was serious when he had said, "Law and order must be maintained at any cost." The mayor might have had a reputation for being a fair man, but the longer the strike went on, Klein thought that sooner or later he would turn against the strikers and there would be real trouble for sure. If he let Ketchen send those men on horseback into the streets, who knew what the consequences would be.

It took a few more minutes to reach River Avenue and find the right apartment block. His earlier conversation at the police station with Gertie Viola had been nagging at him throughout the day and he hoped that maybe in her own home she would be more co-operative and revealing. Klein would merely have to be as charming as he knew he could be, especially with an older single woman.

He walked briskly up the three floors and knocked on apartment number seven. The door swung open on its own.

Klein reached into his pocket for his blackjack.

"Hello, anyone there?"

Silence. Slowly, Klein walked in. The drapes were drawn and it was dark, yet he could see that the apartment was a mess. There were clothes strewn about, and a half-eaten piece of bread rested on the kitchen table along with a cup of cold coffee. Klein peeked inside the bedroom, but Gertie Viola was nowhere to be seen. By the look of it, he thought, she must have left in a rush. He walked to the small wooden table in the living room where there was a pile of newspapers, magazines and letters pushed to one side, close to the telephone.

He pulled up a chair and was about to wade into the paper when he heard footsteps at the front door. Quickly and silently he stood, and immediately moved to his right and against the wall. He reached into his coat pocket and pulled out the blackjack. The footsteps shuffled closer to him. As the person moved forward into the living room, Klein waited patiently. Then as he saw a shoulder, he lunged forward and grabbed the intruder's left arm, twisting it behind their back.

"Hey, what's going on?" a woman's voice shouted. "Let go at once, I'm a police constable."

"Mrs. Nash?"

8

"I THINK IT'S SAFE to let go of me now, Mr. Klein," said Hannah.

Klein immediately released his grip. "Sorry," he muttered. "Hope I didn't hurt you. You can't be too careful in my line of work."

"Mine, too. Now do you want to tell me what you're doing inside Gertie Viola's apartment? I could have you arrested for breaking and entering."

Klein grinned. "You wouldn't do that would you?"

Hannah didn't answer.

"Honestly, I just wanted to speak to Miss Viola one more time. There is something about her story that doesn't sit right with me. Nothing she said. It's what she didn't say, if you understand what I'm talking about."

"Actually, I think I do, Mr. Klein."

"Please, it's Sam."

"What I was saying, Mr. Klein, was that despite what McCreary feels about Metro Lizowski, I too have not been satisfied with Miss Viola's statement."

"I thought MacPherson didn't let you out of the station house to do police work?"

"I'm off duty. On my way home. My block is only a few streets over from here"

"I see. Isn't that breaking police rules?"

A slight smile played at the edge of her mouth. "Perhaps."

"Perhaps?"

Hannah stepped back and rubbed her arm. Then she looked around the room. "I take it Miss Viola isn't here."

Klein nodded. "From the look of things, I'd say she left in an awful hurry. Didn't even bother to finish her snack," he said pointing to the food on the table. He pulled out his silver cigarette case and lit one. "You smoke?"

"No thanks, Mr. Klein. What is it you think you're doing?"

"I was about to look through that pile of paper on the desk. See what I could find out about our Miss Viola."

"I don't think so. I'll file a report on this incident and see if we can find her. Then we'll ask her about her personal belongings."

"Hannah, really. You don't mind if I call you Hannah do you? The strike has the department upside down. Half the men want to walk off the job, and the other half want to break the heads of every striker they see. They won't have time to look for a secretary who probably doesn't want to be found to begin with."

"What makes you think that? I mean about Miss Viola."

"Simple. There's no sign of a struggle anywhere. No blood. The door's not broken. So we can assume that Miss Viola left on her own free will, that she's likely scared about something or by someone and the odds are it has to do with her story to the police."

"I see. You're pretty sure of yourself, Mr. Klein, aren't you?"

"I guess I am. And please call me Sam. Mr. Klein sounds far too formal if we're going to work together on this case."

"Pardon me?"

"Let's be honest, Hannah. You need my help as much as I need yours. I used to count on McCreary to let me know what's going on, but he's not interested in this case. He's certain that he has the murderer locked up and nothing I say or do is going to make a difference."

"That's not what I hear. The story around the department is that you've solved some tough cases in your time."

Klein took a deep drag on his cigarette. "Just doing my job, that's all. But it's true that I've convinced McCreary once or twice that he might be wrong."

Hannah smiled. "I wish I could've seen that."

"Must be a real pleasure working with McCreary."

"I can handle him."

"I'm sure you can."

Hannah shrugged. "Though I'd never admit it to him, he's taugl me a lot about police work, about trusting my intuition."

"So what's your intuition tell you now?"

Hannah reached inside her handbag and pulled out a cigarette c of her own. She opened it and took one out. "I'll have that light nov

Klein quickly lit another wooden match. "You never cease to surpri me, Mrs. Nash."

"Call me Hannah."

Klein grinned. "There was someone else in the office with Simon the afternoon before he was killed and Gertie knows who it is. In fac I'd say she's running from this person."

Hannah inhaled deeply. "I agree. I'll tell you what, Sam, I'm goir to have a look in the kitchen for a few minutes. Why don't you wa here by the desk? And, of course, you know you can't look throug those papers without a warrant."

"Of course. And what about working together, sharing inforn tion?"

"Let's take this one step at time, Sam."

Klein butted his cigarette in an ashtray. "You know, you're notl like McCreary described."

Hannah laughed as she turned and walked into the other r Klein didn't take his eyes off of her until she disappeared aroun corner. Then he sat down and picked up some of Gertie ' private papers.

The Labour Temple on James Street was dark except for one r the third floor. As usual, they were all there for their nightly ass of the situation. They had been meeting like this for more thar since the strike had been called. And tonight's discussion wa ferent than the rest; The revolutionaries, or at least those who ed real change—Bob Russell, Bill Pritchard, George Armstro

Bower and a few others—were pitted against the moderates—Fred Dixon, Bill Ivens and John Queen and Abe Heaps.

"So, earlier in the day, I'm walking down Main Street toward the North End," said Bob Russell, "when I see two women from the neighbourhood, pulling each other's hair out, screaming and kicking like a pair of wild cats. I grabbed them both and tried to break it up. They're scratching and hitting each other. I ask them why they're fighting. They tell me that since they heard the workers are going to win the strike and take over the city, they had gone down to Wellington Crescent to see which of the mansions would be theirs. And sure enough, they had picked the same house."

The other men roared with laughter, everyone except Reverend Bill Ivens.

"You may enjoy yourselves gentlemen, but greed is nothing to laugh at. I was under the impression our current struggle was about creating a better world, the Kingdom of God on earth; a world in which the guiding principles are not money and profit, but justice, equality, and a square deal for every man."

"You're much too serious Comrade," said Russell.

"I wish you wouldn't refer to me like that. We're not here to overthrow the government. We're here to improve the lives of our fellow workers."

"You can think what you want Reverend," said Bill Pritchard, "but this is a revolution. This strike is about change, real change. It's about getting rid of speculators at the Exchange, grain men who fleece our farmers at every turn, managers who keep the profits of labour for themselves. It is about the defeat of the greedy and the cruel."

"Nicely put, Bill," said Russell. "Listen Ivens, you and I will never agree on everything, but let's remember that the fight is out there, with the Committee of 1000, with the army and the Mounties, not in this room. Agreed?"

"Agreed," said Ivens. Would you like to hear my hymn for tomorrow's prayer session?"

"Not now," said Dick Johns. "Bob, I'd like to get this meeting to order. I have no desire to be here all night, again."

"It won't take long," smiled Russell. "Go ahead, Bill. Let's hear it."

Ivens, dressed in a grey suit with a high white collar and black tie, stood and surveyed his friends and associates seated around the table. A few were smoking cigarettes and sipping coffee. He cleared his voice and began: "New learning, science, travel, art. Each in its sphere hath played its part. 'Tis time for change the wide world o'er; as knowledge grows from more to more. Thus, Christ, the 'Man of Galiee,' Thus Socrates, to make men free; Voiced Progress, Liberty and Right; And Truth had conquered over might…"

"Well put," said John Queen. "Fine sentiments. You should end it with that phrase you used the other day. How did it begin? "If you will stand firm…"

"If you will stand firm for a short time, we will bring them cringing on their knees to you saying: 'What shall we do to be saved?'" announced Ivens. "Yes I like that, John. Thank you. I have more work to do on it, but I think it will have the desired effect. You know since I moved to the Dominion Theatre, the Temple services have been full. Jacob, here, has been a big help."

A tall man sitting off to the side nodded. "I did nothing special," said Jacob Bower. "If we can give the strikers some hope, all the better, at least that's what I think." Unlike the other men, Bower had only recently arrived in the city from Halifax where he had been active in Maritime labour organizations. No one knew much more about him, but he had demonstrated a keen eye for detail and a commitment to labour principles that was hard to ignore. For the past week, in fact, since the strike had started, he had been assisting Bill Ivens with the Labour Temple and acting as Bob Russell's lieutenant.

"With all due respect to both of you," said Pritchard, "I don't think prayer is going to solve this."

"You'd be surprised," said Abe Heaps, "prayer can have a remarkable effect sometimes."

"Yeah, maybe for your people, Abe," said Pritchard, "you've been 'chosen,' but real collective action is what's going to change the mind of the bourgeoisie in this strike."

"I think it's still possible for city hall to solve…"

"City hall. You may be an alderman Abe, but the day that council does any good for this city—" said Pritchard.

"Gentlemen, there's nothing more I'd rather do than listen to your great philosophical debates," said Russell, "but I believe we have some work to do this evening. The story in today's *Telegram*."

"You mean the 'Yellowgram,'" said Pritchard.

"Okay, Bill, the 'Yellowgram.' The story in the paper makes it clear that we have our hands full."

"How does it feel to be called 'human rubbish' Bill?" asked Johns. "And Ivens, you're the 'half-mad preacher.'"

Ivens shook his head.

"Forget about the *Telegram*, it's not important right now," said Russell. "My meetings with the mayor, premier and representatives of the Committee of 1000 were not successful. Powers was adamant that there will be no negotiation on the collective bargaining issue until we're back at work."

"What a hard-nosed bastard," said Pritchard.

"He may well be," continued Russell, "but we'd better prepare ourselves for a long struggle. Needless to say, Powers, Gray, or Norris were not impressed with our signs on the delivery wagons. They've already told Crescent Creamery to remove them. Hell, they weren't even our idea, Carruthers came to us."

"So why are we listening to a manager?" asked Johns.

"It doesn't matter," said Pritchard, "everyone in the country knows who's in charge in Winnipeg."

"You assured him that we have no intention of taking over the city or government?" asked Ivens.

"Of course," said Russell. "I repeated it until I was blue in the face that this was no Soviet-style revolution."

"Speak for yourself," said Pritchard.

"Come on now, Bill. You can talk all you want about the evils of capitalism and reforming the system. I agree with everything you do. But we both know that overthrowing the government and replacing it with Bolsheviki rule is not going to happen in our lifetime," said Russell.

"That's not what Lenin and Trotsky said."

"This is not Russia," said Ivens. "This is a civilized British country. And it shall be today, tomorrow and for the rest of this century. You talk like that and the *Telegram* will continue to write trash about us, and they'll have every reason to. This strike is not going to change that, no matter what you think. Don't you agree, Jacob?"

Bower nodded. "I couldn't have said it better myself. Still, sometimes real action is necessary. You got to make sure the bosses know who's in charge."

"I wish Metro were here right now," said Pritchard, "he'd know what to do."

"Lizowski is trouble. Who around this table is surprised by what happened to him?" asked Fred Dixon. "He would've got us all arrested as soon as the strike started. All his talk about the 'violent overthrow of the ruling classes.' I'm sorry to say that he scared me. He scared me a lot."

Pritchard laughed. "That's the trouble with you moderates, Fred, you're scared of your own shadow. Metro was going to make things happen. None of this sitting around a table and jabbering on until two in the morning. He wanted to take this fight to the street."

"And we can still do that," said Russell, "but all in due course. Even if Gray says we can't march, we will anyway. It'll be peaceful, I guarantee that, but we'll continue to march. Hell, it's our democratic right."

"That's more like it," said Pritchard.

"Lizowski got what was coming to him," said Ivens. "He was a disgrace to this movement. Cheating on his wife with that Hebrew woman. No insult intended, Abe."

"None taken," said Heaps. "But I don't make judgments like that. As a matter of fact, I'm well acquainted with Rivka Klein and her brother Sam."

"He can't stay out of trouble," said Ivens. "Or keep his name out of the papers. An immigrant from the North End who doesn't know his proper place, that's what he is."

"Let's say he's resourceful," said Heaps. "Apart from any personal problems, Rivka is truly dedicated to our cause. She's been helping Helen with the Women's Labor League, and the two of them have arranged free meals for our people at the Strathcona Hotel. Isn't that right, George?"

"That's what Helen tells me," said Armstrong. "Although lately I only run into Helen when I crawl into bed at night."

"With Bob's approval," continued Heaps, "we're helping pay for Sam Klein to investigate Metro's case. I've already spoken to Alfred Powers, who's agreed to defend him."

A murmur of surprise swept the room. "That lying capitalist," said Bower. "He's no better than his son."

"He's Metro's best chance. And believe me Bill if you ever wound up in jail facing the gallows, you could only pray that someone like Alfred Powers would be your lawyer."

"And Metro has agreed to all of this?"

"He doesn't exactly have much choice," said Russell.

"MacPherson is ready to string him up for Simon's murder. He needs all the help he can get."

"Now there's someone we won't miss, Bill Simon. I wouldn't blame Metro if he really did slit his throat," said Bower.

"Simon is history. Forget about him," said Russell. "John, Abe and Dick, I want the three of you to come up with some fresh ideas about handling the vets. They aren't all under the spell of that Loyalist Jack Scott. I know there are a lot of decent tradesmen who want to help us win this fight. We can't ignore them. In fact, whether we win this battle or not might just hinge on convincing enough soldiers to join us."

"And what about Ketchen? I hear he's brought in some goddamn machine guns," said Pritchard.

"We don't want violence," said Russell. "So there won't be any need for the guns."

Pritchard laughed sourly. "I know your heart is in the right place Bob, but before this thing is over, blood is going to be shed. I guarantee that."

Even at this late hour, the night air was humid and hot, a bit unusual for late May. Jacob Bower had removed his jacket, but he was still sweating. "Where is that man?" he grumbled. He had been standing in the alleyway just off Bannatyne and Main behind the Imperial Bank for twenty minutes. It had been a long day of discussions and meetings and he wanted to get back to his apartment for some much-needed sleep. He didn't know how much longer he could continue with this charade. It was exhausting playing his part. Five years ago, he had joined the RNWMP with the idea of policing the West, perhaps set-tling down in a prairie town out in Alberta. Instead, he had been recruited for "special" undercover work.

It had been so simple to infiltrate their organization. Not even Russell, as astute a man as he had met, had bothered to check out his credentials. Mind you, it would have done him no good, since opera-tives in Halifax had already created a fake identity for him, complete with contacts from supposed labour leaders and a job record to match. Still, he didn't know how much more Bolsheviki talk he could stom-ach. Most of the time, he felt like lashing out and beating some of those Reds senseless. Pritchard was the worst of them, him and Metro Lizowski. Hanging was too good for them, he thought. They both should be put on the first boat to Russia. Let them spend the rest of their lives living under the Communists if they think it's so much bet-ter than the freedom of Canada.

A small flicker from a cigarette caught his attention in the darkness. "That you?" he called out.

"Yeah, it's me," said John Franklin, emerging from the alley. "Why don't you yell a little louder? Maybe they'll hear you back on James Street."

"The meeting's over, Franklin. You want to hear my report or not?"

"What do you have?"

"They're not going to quit, I can tell you that. Nothing Gray or Norris has said has made the least bit of difference. Russell says that he's going to march, no matter what the mayor says, and I believe him. You'd better have the Commissioner speak with General Ketchen."

"Anything else?"

"Yeah, I'd also put Jack Scott on your list of people to see. He's got to work harder at keeping the vets on our side."

"That shouldn't be too much trouble. He'll do anything I say as long as I keep supplying him with morphine."

"He's that bad?"

"He took a bayonet in the shoulder, poor bastard. Now, anything new about Lizowski or his case?"

"You're awful interested in that, Franklin. I thought our job was to keep an eye on the strike committee."

"I don't have time for games, Bower. What the hell do you know?"

"Hey, don't be yelling at me. There's nothing to tell. Lizowski's got Alfred Powers for a lawyer. The father of Graham Powers. And…"

"And what?"

"And they've also hired a private detective and troublemaker named Klein to do some digging around."

"Yeah, I know that already. Met one of Klein's friends today as a matter of fact. He won't be doing much talking or writing for a while."

Bower peered through the darkness. "So what did happen to Bill Simon?"

"The Bolshevik killed him. That's what happened. Just like the police think. And he's going to be punished as he should be."

Franklin threw his cigarette on the ground, turned and walked back into the darkness. Bower was a decent operative and a clever one at that. The RNWMP were lucky to have someone as talented as him working for them. Yet even Franklin felt the situation was spiraling out of control. He hadn't meant to hurt that reporter, but he had no choice in the matter. All of those questions about Simon. Certain secrets had to be protected, he had promised Bill that.

He had to admit, though, that the secretary's disappearance was troubling. He had only wanted to frighten her to keep her mouth shut. But now that she was on the run, there was no telling what she would do. Desperate people could be dangerous liabilities. It was one of the first rules he had learned as a secret agent. He had to find that woman before Klein did, in case she was ready to talk.

9

MAY 31, 1919, WINNIPEG

To: A.B. Perry, Commissioner
Royal North-West Mounted Police Headquarters
Regina

From: Agent No. 12

Sir:

I am pleased to report that both post delivery and telephone service have been restored in the city. George Watson of the Manitoba Telephones deserves much of the credit for hiring 600 new women and girls to work the telephones. However, the operators have been regulary insulted by many telephone callers. "F-----scab" seems to be the favourite expression from those who believe the women have committed a grave sin.

As per your orders, I have seen to it that Mr. Graham Powers has had access to the "Bolsheviks and Agitators" files. He is determined to bring charges of sedition and treason against several of the strike leaders. But my man inside the Labour Temple assures me that the leaders are as committed as ever to their course of action.

Another matter of concern remains the police force. Yesterday, the Police Commission gave the constables an ultimatum, a foolish act in my view.

They are required to sign a contract that states they will not under any circumstances walk off their jobs in a sympathy strike or be affiliated with any association or organization beyond the civic government. Chief MacPherson seems satisfied, but in my last meeting with General Ketchen he maintained that most police constables were ready to march along side the strikers. Threatening the men in the fashion they have done, will, I believe, accomplish nothing positive. Blame for this must be placed on Alderman Frank Fowler, who has fought with both civic firemen as well as the police. The General has already worked out a plan for the police to appoint 'special' constables, mainly Loyalist veterans, to keep the peace until the labour troubles have ended. It remains to be seen whether they can deal with this in an appropriate manner.

Finally, I continue to watch the Lizowski case closely. Nothing to report at this time, other than legal matters proceeding as anticipated. I expect Lizowski will be officially charged with the murder of Bill Simon within the week. His trial, however, may have to be delayed until after the labour problems have been settled.

"SHAILEK, YOU WANT SOME COFFEE?" There was no reply. Sarah's husband was sitting by the kitchen table and staring out the window. "Shailek," she repeated, "I'm talking to you."

At that, Klein turned to his wife. "Sorry, Sarah, I didn't hear you."

"Didn't hear me? You must be daydreaming."

"Just thinking about the case, that's all." That wasn't the whole truth, Klein thought, but that was all he was prepared to say. Since he had returned home last evening, Klein could not get the image of Hannah Nash from his head. This was both unsettling and odd. There had been no other woman in his life than Sarah since his marriage, and he expected there never would be. Apart from the normal kinds of arguments over money and family, they were happily married. Sarah was still as beautiful as the first day he had met her back in 1911. And yet, he found this woman police constable strangely compelling.

"What did Alfred's message say?" asked Sarah.

"I'm speaking with Lizowski later this morning. See what he has to say about things."

"Well, I'm sure he can't be happy spending time in jail when there's so much going on in the streets. I hear the veterans are marching to see Norris this afternoon, even if it rains."

"He should've thought of that before he messed with someone like Bill Simon."

"You sound as if you've already decided he's guilty."

Klein shrugged his shoulders. Unlike most of his cases, he had come to realize he didn't particularly care what happened to his client. He seemed like a bad element and, truth being known, Klein wasn't happy about the relationship between Lizowski and Rivka. "Maybe he is guilty. Nobody on the streets has heard anything different."

"And here you've always told me never to make up your mind too quickly about a murder case until every question has been answered. Has it?"

"I guess not. But I'm telling you, Sarah, it doesn't look good. I don't know, maybe Maloney will find something out for me that'll change my mind. So far the only thing that troubles me is why someone's going to so much trouble to stop me from investigating."

"You mean that guy in the park?"

"Yeah, him. If Lizowski is guilty, why threaten me?"

"Well, then, there's more to this than meets the eye."

"Maybe," said Klein lighting a cigarette.

"Maybe," added Sarah, "this has something to do with Rivka?"

A loud knock on the door of the apartment interrupted them.

"Who can that be at this hour?" said Sarah.

The knocking grew louder. "Sam, Sarah, please open. It's Rivka."

Sarah unlatched the door and opened it. "Rivka, what are you doing here?"

"I'm sorry, Sarah. I have to talk to Sam."

"You could've used the telephone."

She shook her head. "And talk to those shiksa scabs. My God, do you think I would do that? I won't pick up a telephone until the strike has ended, one way or the other."

"What's all the commotion about?" asked Klein.

"It's Rivka, she has to talk to you. And, she couldn't use the telephone," said Sarah, rolling her eyes.

"You can both think what you want," said Rivka, "but I don't support scab workers, not ever."

Klein took one last drag on his cigarette and then butted it. "So, you got some news?"

Rivka sat down and took a deep breath. "Late last night, the police searched Metro's house. Scared his wife and son half to death."

"How do you know about this?"

"I know, trust me. Oh, what does it matter? One of the constables, Jeb Kenzie, told me. I know his sister, and besides, he's ready to join us."

"So what happened? What did they find?"

Sarah set a mug of hot coffee down in front of Rivka.

"Thanks, Sarah. What did they find? Everything. His books, pamphlets, strike plans, and letters from Russia."

"Letters from Russia, you've got to be kidding."

"Don't look at me like that, Sam. About a year ago, Metro started a correspondence with a cousin, Maxim Dzerzhinsky, a journalist in Petrograd. At first, Maxim was against the Bolsheviks or certainly wary of their rule. But like others, he's been forced to see the world through Lenin's eyes. He now writes for Pravda, and moves in the highest circles. He's interviewed Lenin, Trotsky and Stalin. He's visited the troops fighting the White Army."

"How do the letters get to Canada?"

"Through the socialist underground in Paris. Maxim was ordered to make contacts with supporters in North America. He naturally thought of Metro. I think he's also contacted someone in Seattle."

"What exactly did the police find in the house, Rivka?"

"Revolutionary pamphlets, newspaper articles, Maxim's letters. It's all in Russian, they'll never figure it out."

"I thought you were smarter than that. It'll take them an hour to fetch someone from the North End who'd be glad to translate it for them. There's something else, isn't there?"

Rivka nodded, her eyes welling with tears. "Metro had several guns. He…he said he bought them in case he needed them—"

"He needed them for what? For the bloody revolution?"

"Don't yell at me."

"Shailek, please," said Sarah.

"I'll yell, when I have to. Have you any idea what'll happen now? Either of you? Not only will your friend Metro be charged with Simon's murder, but they'll also charge him with sedition and treason, and for conspiring to take over the country. What do you think a jury, a good Canadian jury, is going to decide? And I assure you none of them'll be comrades from the factory. They'll convict him in twenty minutes, no matter what evidence I can dig up or what magic Alfred can spin in the courtroom. This case is over. Tell me why in the hell I should waste my time on it?"

"Because I want you to. Isn't that enough?" asked Rivka, her voice breaking. "Damn you Sam, I ask nothing from you. Once in your life…"

Klein stood up and marched toward the front door.

"Daddy, where are you going?" asked Freda passing her father in the hallway.

But Klein did not respond.

"It's nothing to worry about, Freda," said Sarah. "Come give Auntie Rivka a hug. I think she needs one."

"What else does it say?" demanded MacPherson.

"Hey Chief, I'm doing this as fast as I can," said Igor Gusev. "It's not like I read Russian every day." Gusev owned a junk shop on Selkirk Avenue and had some past dealings with McCreary, mainly about selling stolen merchandise. He had been born in Winnipeg, but his parents had immigrated from a village in Russia and as a young boy he had learned to speak Russian before he spoke English. As soon as McCreary had seen all of Lizowski's Russian writings and documents, he had sent two constables to bring in Gusev.

"Okay. Here's how this passage goes: 'The spiders are the masters, the money-grubbers, the exploiters, the gentry, the wealthy, the priests, pimps and parasites of all types. The flies are the unhappy workers, who must obey all those laws the capitalist happens to think up—must obey, for the poor man has not even a crumb of bread.' It is from a pamphlet called Spiders and Flies by Wilhelm Liebknecht."

"Sounds German to me," said MacPherson.

"German, Russian, Galician, Hebrew, it's all the same. Aliens who shouldn't have been allowed in this country from the beginning," said McCreary. "Who do you think's behind this strike?"

"Oh, let's see, Russell, Ivens, Pritchard, Armstrong. Good British stock, that's who," said Hannah Nash. "You should stick to being a detective, McCreary, and forget about politics."

"You don't know what you're talking about," McCreary said, with a wave of his hand.

"Will the two of you stop, please," said MacPherson. "Mr. Gusev, continue. What is this one?"

Gusev studied the pages for a moment. "It's by him."

"Him?"

"Lenin."

"And it says?"

"The title is 'How to Organize Competition.' It was written in December 1917. See, here's the date."

"Go on," said the Chief.

Gusev read quietly to himself for a few minutes. "He calls for a 'war to the death against the rich, the idlers' and the parasites.' He writes that every town and village in the country should find a way of 'cleansing the Russian land of all vermin, of scoundrel fleas, the bedbug rich,' and so on. 'In one place they will put into prison a dozen rich men, a dozen scoundrels, half a dozen workers who shirk on the job. In another place they will be put to cleaning latrines.' And it goes on like that. 'In a fourth, one out of every ten idlers will be shot' and so forth."

MacPherson shook his head. "You read about the upheaval in the newspaper, but when you hear this right from the Russian, well, I'll tell you it scares the living daylights out of you."

"It's supposed to. And, that's what's going to happen in this city," said McCreary, "They can't wait to arrest everyone who doesn't agree with them and then shoot them down like you would a pack of wild dogs."

"What about these letters?" asked Hannah.

"They all seem to be from someone by the name of Maxim," said Gusev. "The first one's dated from November 1917. The last arrived two months ago. From what I can gather, there are some instructions on how to proceed, how to challenge the capitalists, how to make the world socialist revolution a reality, and there's a few comments about…"

"About what?"

"Explosives and dynamite."

"It's a bloody blueprint for a war, that's what it is," said McCreary. "Why wait for a trial? Even if he didn't kill Simon, that bastard ought to be strung up right now."

"McCreary, enough of that kind of talk. What about the guns?"

"Nothing fancy," said Hannah, picking up one of the pistols. "Two older Colt revolvers and one rusty shot gun. I've seen worse."

"Yeah, well what do you think a man like Lizowski was planning to do with these weapons? They sure aren't for hunting squirrels," said McCreary.

"Here, look for yourself, McCreary," said Hannah throwing one of the pistols at her partner. "This isn't going to bring down the government. I'm certain that when and if we check Mr. Simon's home, we'll find a few hunting rifles that could do a lot more serious damage than these."

"That might be the case, Mrs. Nash," said MacPherson. "But together with these pamphlets and letters. I'd say that Lizowski's guilty of sedition and treason, and he likely killed Mr. Simon. Who knows, he was probably his first target. That would make sense, right? Bill Simon was a wealthy man with a nasty temper. Why not get rid of someone like him first, if you're trying to make a point?"

"It does sound possible," said Hannah. "I'd like to investigate further. I'd still like to speak with Mr. Simon's secretary."

"Who cares about her," said McCreary. "We don't need her now. This case is over."

The Chief hesitated. He didn't rise to the top of the department by being rash. "Keep searching, Mrs. Nash. See what you can find. Give it a few more days of work, but that's all," he said. "I'd imagine that when Graham Powers sees what we've found, the government will want to push ahead with the sedition charges right away."

"Give him one trial for everything, the murder and the conspiracy. I can't wait to see how long it takes for the jury to deliver a guilty verdict," said McCreary.

"Easy, McCreary. Let's take this one step at a time. No need to cause a riot quite yet. I'll let General Ketchen know about what we've found and he can take it from there," said MacPherson.

"What about Fowler's ultimatum?" asked McCreary.

"He's given me until June 9th to talk to the men. What about you two?"

"I have no problem signing an oath of allegiance," said McCreary. "I got no intention of ever going out on strike."

"And you Mrs. Nash?"

"I don't know. That's an honest answer. I have to agree with McCreary, I'm not thrilled at the idea of striking. And yet…"

"And yet, what Hannah?" asked McCreary.

"Life's not so black and white, that's all. These men work hard for their families. They ought to be paid properly and treated fairly. I don't know about you, but I don't think anyone should have to work twelve hours a day. Not even you."

"You're being naïve."

"Am I? My husband worked like a dog his whole life at that lumberyard. Where did it get him? Nowhere. Dead at thirty-eight. You know what his employer did, the great Mr. Jenkins? He sends me twenty-five dollars to help with the funeral expenses. That was the last time I heard from him. When Ted got sick, all he cared about was that Ted return any of the company's equipment and account books." She shook her head. "I became a policewoman to fight for those who can't fight for themselves, and that's what I aim to do."

"Suit yourself," said McCreary. "But that sounds a little Red to me."

10

KLEIN WAS STILL seething by the time he arrived at the Rupert Street Station. He had his doubts about Lizowski from the start, now he was certain that the man was a lost cause, no matter what his sister thought. She was blinded by love, that much was clear to him. Graham Powers and the other members of the Citizens Committee, not to mention the Mounties and the federal government were going to jump all over Lizowski. He was the symbol of evil they had been searching for, the socialist who would stop at nothing to fulfil his dark plan.

J.W. Dafoe would attack Lizowski in the pages of the *Free Press* when he got hold of the material from Lizowski's house. Only last week, when the newspaper started running again, after being closed down for five days, Dafoe had denounced the strike and its leaders. They were, in the editor's view, revolutionaries intent on following 'the doctrines and practices of Lenin and Trotsky, the High Priests of the Winnipeg Reds who were responsible for this conspiracy.' And Klein was sure that Graham would be more than happy to let Dafoe have a look at Lizowski's propaganda, as long as he could count on the *Free Press* painting Metro Lizowski as "Canada's Lenin." And there did not seem to be any doubt about that.

He saw Hannah leaving the Chief's office and his heart jumped.

"Sam, is that you?" she asked. "What are you doing here?"

Klein cursed his foolishness. Anyone would think he was a mooning teenager. "How bad is it?" he said in a gruffer voice than he intended.

"It's bad. It looks as if Lizowski had plans to begin a real revolution. There's pamphlets in Russian, writings by Lenin, letters on the plans for the 'world domination of socialism' and much more. And we also found a few guns."

"I heard."

"Mind if I ask from who?"

"I got my sources."

"They're going to come after your sister Rivka, you know that?"

"It's crossed my mind. She'll be fine. She's a tough woman."

"I'm sure she had nothing to do with it."

"Yeah, well, Graham Powers might see it differently."

Hannah smiled. "So, what are you doing here?"

"Alfred Powers has arranged for me to speak with Lizowski, though at this point I don't know why I should bother."

"I'm surprised the Chief agreed to that."

"Alfred can be very persuasive. Besides, he still has a few friends in high places."

"You want me to come along?"

"No. Let me talk to him on my own. How about we meet for lunch later. I hear Molly's on Smith Street is still open."

"I suppose….I suppose that would be acceptable."

"I should be about an hour. How about one o'clock? And then we can compare notes. You find anything more about the missing secretary?"

Hannah shook her head. Her mouth was dry. She wasn't quite sure why she agreed to meet Klein for lunch. But it was about the case after all. There was nothing inappropriate about that.

Klein walked down the stairs into the cell area, wondering what in the hell he was doing. He couldn't stop himself. It was as if his mouth had a mind of its own. Hannah was attractive, but it was something else about her that appealed to him. He couldn't quite put his finger on it. All he knew was that when she smiled at him, as rarely as that had happened, it made his blood rush a bit faster. This had nothing to do with Sarah; he loved his wife as much as he ever did. For some reason, he just wanted—in fact he needed—to get to know Hannah Nash better. Besides, he thought as he knocked on the jail door, maybe she could help him unravel this case.

How many times in the past eight years had Klein found himself in the dank, dark and musty Rupert Station cellblock, visiting clients who invariably claimed they were innocent? And sure enough, sometimes they were. Persistence was the key to solving many cases—that and a lot of faith. Who knows what would have happened to Alfred Powers back in '14, if Klein had not kept digging for the truth about his wife Emily? At the same time, he also accepted that many of his clients would (and often did) lie to their mothers and priests if it meant getting out of jail. True, the police made mistakes, but nine times out of ten they were usually right about an arrest. It had taken a long time for Klein to accept this bit of wisdom.

He found Lizowski in his cell sprawled out on his cot. The stench in the jail block was as pungent as ever.

"Don't worry, Klein, in a few moments you'll get used to the smell. At least I did," said Lizowski as he sat up. "Powers said you'd come by today."

Klein stood on the other side of the barred door. "I'm not sure why. Yesterday I thought there might be some hope, but not now. You know what they found in your house last night?"

Lizowski shrugged. "Doesn't mean I killed Simon."

"Maybe not, but it sure doesn't help your case either. Even if they don't make the murder charge stick, you'll be charged with sedition and treason. One way or the other you're going to spend a long time in jail, if they don't hang you first."

"You come to cheer me up, Klein? You're doing a good job so far. Listen, I didn't kill Simon. I was in his office earlier that day. We did have a bit of an argument. Christ, he offered me all of this money to have the strike called off. I told him he couldn't buy me or anyone else in the unions off."

"What did you do after you left Simon's office?"

"I never saw him again. I went home."

"Don't lie to me, Lizowski. My sister already told me that you were at her place around five. What about before that?"

"I had some work to do on the strike. I stopped by the Ukrainian Temple on Pritchard Avenue and then met Rivka."

"Simon's secretary says she saw you in the barn beside the car."

"She's a damn liar. I wasn't there. Ask her again."

"Seems Miss Viola has taken a holiday, but I'm trying to locate her."

"Then why don't you find that bastard who was with Simon in his office earlier that day. He'll tell you what happened. He's a big guy with a thick black moustache. He was wearing a dark bowler hat. He practically strangled me. As mean an asshole as I've ever met."

It sounded to Klein as if Lizowski was describing the same man who had attacked him in Victoria Park. But he shook his head. "Yeah, well, that could be half the men in this town."

"I'm telling you Klein, he was there. You got to believe me."

"That remains to be seen. Tell me Lizowski, were you really planning to turn the strike into a full-scale revolution?"

Lizowski stared at Klein, trying to gauge if the question was sincere. "I think this country needs to make some serious changes. There are only a handful of people who have most of the money and the power. It has to stop at some point."

"Well, that's how things are. I'll take capitalism any day, even with all of its problems, rather than live under Bolsheviks."

"What do you know about it?"

"I know enough. Freedom's a precious thing, Lizowski. But I don't think you've figured that out yet. Maybe after a few years in jail."

"I thought you said I'd end up hanging from a rope?"

"You just might. But…"

"But you'll help me?"

"Trust me, I don't care if you rot in here for the next ten years. I'm doing this for only two reasons. Because Alfred asked me to, and…."

"And Rivka?"

"Yeah. Because of Rivka. God knows why she cares so much."

Lisowski hesitated. "How is she?"

"As good as can be expected. She's worried about you."

"Tell her I'm fine."

Klein scowled. "Should I pass that message on to your wife as well?"

"They let my wife see me yesterday as a matter of fact. Don't condemn me Klein for loving your sister."

"Oh please, Lizowski. She thinks you're going to leave your wife and then the two of you will live happily ever after. You and I both know that's not going to happen. That the only person who's going to get hurt is Rivka."

Lizowski was silent for a moment. "You've never been tempted, Klein? Never looked at another woman?"

"No, never." The words came out of Klein's mouth, but he wasn't sure he believed them.

"You don't sound so convincing."

"I don't give a damn what you think."

"It happens. I don't know why. Maybe Rivka gives me something my wife doesn't. And I don't mean only in the bedroom."

"I don't want to hear any more of this."

"All right, no more about Rivka. I'll accept the punishment for my political work, but not for a crime I didn't do. You have to believe me."

Klein did not think that Gertie Viola had told him the truth about what had transpired that day in Simon's office. And there was also the mystery man Lizowski claimed he fought with and who might be the same man who threatened Klein at Victoria Park. Something was missing, but he needed more time to think. Maybe Maloney would turn up trumps. He had promised to get in touch with him later in the day.

"I want you to do me a favour, Lizowski."

"What?"

"You tell Graham Powers that Rivka had nothing whatsoever to do with your plans for a revolution."

"She did know something about it."

"I don't care, you tell him she was completely innocent."

"You think they're going to arrest her?"

"This city has been turned upside down. Strikers everywhere. There are a lot of prominent and powerful people who are very scared. Anything is possible. But I do believe they'll bring her in for questioning. I'm going to speak with Graham Powers and see what I can do."

"Will he listen to you?"

"I don't know. We go back a few years. I helped him and his family out once. I think he owes me."

"Mr. Klein, are you in here?" It was Hannah Nash down the darkened hallway.

"Over here," said Klein. "I was just leaving."

"I have to speak with you, but privately."

"Something wrong?"

"Come with me."

Klein followed her out past several empty cells, through a thick wooden door and into a hallway. "Okay, Hannah, we're outside. What is it? Did you find the secretary?"

"No, it's not about her."

"Then what?"

"Two hours ago, a constable out on patrol in Point Douglas found a dead body behind one of the brothels on Annabella Street. The person was pretty beaten up. It looks as if he was killed somewhere else and dumped in the yard."

"And what does this have to do with me?"

"Sam, I'm sorry to have to be the one to tell you this, but we've identified the body and McCreary says he was a friend of yours."

"A friend of mine?"

"A reporter from Toronto. McCreary says his name is Maloney, John Maloney."

II

"I WANT TO SEE HIM," said Klein. His tone was angry. He had made his way to the second floor of the station and into the detectives' small offices. Even with the few windows in the room open, the air was stale and smoky. A group of men huddled around one desk were examining what looked to be a new typewriter.

"Take it easy, Sam," said McCreary. "Here sit down for a moment. You want a cigar?" He opened a box of Roxborough's that he always kept close by amidst the ever-expanding pile of paper surrounding him.

"No, I don't want any of your cheap cigars, McCreary. I just want to see Maloney for myself."

"Trust me," said McCreary, lighting up, "it ain't a pretty sight. He was beat up bad. Probably died from being kicked in the head, at least that's what Doc Macdonald told me."

Klein shook his head. "He had a wife and two kids."

"I'm sorry about that Klein. He was a real pain in the ass when he was working for the *Trib*, but he was a straight-shooter."

"Yeah, he was that. Someone's going to have to send a telegram to the *Star* and his wife."

"We were just about to do that."

"That's good. Shit, Leila is going to take this hard. How in the hell is she going to manage?"

93

McCreary shrugged. "Any idea what he was doing in Point Douglas?"

"Doing me a favour, that's what. The *Star* sent him here to cover the strike. I saw him at Victoria Park the other day, when I was attacked."

"Go on."

"He said he had an idea about who attacked me. Said he was going to look into it. That's the last time I saw him."

"I guess he found whoever it was he was looking for."

"I guess so, McCreary. This guy had a thick neck and a heavy moustache. I'd never seen him before. He was big, over six feet. Sound like anyone you know?"

McCreary shook his head. "The strike has brought a lot of strange characters to the city. If this person was the one who killed Maloney, he's probably long gone by now."

"I don't think so. I think that this has something to do with the Simon case. That's why that asshole went after me and why he murdered Maloney. Trust me, I'll find him one way or the other."

"Easy Klein. Didn't you tell me once that an angry detective was a useless detective?"

"I can handle myself, don't worry about it."

"That's exactly what I'm worried about. You're also jumping to conclusions if you ask me."

Klein checked his watch and cursed. "Do me a favour, McCreary. I was supposed to meet Hannah later for lunch. Tell her I won't be able to make it."

"You're meeting Hannah for lunch?" McCreary raised an eyebrow.

"What of it? We were going to talk about the Simon case, that's all."

"I didn't say anything, Klein. Why are you getting your back up?"

Klein was in no mood for McCreary's sarcasm or his advice on what he should or shouldn't do. His head told him to calm down and think about things clearly, but in his gut he felt a conflicting mass of emotions—sadness, pity, and a great deal of anger.

Over the years, he had come to like Maloney and regard him as a friend. They had met under difficult circumstances during the Blood Libel case of 1911, yet they had forged a curious bond. Klein now recalled with some amusement how Maloney's stories in the *Tribune* had caused a riot on Selkirk Avenue. At the time, of course, he was furious with him, but that single event had been the beginning of their odd partnership. While he worked for the *Tribune* and later the *Free Press*, Maloney was one of the best sources of information Klein had, even if he often put his job as a reporter before any other consideration.

"The only loyalty a reporter has," Maloney once told him, "is to his story." Klein never quite understood that sentiment, but he came to grudgingly respect Maloney's professionalism and his desire to seek the truth.

He knew that when this case was over he would have to write to Leila, explaining what had happened. He wanted to tell her that her husband had not died in vain and that his death was not meaningless—even if that's how Klein now felt. He wanted to be truthful and assure her that justice had been done. For that to happen, however, Klein had to find the bastard who attacked him in the park and probably murdered Maloney.

"Scott, you look pathetic," said Franklin. "That booze is going to kill you someday."

"You got what I asked for?" asked Jack Scott.

"I got it, but first we have a few things to discuss."

Franklin had insisted that Scott meet him in the last row of the balcony of the Lyceum Theatre. A few dollars had taken care of the theatre's manager who, following a slow week, was more than happy to comply with Franklin's request for privacy. True, the Strike Committee had permitted the theatres in the city to remain open, but that did not necessarily mean that people were in a mood to attend. The majority of the striking workers had no extra dollars in their pockets for entertainment. Besides, they were too busy preparing for the next escalation of the strike.

Franklin leaned back in a plush red seat. A row of glass chandeliers hung overhead. The theatre was dark, except for a narrow beam of light emanating from a small crack behind the stage curtains. The theatre, usually filled with laughter and revelry was silent.

"What is it you want?" asked Scott, rubbing his arm.

"You look like you're in pain." said Franklin.

"What do you know about it? What the hell were you doing during the war?"

Franklin did not reply.

"I took a bayonet in the shoulder. That Hun wanted to kill me and he would've too if my buddy hadn't shot him first. It hurt like hell then, and has every day since. That's why I need the medicine, but you know that Franklin, don't you?"

"You're a brave man Scott, a real credit to your country," he said reaching into his pocket and pulling out a small vial. "There's more where this came from as long as you can assure me you're winning the battle with the veterans."

"I've already told you. My men are working on it. I only got so much power, Franklin. Some of the vets have fathers and brothers among the strikers. They're sympathetic to the cause and there isn't much I can do about that. We aim to disrupt their march and rally today. I'll tell you this, though, none of them, even the ones who like the unions, will tolerate any Bolsheviks or aliens leading them. That's where they draw the line. They didn't see their buddies die in the mud and trenches for nothing."

"Well, that shouldn't be a problem. When they read about Lizowski's plans for a revolution in tomorrow's *Free Press* and *Telegram*, I think your work will be a lot easier."

"He killed Simon like they say?"

"Yeah, he did it all right. But you never mind about that." Franklin handed him the vial of morphine. "You just keep those men on the Loyalist side, keep reminding them why they risked their lives overseas. Then this war will be won."

Scott grabbed the vial, and prepared to leave.

Franklin laughed.

"You find this funny?"

"I was just thinking what Bill Simon would have thought about my dealing with you. He didn't have a lot of patience for defects. Said they ruined the natural order of things. You are, I believe, what he would have referred to as 'poor breeding stock.' You're not married are you? "

Scott stood up and clenched his fists.

"You really don't want to start trouble with me," said Franklin, "Unless you want to lose all feeling in your legs, that is. Then you'll be even more useless than you are now."

"Do your superiors have any idea what a miserable son-of-a-bitch you are?"

"Actually I don't think so. I get the job done, so they don't ask a lot of questions."

"Maybe I'll let them know one day."

Franklin stood up and towered over Scott. "That day, my friend, just may well be your last. Think about it."

McCreary had been right. A visit to Doc Macdonald's office had turned up nothing worthwhile. And seeing Maloney on the Doc's table like a slab of meat made Klein sick to his stomach. His friend deserved better than that. Macdonald had told Klein that Maloney had been beaten to death, probably sometime late yesterday evening. As for McCreary and Hannah's speculations that Maloney had been killed somewhere else and then dumped in the yard on Annabella Street, Macdonald was not as certain.

Klein decided that he first needed to visit the site where Maloney had been found and then go to the boarding house where Maloney had been staying. Maybe, just maybe, something the police missed would turn up. He never did have much faith in the investigative skills of Winnipeg constables or even in the "plain clothes" men—with the exception of McCreary, of course. Under normal circumstances, they were often sloppy, and missed clues and evidence. Look how long it had taken them to find Cecil Sage's missing coat buttons. Yet given the stress of the past few weeks, and the recent ultimatum made by civic authorities—which Klein felt was eventually going to lead to a massive police walkout—he reasoned that their search of the yard was done quickly and without much care. Who knows if they had even bothered to check through Maloney's personal belongings at the boarding house?

As Klein reached Main Street, he could see through the drizzling rain the mass of veterans marching toward city hall. What seemed to be an endless stream of men passed by him. There were probably close to 10,000 former soldiers in the street that day, he estimated. They carried an array of signs and banners, large and small with such slogans as: "End the Strike Now," "Collective Bargaining is Our Right," and "Down with the Profiteers."

Leading the charge was Roger Bray. Even if he was a short man, every step he took had a purpose not lost on those who followed him. As the group approached city hall, Bray ran up the front stairs to greet Mayor Gray. Caught up in the excitement, Klein followed behind to watch this spectacle.

Bray raised his hands and immediately the veterans quieted down. "Mr. Mayor, this strike must end," he said, sounding like the English Methodist preacher that in many ways he still was. "The strikers' demands must be met." At that, the men cheered. "Call off the Citizens Committee of 1000. They represent the same bunch of boodlers who plundered this province and city. Do we need men connected to crooks like Joe Flavelle?"

"No!" the men chanted, loudly booing munitions czar Joseph Flavelle's name.

"These men on the committee, what were they doing during the war? I'll tell you, they were purchasing real estate worth thousands of dollars and have made money out of the innocent, while we were over there defending the land we love."

Again a loud roar emanated through the throng of ex-soldiers.

"You're nothing but a Bolshevik agitator, Bray, go back where you came from." Immediately, hundreds of heads turned. It was Jack Scott and his group of Loyalist soldiers. They were standing on the far side of Market Square opposite city hall. The signs they held were of a different vein: "Down with Bolshevism" and "Deport Undesirable Aliens."

Seeing Scott, Mayor Gray immediately called out a contingent of armed constables.

"You're welcome to join us Scott," said Bray. "Listen to what we have to say before you condemn us."

"I didn't fight overseas to defend the likes of you," Scott shouted back. "All of you listen to me. Do you want this city run by a Soviet government? Because that will be the end result, I guarantee it."

"That's not true," said Bray. "All we want is a fair wage and recognition of our unions' rights. Do I look like a Bolshevik, Scott? I'm not even the 'English anarchist' that the *Free Press* calls me. I am here to fight for justice."

"You tell him, Roger," cried out a voice.

At that, Gray ordered the police to disperse Scott and his group. They did so, but not before there was some violent pushing and shoving.

"I must say to all of you," said the mayor, "that Mr. Scott is right. This strike must end today. It's wrong and cannot succeed."

Now the large crowd of veterans jeered and moved closer to the front steps. Bray did not want any trouble and held his hand up again.

"I'm prepared to sit down and meet with Mr. Bray, but I'm not promising you anything. And I want all of you to know this as well; if there is trouble I won't hesitate to ask General Ketchen for help."

Standing far back, Klein watched Bray and the mayor. He could only shake his head. Gray just did not get it. These men would not be frightened by threats of martial law, or dissuaded by the likes of Jack Scott. They would have their day, of that Klein was certain. The city was on the verge of an explosion, worse than anything that had ever taken place in its history. Only blind politicians like Premier Norris and Mayor Gray refused to see that. Or if they did see, they did not want to admit it to themselves because they could not deal with the potential consequences.

Klein was beginning to realize that this strike was not an event in which he could continue to sit on the fence. The world was changing fast. The rigid class system that had characterized life in the city for so many decades was no longer acceptable for the vast majority of its citizens. Why should a small group of men control the commercial, political and social existence of the city? Wasn't the New World about equality and opportunity for everyone, not just the wealthy? Winnipeg's working class may not want a Soviet-style revolution Klein thought, as he slowly walked toward Point Douglas, but they did want real change. And the property owners and business elite who ruled the city like lords for so long had better get used to the idea, or matters were going to get a lot worse than they already were.

12

THE RAIN WAS COMING DOWN hard as Klein turned the corner on Sutherland to Annabella Street. Looking around at the small wooden houses that lined the narrow street, Klein thought the neighbourhood appeared a bit more run-down than usual. Some of the homes had broken windows and doors, and junk was piled in the high grass.

Much to the consternation of many morally-minded Winnipeggers, the area around Annabella Street still had a reputation as the country's most infamous red light district—and rightly so. Ever since Chief MacPherson's predecessor John McRae had worked out an arrangement with the local madams nearly a decade earlier, the number of brothels in Point Douglas had multiplied. Occasionally, some of the women who plied their trade got into trouble—roaming the streets wearing only their undergarments or drinking and cavorting on their front porches. Over the years more than one prostitute was caught with opium, or more frequently, was the victim of a violent crime perpetrated by a client who did not want to pay. For the most part, however, the authorities tended to look the other way. And as long as such madams as Klein's former boss, Melinda Hawkins, still renowned as "Queen of the Harlots," paid their property taxes and kept their girls in line, life in Point Douglas went on.

"You got lots of luck, Hilda," said Klein lighting a cigarette. "Any objections to me looking around the back yard?"

"Go ahead. I need this like a *loch in kop*."

"You ever think about getting this yard cleaned up, Hilda?" asked Klein as he made his way around to the back of the house.

"It's on my list of things of to do," said Hilda. "By the way, feel free to stop by for a visit later. I'm sure a few of the girls would love to see you."

"And I'd love to see them too, but I have this case."

"Sarah'll never know," said Hilda returning inside. "Think about it."

Klein would have agreed that there was no better way to kill an hour or two than flirting with the lovely ladies of Annabella Street. As a group, they were charming, entertaining, and always clad in as little as possible. Black corsets, silk nightgowns, shimmering nylons, and high-laced pumps were particular favourites. It kept their customers happy and coming back for more. Compared to the rest of the women in Winnipeg, the ladies here were an unrestrained bunch who enjoyed life to its fullest. Pleasure was their business—for the right price, of course. True, some, but certainly not all, of the girls had been coerced into prostitution by debt, pimps, or opium addiction. That too was the nature of the profession and Klein had been around Annabella Street long enough to know that this was just how things were. Sarah had got out and so too had other girls.

The women would have to wait, Klein thought, as he waded into the tall grass. The yard was a mess. There were wet and musty cloth sacks piled in one corner beside a stack of decaying and rotten wood. On the other side of the yard was the remnant of what Klein assumed to be the backyard privy. Most everyone in Winnipeg, including the brothels in Point Douglas, had had indoor plumbing for several years now. That meant a toilet but no bathroom; the bathtubs were in the kitchen close to the tub by the stove that slowly heated the water. The yard was littered with dog waste. Some day, thought Klein, the city inspectors would get tired of their free "gifts" and would close this place down.

Maloney's body had been found close to the old privy. Klein poked around for a few minutes, but quickly concluded that he was not going to find anything useful. Besides, the smell was impossible to take.

Maybe he'd have more luck in Maloney's room at the boarding house. He would visit with Melinda and then get back to work.

"You looking for something, Sam?" The voice was soft and pleasing.

Klein turned around. Before him stood Amanda Thomas, Hilda's star attraction and chief moneymaker. Gossip had it that she had even surpassed Sarah as the most desirable whore in the city. She was twenty years old, dark, and as beautiful a woman as Klein had ever seen. If you didn't know better, she could've passed for a younger version of Gloria Swanson. Her red chemise hung loosely open over her voluptuous figure. She was wearing a white lace corset, black nylons that were fastened to the bottom of the corset by four button-hooks, and black high-heeled pumps with intertwined laces that encircled her ankles.

Klein sighed. "Amanda, you're looking as lovely as ever."

"Why, thank you Sam. You should come by more often. We could get to know each other better."

"Yeah, Sarah would like that. What's that in your hand?"

"You mean this?" she said, holding up small black notepad. "Here's the thing, Sam, after the police took away that dreadful body, I was out having a cigarette and lo and behold I came across it."

"Can I see it?"

She moved closer to him. Her lilac perfume was strong and enticing. "I could let you see it...for a price."

"Just let me see it, Amanda."

She laughed. "Oh very well, Sam. I hear you used to be a lot more fun in the old days, at least that's what the girls at Melinda's say. Now look at you, you've become an old married man."

Klein grabbed the notepad out of her hand. He leafed through the pages. Sure enough, it was Maloney's. He felt a surge of excitement. "Thanks, Amanda. I appreciate this."

Klein walked around to the front of the house and stopped for a moment beside the gate leading to Melinda's to examine the notebook. There were a few pages with scribbled notes on them. Most of them dealt with matters concerned with the strike. It seems that Maloney had interviewed both Bob Russell, for the strikers' point of view and George Runciman for the businessmen's perspective on the dispute. Klein would have to make a point of speaking to both of them. He turned several more pages until he came to one on which Maloney had scrawled: "Agent 12. Wire Perry. Regina." Then near the bottom of the same page was written: "J. Bauer, Sunday at noon."

He took a deep drag and stared at the words for a minute or two trying to decode Maloney's notations. Some of the writing seemed obvious. Klein figured that by "Perry" Maloney must be referring to Aylesworth Perry, the Commissioner of the RNWMP whose office was in Regina. He was a virulent opponent of the strike, and saw no difference between legitimate labour grievances and a full-scale Bolshevik revolution. Why had Maloney wanted to speak with him, Klein wondered? Perhaps it was about the Mounties's plans to assume responsibility for policing the city, should Winnipeg's constables walk off their jobs. Or maybe it was about Perry's strategy to ensure that the strike would soon be quashed. Confirming Maloney's intentions with Perry, however, would be difficult to determine. The Commissioner, Klein knew, was not an easy man to deal with, nor did he have time to answer questions from a private detective. He would have to speak to Alfred Powers about this. Powers had a real talent for opening doors that were closed to almost everyone else.

The "J. Bauer" noted at the bottom of the page was more difficult. Klein ran the different Germans he had encountered over the years through his head. He couldn't remember any Bauers. As he mouthed the name, he suddenly remembered a Jacob Bower to whom Klein had been introduced by Rivka at a labour gathering about a week before the strike had started. He seemed like a nice enough fellow, genuinely interested in fighting for workers' rights. From what Klein heard, he had fully supported the strike and had been active in pushing for as radical a program as possible. What would his connection be to the Commissioner?

Finally there was the reference to "Agent 12." Klein found that intriguing. For weeks, the city had been rife with rumours about secret Mountie operatives spying on the labour organizations. Klein did not doubt for a moment that the stories were true.

The war and all of its many consequences had made the authorities overly suspicious, almost terrified in some instances. It was an irrational fear often incited by new and dangerous, or at least perceived to be, political voices. Anarchists and the international threat of

Marxism topped the list. So-called patriotic Canadians in Winnipeg and elsewhere, had applauded the federal government's imposition of the War Measures Act in 1914 that essentially transformed the country into a dictatorship run out of Ottawa. They had wholeheartedly approved of the deportation of nearly nine thousand "enemy aliens"— Germans, Ukrainians, Austrians and Turks—to camps in northern British Columbia, and Ontario. They accepted without question the censorship of newspapers and books, and believed the propaganda the government fed them. If liberty for all was a casualty of the war, so be it.

Now these good Canadians looked around and wondered what those four years of bloodshed and death had truly accomplished? Europe was in ruins, centuries-old monarchies had been toppled, and nations were destroyed. Even now, world leaders were meeting in Paris to redraw the map, but many doubted that they would be successful. Just as the war had spurred on voices of the left, it had also given a new impetus to those on the right, those who wanted to preserve and control the old order.

Among them were conservatives and nationalists in Germany, Italy, France, the United States and Canada who resented democracy for all of its many weaknesses, detested wide-open immigration policies, and believed that Jews, among others, were conspiring to take over the world. Popular authors wrote alarmist books on the subject. Many adhered religiously to the principles of Social Darwinism—based in large part on the writings of Herbert Spencer rather than Charles Darwin himself—that stated that the strong would inherit the earth. This, in turn, led many of them, like Bill Simon, to the eugenics movement, with its promises of creating a better, stronger and more intelligent race of humans.

Klein had read about all of this in the papers. Admittedly, he did not understand some of the finer points in the on-going debate about natural selection, but he did know something about the power of hate, especially when it was driven by baseless fear. How many times he had been called a "kike" or a "Hebe." More troubling, in many ways, were those moments when he had been dismissed with a wave of a hand, treated rudely by a clerk or businessman, and looked upon with disdain by complete strangers merely because he was a Jew. And so, when he heard that the RNWMP had launched a clandestine campaign to infiltrate and stamp out Bolshevik groups and anyone else who threatened the "Canadian" way of life, he merely accepted that this was the government's latest strategy to preserve the world as they defined it. Who exactly "Agent 12" was, and why Maloney wanted to see him, Klein would have to answer for himself.

A shattering of glass broke Klein's concentration.

"Get out and don't come back, you asshole." It was Melinda and by the sound of it, she wasn't too happy.

Klein immediately moved towards the front door of the house to investigate. As he did so the door opened and Melinda, dressed in low-cut black satin, her ample breasts barely restrained by her matching corset, stormed out holding a troublesome client by his collar. The man was conscious, but listless and appeared to be drunk.

"Sam, you're a sight for sore eyes," she said. "You want to help me deal with this crook?"

"What did he do?"

"What didn't he do? He drank my best whisky. Do you know how much I had to pay the Bronfmans for that? Then he spent time upstairs with two of my girls, then told me he didn't have any money to pay. It's this bloody strike, Sam. They come here because they don't have anything else to do, but most of them don't have any cash in their pockets. This isn't the first time this has happened."

"Here, Melinda, let me deal with him." Klein took hold of the man's arm and led him toward the gate.

"Say, aren't you Sam Klein?" the man mumbled.

"Do I know you?"

"I don't know. Scott is the name, Jack Scott."

"Sure, I've seen you around. You're the one who caused all of that trouble at the police station the other day."

"That's me," Scott said proudly.

"So how come you can't pay your bill here?"

"I told your friend that I'd return within the hour with the money, but she didn't believe me, the whore."

"Watch your tongue, Scott."

"So she hits me on the head with a shoe, for Christ sakes."

Klein smiled. He had seen Melinda's hot temper many times in the past. She had a well-deserved reputation for being a woman of pleasure and delight, but there was a darker, more authoritarian side to her as well. None of her girls would dare cross her; they knew too well the sting of the back of her hand.

"You must've had quite an afternoon, Scott. Where do you live?"

"A rooming house on Euclid Street. Why?"

"Tell you what, Scott. This is your lucky day. You don't want to make an enemy of Melinda. She's got too many friends at city hall, and in places you wouldn't want to visit alone at night. So how about if I come with you to your house, get the money, and I'll deliver it to Melinda personally?"

Scott nodded unsteadily. "Yeah, sure. Why do you want to help me, Klein? I hear you're working for that Red Lizowski."

"So what of it? From what I hear you're a pain in the ass who wouldn't lose any sleep if Lizowski hung for a crime he didn't do. But I think you and I should talk about a few things. I'd like to hear more about your Loyalist group, your plans for the next few days, things like that. Maybe you've had some dealings with the Mounties or know something about their operations? I bet you have lots to say, Scott."

"I don't know what the hell you're talking about, Klein and I got nothing to say to you. You're a damn Red."

Klein laughed. "I may be a lot of things, Scott, but I assure you I'm no Red."

The two men began to walk towards Euclid Street. Scott took slow, careful steps. "You haven't got a clue just how dangerous this strike is, do you?"

Klein ignored the question. "Tell me, you ever meet a reporter from Toronto named Maloney?"

"No, never heard of him. Why?"

"Just curious. And I guess you wouldn't know anything about Mountie agents either?"

"Why would I? I'm a soldier with no job, and few prospects. And I got this pain in my shoulder from a German bayonet that won't go away. Say, how come you never served, Klein?"

"It's a long story. Who organized your group anyway?"

"The Loyalists? Bill Simon did that. He gave us a bit of cash to rent a hall down on Hargrave. It was probably the last thing he did before Lizowski murdered him."

"Simon was a busy guy, wasn't he?"

"I wouldn't know anything about it."

"Tell me, Scott, maybe you've seen someone I'm looking for at one of your meetings. He's tall with a really thick neck and big black moustache. And mean. You'd remember him if you ever met him."

Scott's face blanched. "I don't know anyone like that."

Klein was not a big believer in fate, but he had to admit it was often curious the way things worked out. Scott may've been a cheat, but he was no fool. Klein's gut instincts told him that Scott knew more than he was willing to tell. Once they arrived at the rooming house, Klein decided that he and his new friend were going to talk about Maloney, Gertie Viola, Bill Simon, the Loyalist Veterans Association and anything else on Scott's mind. Who knew what information he had stored in that head of his?

13

RIVKA COULD NOT KEEP UP with the demand. She had been working non-stop since six that morning, making cheese and egg sandwiches, and boiling water for tea. Twice already, she had run out of supplies and had had to wait for volunteers to deliver more food. The line of people passing through the Oxford Hotel was steady. They were feeding 1,500 strikers a day now, double the number from the first week over at the Strathcona. Rosenthal had let them stay there for ten days before he succumbed to the pressure of the Citizens' Committee and told the women they had to find other premises for the Labour Café. Everyone had been upset with Rosenthal, but not Helen Armstrong. She shrugged her shoulders and moved on.

There were few women who impressed Rivka as much as Helen did. No one was as devoted to the movement as she was—no one worked harder for the cause. And unlike many women in the city, Helen did not care what someone's last name was, where they were born, or what their religion was. "If they're fighting for their rights as workers against the capitalist class," she would say, "then I'll stand with them." And she did.

Ever since Helen had been elected president of the Women's Labour League two years ago, she had been indefatigable. She helped the Hello Girls in their struggle for wages, and marched on the picket line with the poorly paid women clerks at the F.W. Woolworth's stores. She spoke whenever there was a labour rally. She pestered the Trades and

Labour Council until they took action to improve the conditions of a group of railway workers, who had been imprisoned at Stony Mountain Penitentiary for supposedly violating their employee contracts. She battled the conscription forces single-handedly, and started organizing Winnipeg's housemaids into a union; and when the strike began she opened the Labour Café. Any women on strike were entitled to three square meals a day, while the men who came looking for food were supposed to make a small donation. Helen, however, never turned anyone away.

"Here's a few more bags of coffee, Rivka," said Helen. "Should keep us until tomorrow at least." She placed the sacks on top of the table where Rivka was working.

Rivka grinned. "What are you doing here? I thought you were in jail."

Helen laughed. "You think they were going to keep me in jail for very long? I know my rights."

"Are you going to keep at it?" As soon as the words had left Rivka's mouth, she knew it was a foolish question. Two days ago, Helen had been arrested in front of the Canada Bread Company plant for inciting the female employees to join the strike. The owner had her arrested for trespassing.

Helen smiled and touched Rivka's arm. There were bags under her eyes and she looked tired, but determined as ever. "You really want me to answer that?"

"Of course not. Now tell me, is the line any shorter?"

"Afraid not. There's a lot of hungry people out there. And if they're willing to fight for unions and wages, I'll keep feeding them."

Here was Helen's one blind spot. It wasn't as if most of the workers had actually understood what a general strike entailed, or how much they and their families would suffer as a result of the labour action. Rivka had already witnessed plenty of bitter arguments between husbands who had obediently walked off their jobs, and their wives who now equated the strike with hunger and no money. "You're taking food from our children," they'd shout, and the hapless men could only promise that in the end all of this would be worth it. But they never sounded very convincing, at least in Rivka's view. Whenever she brought this up with Helen, though, she got nowhere. Militancy was bred into Helen and she stood by her husband George, and everyone else on the Central Strike Committee.

"How are you keeping up?" asked Helen.

"I'm fine, all things considered."

"Have you heard from Metro?"

"Only once, but my brother Sam is working on the case. He's no strike supporter, but he'll do his best."

'I'm sure he will, my dear. I've heard some interesting tales about him. Besides, if anyone can get out of this jam, it's Metro."

It was curious, thought Rivka. She knew that Helen was a friend to Metro's wife Sylvia, and that she could not have approved of Rivka's behavior, but she never said anything about it. Helen had discovered their affair by accident one day when she saw them together on the street arm in arm. When Helen had finally asked Rivka about it, she couldn't lie and told her everything. Helen had merely nodded, offered no advice, and made no judgements.

"I know you don't want to hear this Rivka, but we have to find another place and soon."

"Tell me you're kidding."

Helen shook her head. "Seems the capitalist committee got to Stevens as well."

"So where do we go from here? Pretty soon, we'll run out of hotels."

"Already talked to people over at the Royal Albert. They said we can move there in three days if we want."

"You never cease to amaze me, Helen."

Their conversation was interrupted by the sound of breaking dishes.

"What are you doing here, you bloody scab," a woman shouted.

Helen and Rivka rushed into the main dining room to find a young woman holding a kitchen knife in her hand. She was standing facing another woman. A small crowd had gathered.

"What's going on here?" Helen demanded.

"She's a bloody scab," said the woman with the knife. "I saw her go into the Manitoba Telephone the other day. She's been working the phones."

"Is that true?" Helen asked the other woman.

"I…I have kids. We got no food. I just didn't know what else to do. It was just one day. I'm not going back, Helen. I swear."

Helen walked up to the woman and took the knife from her. "You go sit somewhere else. Now." Reluctantly the woman did as she was told. "You can stay," Helen said to the other woman. "We all make mistakes. If you have any more food problems, I want you to come directly to me. Just don't cross the picket line, not ever. If you do, we all lose. Do you understand what I'm saying?"

"I think so."

"Good, now sit down and finish your meal. And take a few sandwiches for the kids."

Workers in the room continued to mill around the table for a few more moments, then returned to their chairs and food. Things had quieted down when the main door swung open and in marched five burly constables. Helen immediately approached them.

"You ready to fight for your rights, gentlemen?" she asked.

"You Armstrong?" asked one.

"That's me. What do you want?"

"We're here for Rivka Klein. Where is she?"

"What do you want her for?"

"Where is she, Mrs. Armstrong?"

Rivka stepped forward. "I'm Rivka Klein, what's going on?"

Three of the constables immediately encircled her, hovering as if she were a dangerous animal.

"Rivka Klein," said the cop who initially had been speaking with Helen, "you are under arrest for sedition and conspiracy to aid in an insurrection."

"You must be joking," said Helen.

"I assure you Mrs. Armstrong, this is no joke."

One of the constables standing beside Rivka grabbed her arms and put them behind her back. Another one fastened handcuffs to her wrists.

By this time, the crowd in the dining hall had grown large and angry. "Hey, leave her be," said one man.

"If you had any guts, you'd join us, not arrest her."

As the crowd drew closer, two of the constables removed their revolvers from their holsters.

"What are you going to do, shoot us all, you scab?" shouted a woman at the back.

"Here, look at these children," said another woman, pushing a young boy and girl forward. "These kids haven't had a decent meal in days. If it wasn't for women like Rivka."

"Move back, all of you," said the constable. He did not raise his voice, but it was firm.

"Helen, please," said Rivka, "I don't want anyone hurt. Tell them to move back."

Helen looked at Rivka for a moment. "You're right, of course, my dear." She kissed Rivka on the cheek and hugged her for a moment. Then the police led Rivka towards the door. "Get word to my brother," said Rivka. "He'll know what to do."

"I promise," said Helen. "And be strong. There's nothing they can do to you."

"I know," Rivka whispered as she stepped through the doorway.

Klein's 'discussion' with Jack Scott had gone nowhere. In fact, all he had got for his trouble was the $25 Scott owed Melinda. No matter how persuasive Klein had been, Scott was not talking. He was scared about something, or someone, Klein figured, but he could not get it out of him. And he wasn't about to get too rough with Scott—at least not yet. The one valuable piece of information he had learned was that Scott was a morphine addict. Scott had desperately tried to hide the used syringes scattered throughout his room, but it didn't take long for Klein to get him to admit to his addiction.

"Don't judge me, Klein," Scott had told him. "I served my country proudly, and would do it again. Just a bit of bad luck this wound, and the morphine helps me forget the pain."

Klein wasn't judging him. Truth be told, he was almost envious. He never would be as patriotic as Scott was, and he was not anxious to die in Europe protecting the British Empire, yet it hadn't been easy not going to war. No matter that he had a legitimate reason or not, he still had to endure the stares in the street, the whispering behind his back, and the taunts from young men and women like Scott who saw the world through a narrow lens. You either performed your duty to your country, or you did not. For them, there was no middle ground.

Klein wasn't finished with Scott yet, but there did not seem to be any reason to bother him anymore for today. He had given Klein the $25, albeit reluctantly, and Klein had left, telling him that they would talk more in the days ahead. Scott told Klein he was a bastard, and that was the end of their conversation.

Thirty minutes later, Klein was back at Melinda's on Annabella Street to make his delivery. He found his former boss sipping tea in her ostentatious parlour—red velvet drapes, overstuffed turquoise couches, and the newest addition, dark green striped wallpaper. Melinda may have been a savvy Madam, but her taste in furniture and interior decorating left much to be desired.

She was speaking to a young redhead, a prospective employee. The woman was wearing a shorter than usual skirt, and her ankles were clearly visible. Despite the fact that this was the latest in ladies' fashion, a majority of women in Winnipeg still preferred skirts that hid their ankles. She wore powder and cosmetic paint on her face, another indication that she was a woman of style. The perfume of both women permeated the air. The odour was powerful and intense, and Klein found it appealing.

"Sam, you got my cash?" asked Melinda.

"I got it," said Klein, handing her the money. "You think I was going to steal it from you?"

Melinda ignored the friendly jab. "Sam, allow me to introduce you to my guest. This is Roslynn Denning from New Orleans. She used to work for a friend of mine down there. Says she needed a change of scenery."

"Nice to meet you Miss Denning."

"A pleasure Mr. Klein."

"You know my name?"

"Roslynn's come prepared," said Melinda. "She's done a bit of research on me, the business and, I guess, you too."

"You planning on staying here very long?"

"Depends if Melinda gives me a job, I suppose," she said with a slow smile.

"Don't worry honey, you got the job. I figure that you'll draw them in. Once this damn strike ends, things might just get back to normal around here. I could use a new attraction."

"And does that mean I'll be seeing more of you too?" asked Rosylnn, as she stared at Klein.

"Oh, I like to visit every once in a while. My wife and Melinda are partners in a cosmetics shop."

"Ah yes, that would be the Sarah I've heard so much about."

"Sam's spoken for, honey," said Melinda. "He's what we call a family man."

"The best kind for business, where I come from," said Rosylnn.

Klein bid farewell to Melinda and wished Rosylnn well in her new job. Looking her over, he suspected that she was very good at what she did.

It was nearly one o'clock and he had promised to meet Alfred at Dolly's on Hargrave for lunch. Dolly, too, had defied the strike committee and had stayed open throughout the labour conflict. A Winnipeg institution, Bob Russell and the other leaders had opted to leave her alone. They needed somewhere to eat as well.

Except for the smaller crowds, and a few closed shops and stores, Main Street looked like its old pre-strike self. The Citizens' Committee volunteers had worked hard to clean up the garbage. It was probably, thought Klein, the first manual labour some of them had ever done. He couldn't get over the sight of the sons and daughters of the wealthy manning gas pumps, and sweeping horse manure off the streets. Still the traffic of automobiles and horse-carriages was lighter than usual, at least at this hour, and the streetcars remained parked in the garages. Klein had heard that the mayor and aldermen were desperately trying to get the streetcars running again, yet negotiations with representatives from the Winnipeg Electric Railway Company and the Street Railway Union had accomplished nothing. The Company refused to use strikebreakers for fear of causing a riot, and the union took its orders from the Central Strike Committee. For the time being, most

Winnipeggers were going to have to walk, or use the jitney transport service provided by the Citizen's Committee for its supporters. More than fifty automobiles were conscripted to taxi people around the city.

As Klein reached the corner of Portage and Hargrave, he could see small groups of women window-shopping at Eaton's department store across the street. In many cases, their husbands followed along pushing baby carriages, or holding the hands of small children. In front of each window also stood a guard with a wooden baton. The Eaton Company had objected to the strike from the start, and had shipped in scab labour from its Ontario stores. It had promised its Winnipeg employees a $4 salary increase if they remained on the job, but many had sided with labour. During the past week, two or three store windows had been smashed by angry strikers, or perhaps by returned soldiers who had drunk too much still-made whisky. In any event, Eaton's, the most popular place to shop in the city, was now off-limits for many Winnipeggers, who wouldn't be caught dead in the department store for fear of the consequences from their fellow strikers.

"Sam." Dolly greeted him as he walked into the restaurant. "You look like you really need a cup of coffee. Life not treating you well these days?"

"Dolly, you don't know the half of it. I'll have that coffee, black. You seen Alfred Powers?"

"Sitting over there in the corner and he's got a lady with him."

Klein spied Powers at the back of the room. At the table with him was Hannah Nash.

"Sam, glad you're here," said Powers. "Mrs. Nash was just filling me in on a few things. You two know each other, I believe?"

Klein nodded to Hannah who cooly returned the gesture.

"Yes, Mr. Klein and I have met," said Hannah.

"Does McCreary know you're talking to the enemy?" asked Klein.

"I don't report everything I do to him, but if you must know, the Chief gave me permission to meet with Mr. Powers. We were just speaking about Miss Viola."

"The disappearing secretary. Any luck?"

"Not yet, but Chief MacPherson informs me that the Mounties are searching for her and they have reason to believe she may be out west somewhere. Apparently she was spotted on a train leaving Regina. I'm confident we'll find her soon."

"And then what?"

"And then we'll find out why she ran away."

"And from whom she was running," added Powers.

"You realize that she may stick to her story, Mr. Powers. That she saw your client with Mr. Simon on the day of the murder."

"Maybe, but I've heard Sam's opinion on this, and I agree with him that Miss Viola has more to tell."

After a moment's hesitation, Klein sat down at the table in the seat next to Hannah as Dolly brought him a cup of coffee. He reached across for a stick of sugar, and as he did, his hand lightly brushed against Hannah's. She glanced at him, but did not say anything, and he pretended not to notice. For a moment, there was an awkward silence. Klein sipped his coffee, then took out his cigarette case.

"Have you had a chance to write Leila Maloney yet?" asked Powers.

"Not yet," said Klein, "I want to be able to tell her that the murderer has been caught. And I'm not any closer to doing that than I was yesterday."

"We've been through the neighbourhood twice," said Hannah. "No one saw anything, at least that's what they're saying."

"You think the constables' hearts are in their work, Mrs. Nash?" asked Powers.

"I honestly don't know. I do know that morale in the department is terrible. The Chief is trying to remedy the situation, but threatening the men was foolish," said Hannah.

Powers scowled. "This city is run by foolish men, that's why we're in this situation."

"You were the last great mayor, Alfred," said Klein.

"Don't I know it."

"What are you going to do, Hannah?" asked Klein.

"I'm not certain. I haven't made up my mind yet. As I told you I'm sympathetic to the strikers, and I can definitely appreciate some of their demands. Who doesn't need more money at the end of each month? I've heard of the mayor's plan to recruit soldiers from the Loyalists to patrol the street. That would be a terrible mistake."

Powers shook his head. "Before this business is over, blood will be shed. And it will be on the hands of Gray, Norris and…."

"And Graham?" asked Klein.

"Yes, and my son Graham. God, I don't think I've ever felt more distant from him than I do at this very moment."

"He's just doing what he thinks is best, I suppose," said Hannah.

"Well, I thought I taught him better than that."

Klein lit a cigarette. "Alfred, you think after what they found in Lizowski's house we have a chance? I have to tell you that after today I'm getting kind of worried about turning up anything. And if the police don't find that secretary."

"I shouldn't be here for the rest of this conversation," said Hannah, standing up.

"No, it doesn't matter, Mrs. Nash," said Powers.

"That's kind of you, Mr. Powers, but I should be getting back to the station. McCreary will think that I disappeared as well." She looked at Klein and touched his shoulder for a moment. "Before I go there is something I have to tell you, Sam. I hate to be the bearer of bad news again. It seems to be becoming a habit."

"What is it?"

"When I was leaving the station, I heard McCreary talking to the Chief. The order has been given to arrest Rivka."

Klein's face tightened. "For what?"

"From what I understand, sedition and conspiring to start an insurrection."

"I didn't think they'd actually do this."

Powers put his hand over Klein's. "They're just trying to scare Lizowski into confessing, Sam. That's all. They know she didn't do anything. Hell, Lizowski wasn't planning a revolution. If he's guilty of anything, it's having illegal propaganda. And that's a questionable crime at best. Who knows how that material ended up in his house."

"I'm going to the station," said Klein.

"I don't think that's a good idea," said Hannah. "They won't let you see her, at least not yet."

"I have to do something. I'm not sitting here while my sister is in jail."

"Trust me, Sam, I'll make sure nothing happens to her," said Hannah. "Will you trust me?"

Klein shrugged. "Thanks."

"Come on Sam," said Powers. "I know how we can put a stop to this right now."

"Graham?"

"Exactly. Let's go pay an unannounced visit to my dear son."

14

"WHAT'S ALL THE commotion?" Hugh Lyall asked. "It sounds as if we're under attack."

"Nothing out of the ordinary these days I'm afraid," said Graham Powers. "A few of the strikers got into an argument with the boys we hired to watch the front door. Seems they had a difference of opinion about the current situation. One of our boys ended the discussion by jabbing an axe handle into the stomach of one of the Reds. Don't worry, he'll live."

"Graham, I'm getting a little concerned. There's been too many of these incidents and I don't think MacPherson is going to listen to Gray."

"The mayor can handle things," said George Runciman, joining Powers and Lyall in the Board of Trade's wood-paneled lounge on the main floor.

"I agree with George," said Powers, "and I've already spoken to Gray. He's got a plan in place to deal with the police. I think he's up to the job. If they won't agree to Gray's terms, he's prepared to fire them all."

"Then what?'

"Then he'll listen to what Ketchen and Perry have been telling him to do. Have a bit of faith, Hugh."

"Speaking of faith," said Lyall. "I miss Simon. Bill would've been a real source of strength in dealing with the socialist rabble. By the way, you didn't finish telling me about what Meighen had to say, Graham."

"I've convinced him that the government has to pass more stringent immigration laws to deal with the Bolsheviks. They're threatening this city and the entire country. I'm confident that this will happen within the next week, probably by order-in-council. He's also agreed to arrest the strike leaders as soon as possible," said Graham.

"And then what?" asked Lyall.

"Then we'll deport some of those bastards, and the rest we'll charge with sedition. After that, I guarantee this illegal strike will be over and we'll hear no more from Russell, Ivens, Pritchard and the rest for some time. This city will once again be ours, as it should be."

"I guess that goes for Lizowski too?" asked Runciman.

"Don't concern yourself for one more minute about that Red," said Graham. "He's as good as hanging from the end of a rope. Frankly, the evidence may be circumstantial, but it won't make one bit of difference to the jury. When I'm finished with them, they'll want to lynch that Bolshie themselves. We won't have to bother with the sedition or conspiracy charges, because he won't be alive for a second trial. Trust me."

"I hear the secretary's gone," said Runciman.

"We'll find her. I have the Mounties looking for her. She'll testify, I promise you."

"And what about your father and Klein?"

Graham sighed. "I'm afraid this is one case that the great Alfred Powers is going to lose. And as for our Hebrew detective, he may be distracted by other things. Klein's not going to save the day this time. There won't be any last minute miracles."

"From what I heard, he's relentless, Graham. How do you aim to stop him?" asked Lyall.

Graham smiled and checked the time on his gold pocket watch. "His sister was arrested about an hour ago."

"Hmm. He isn't going to like that."

"Too bad. He should've thought of that before he joined the other side. Besides, she's been having an affair with Lizowski for months."

Lyall's eyes widened.

"You haven't been keeping up with the gossip, Hugh. Too busy making money? You heard me, Rivka Klein and that bastard Lizowski. He's been cheating on his wife."

"So what did you charge her with, Graham? Having relations with a married man?" asked Runciman with a snicker.

"No, how about sedition and conspiring to start an insurrection."

"You can make a case for that?"

"I don't know. But that has nothing to do with it. I suspect that Rivka had no idea what her boyfriend was planning. I've known her for a long time. A decent enough woman, though she's got some strange political views. A bit too much of a socialist for my liking."

"If she's innocent, why arrest her?" asked Lyall.

"To keep Klein pre-occupied, I'd guess," said Runciman.

"Exactly," said Powers. "He'll be so angry that he won't have time for the Lizowski case and that, gentlemen, will be that. I figure I'll keep her locked up until the strike is over and then let her go. Who knows, she may just have some information we can use against Lizowski?"

"And if that doesn't work?"

"You don't worry about that, just leave Sam Klein to me."

"Don't run too far ahead, Bernice," said Sarah.

"I'll get her Mama," said Freda. "Don't you worry."

"You're a good girl, have I ever told you that, darling?"

"All the time," said Freda with a wide smile, as she chased after her younger sister.

Sarah was dressed in a black and white check skirt, with a matching jacket. The outfit was a little hot for this time of the year, but she ignored any discomfort. Style, rather than comfort, always came first. Her long brown hair was tucked under her summer hat, accentuated by a black lace veil that was pinned at the back. She was out for a stroll with her daughters and that demanded a certain elegance. In fact, their destination was not Carsley's for a new hat or lunch at Eaton's Grill Room, as her outfit might have suggested, but instead the P & B grocery store on McGregor Avenue. Sarah could have had her order delivered right to the apartment by one of the many boys who toiled long hours for P & B carting groceries all over the city. But she needed to get out. She needed to be seen.

Thankfully, Mr. Patterson at the store still permitted her to get her groceries on credit, although he did expect to be paid something at the end of each month. This is what it had really come to, thought Sarah, as she eyed her girls playing down the block. In another lifetime, she had been a woman of glamour and style, a woman desired by every man in the city. Now, look at what she had become. She was a housewife and a mother, pregnant again, and living from month to month, constantly scrounging for money.

She was, of course, happy with her daughters, with the prospect of having another child, and with Sam. It certainly wasn't his fault that they struggled financially; he was hard working and a good man. And she genuinely loved him, no different than she had from the first day of their marriage. It was merely that she knew that life could be better. The past few weeks had been terrible. After speaking to Melinda, they had decided that it was best to close the cosmetics shop until the strike ended. The entire labour mess made her ill. No matter how many times Sam or Rivka explained it, she saw no purpose to the unions' fight. Any businessmen she knew would never comply with their workers' wishes. Talk about turning the world upside down.

As she approached Bernice and Freda, who were throwing little pebbles at each other, a large man suddenly appeared. Normally, Sarah enjoyed chatting with anyone out for a stroll, but there was something about this person, the look on his face perhaps, that did not sit well with her. Instantly she gathered the girls toward her as the man stopped only a few feet in front of them.

"Good day Ma'am," said John Franklin, "nice weather, isn't it?"

"Yes it is," said Sarah.

"Out for a walk with your daughters? A perfect day for it."

"I thought so." He was indeed a big man with a thick neck and bushy moustache, but he seemed gentle enough. Maybe her instincts were wrong this time.

"And what are your names?" Franklin asked the girls.

"I'm Freda, and this is my sister Bernice."

"Nice names. Would you like some candy?" He pulled out a few sticks of black licorice. "Try this."

Freda looked at her mother.

"Go ahead, but give some to your sister." Freda took the candy and broke off a piece for Bernice.

"Are you new to the neighbourhood?" asked Sarah.

Franklin's smile disappeared. "This neighbourhood? Full of Jews and Galicians? I don't think so, Mrs. Klein."

Sarah gasped. "How do you know my name?"

"You really are as beautiful as they say, even if you are going to have another baby."

Sarah felt light-headed. "What is it you want? Who are you?"

"Let's say I'm a messenger."

"What are you talking about?"

Franklin reached down and lifted Bernice up.

"Put my daughter down, right now."

Bernice began to squirm and whimper.

"Listen to me carefully, you Hebrew bitch," he said to Sarah. "You tell your husband that this is his last warning. I thought I'd made myself clear at the park the other day. He had better stop his investigation on the Lizowski case or I might just pay you and the girls another visit. And next time I won't be so friendly."

"Give me my daughter," snarled Sarah, grabbing Bernice from Franklin's arms. "Leave us alone or I'll yell for the police." Her voice was shaking.

Franklin tipped his bowler hat. "Remember, pass on the message to that stubborn husband of yours. Tell him I said he should be smart and move on. I'd really hate to hurt those two little girls."

Sarah took Freda's hand, and holding Bernice, she started walking as fast as she could away from Franklin. Sarah's stomach churned and she felt as if she were about to faint. She glanced behind her and could see that Franklin was gone. She stopped for a moment and placed Bernice back on the ground. She had to speak with Sam immediately. As she looked at her daughters, she shuddered again at the thought of her conversation with that vile man. It was the frozen look in his eyes as he spoke to her that was truly frightening. She was certain that if Sam did not comply with his demands, he would return and he would hurt her and the girls as he had promised.

"We're here to see Graham Powers," said Klein.

Klein and Alfred Powers were standing on the sidewalk in front of the Board of Trade Building. A row of automobiles was parked diagonally behind them and a group of four men stood in front of the main entrance. The traffic of automobiles and horse-pulled wagons on Main Street this time of the evening was fairly light. Klein noticed one Coca-Cola wagon clipping along. The driver looked nervous, as if he knew he was committing a sin by making his deliveries during the strike.

"I got orders not to allow anyone into the building without Mr. Powers's say so." The biggest man was holding a wooden club in his hand.

"You go tell Mr. Powers that Sam Klein is here to see him."

"You're Klein?"

"That's right. You have a problem with that?"

"You're the Jew who's trying to get that Bolshevik out of jail. Did you hear that fellows?" The other men moved closer.

Klein took his hands out of pockets. "Say, what's your name?"

"Rutter."

"I don't want any trouble, Rutter."

"Turn around and leave and I guarantee there won't be any trouble, at least not now." Rutter tapped Klein on the shoulder with his club.

Klein glanced at Alfred. "Sorry Alfred, this will only take a moment. You might want to stand back." Without another word, Klein swiftly snatched the club out of Rutter's hands and pushed it under his neck as he backed him into the door.

"Stop, you're choking me," Rutter coughed. The other men moved closer.

"I wouldn't do that if I were you," said Klein, "unless you want Rutter here never to talk again."

Rutter waved his friends away. "Do as he says," he gasped.

"Now, Rutter, I'm going to release you and you're going to stand aside so me and my friend can walk peacefully inside the building. How does that sound?"

As Rutter nodded, there was a discreet cough behind them.

"Hello there. I thought you were Reds." It was Graham Powers.

Klein pushed Rutter into his friends, but he held on to the club. Rutter got up and appeared ready to charge again.

"That's not necessary, Albert," said Graham. "I think you and the boys can take a few hours off."

"This isn't over between us," said Rutter.

"Yeah, I think it is," said Klein.

"Are those thugs necessary, Graham?" asked Alfred Powers.

The younger Powers smiled but didn't offer to shake hands. "Father, good to see you too. And as a matter of fact, twice now, groups of Bolsheviks on orders from the gang at the James Street Soviet have attacked the premises."

"The James Street Soviet?"

"That's what it is, Father. And you…?"

"Yes?"

"You're one of them. How could you have taken on this case?"

"I'm defending a man on a murder charge. That's what I do. There's nothing political. But I will tell you this. You and the rest of your pompous friends on the Committee have set back relations with labour thirty years. This city may never recover from the strike."

Graham looked around the empty street. "I'd invite you in for a cigar and whisky, but I don't think the men inside would understand."

His father smiled thinly. "I guess we all have some sort of a picket line we can't cross."

"It's necessary to take a stand sometimes, didn't you teach me that?"

"Yes, but I also taught you about respecting others and being tolerant of another man's opinion."

Graham shrugged. "Times are different, attitudes change."

"Is that why you've had my sister arrested, Graham?" asked Klein. "You know she had nothing to do with Lizowski's cock-eyed plans."

"First, Sam, you give me more credit than you should. The Chief ordered the arrest of Rivka, not…"

"And you had nothing to do with it?" asked Alfred.

"It was his decision, but if you must know, I believe she has to be properly questioned. No one has charged her with anything yet."

"This is bullshit, Graham. You're going to railroad her just like you're railroading Lizowski on the Simon case," said Klein.

"Maybe she should've thought of that before she got into his bed."

Klein shook his head. "I told you there was no point to this, Alfred."

"I want to see Rivka, Graham, and I want you to arrange it," said Alfred.

"Perhaps later."

"It's a good thing you're mother isn't alive to see this. She'd be as ashamed of your behaviour as I am right now."

"Ashamed? Why? Because I care about the future. Because I'm prepared to do something to preserve the world for my children and theirs. Do either of you know what's going on in this city?"

"Yes, some hard-working people want better wages and respect for their unions," said Alfred.

"Wake up, the international Communist threat is real. Anarchists are setting off bombs in New York. The human race is fragile as it is. Rich marrying poor, Negroes with white women, Jews with Christians."

"My God, Graham, stop. You sound like Bill Simon."

"Nothing wrong with that, father. Whatever his faults, Bill knew what he was talking about. He made sacrifices neither of you will ever understand. He believed that he had a responsibility for the future of human evolution, and he aimed to do something about it."

"What exactly did he do?" asked Klein.

"Nothing. I've got nothing more to say. If you'll excuse me Father, I have some gentlemen waiting."

Alfred Powers remained silent for a moment as Graham returned inside the Board of Trade Building.

"I don't know what to say, Sam."

"You got nothing to apologize for, Alfred. He knows what he's doing."

"It's as if he's become another person. I don't know my own son. He's a complete stranger."

Klein offered Powers a cigarette, which he took. Standing on the Main Street walkway as several automobiles puttered by, both men smoked silently for a few minutes.

"I think we're in trouble, Sam," Alfred finally said. "The strike will end soon enough and then they'll deal with Lizowski, and quickly I'd wager. We're running out of time."

Klein nodded and took a final drag on his cigarette. He knew Alfred was right but he couldn't bring himself to agree, at least not out loud. Not yet. The question really boiled down to why would someone kill Bill Simon at all? What was the motive? Was it because of his antagonism toward the unions or was it something else entirely? That would have to be Klein's next avenue of inquiry. Because Powers was right, they were running out of time.

Graham Powers knew that his father would never understand the pressures and concerns that governed his actions. That was why he missed Bill Simon so much. They may not have been the best of friends, but at least Simon saw the world through the same lens as Graham. Sitting by himself in the Board of Trade office, he poured a glass of whisky and reviewed the latest correspondence from Meighen in Ottawa. As he had hoped, the proper legislation that would give him the power to dispense with the strike and its meddlesome leaders would be implemented shortly. This revolution would be over soon.

"Can I join you?"

Graham looked up into the cold eyes of John Franklin.

"Been busy today Franklin?"

"I'm doing my job, just like you wanted."

"And what about that reporter, Maloney? What the hell happened?"

"I don't know what you're talking about."

"You had nothing to do with that reporter's death? Is that what you want me to believe?"

"You can believe anything you want. But I'm telling you I don't know anything about it."

"I doubt Perry will be pleased about this."

"There's nothing for him to know. I've been filing my reports on time. All proper, just the way he likes it."

"You got it all figured out, don't you? Well, I don't like it, not for a moment. I've never been party to a murder before. I know these are dangerous times but..."

"Listen Powers, you don't know anything. You've got nothing to tell anyone cause no one murdered nobody."

"Right. And what about Bower? Have you heard from him lately?"

"They don't suspect a thing, those damn stupid Reds. They think he's one of them."

"You know that he'll be discovered. It's inevitable. I wouldn't want to be in his shoes when Russell and Armstrong get a hold of him."

"Don't concern yourself with Bower. He's not important to the larger plan."

"I suppose not. And Klein. I don't want any accidents to happen to him like Maloney. Do you understand? We've arrested his sister. That should keep him busy for the time being."

"I understand. I might just scare him a bit, that's all. Keep him off balance. You'll have to trust me."

Graham gulped his whisky and wondered how he had got so entangled with a despicable character like John Franklin. Here was a man of low morals and character, a man who was meant to follow orders rather than give them. Did it matter that he shared Graham's political principles and was as dedicated to the cause? Maybe Franklin was telling the truth about Maloney, maybe he didn't have anything to do with it. Graham reached for the bottle of whisky and poured himself another glass. There would be no answers to any of these questions today, and perhaps under the circumstances, it was better not to contemplate them at all.

15

"WHERE IS SHE?" demanded Klein. "Where's my sister? I want to see her now." He was back at the police station accompanied by Alfred Powers.

"Easy, Klein," said McCreary. "Nothing has happened to her. We haven't even had a chance to speak to her yet. She's sitting alone in a room on the second floor."

"Where?"

"Can't do it, Klein."

"You have to believe us, Sam, no harm will come to Rivka," said Hannah.

"Mr. Powers, are you acting as her lawyer?" asked McCreary.

"I am," said Alfred.

"You can see her in about twenty minutes if you like, but just you. That's the orders I got. Sorry Klein."

"This is a crock, McCreary, and you know it. Rivka is as guilty of being involved in a Bolshevik conspiracy as I am or you are. Can you at least keep her name out of the papers? I mean if Dafoe or Colonel Porter get wind of this…"

"I'll do what I can. But I can't promise you anything. This is way beyond my control. You have no idea how afraid some of the people are around here. They really believe that the city is about to be taken over by the Reds."

Klein waved his hand in disgust. He knew that McCreary's interpretation of what had transpired was more or less correct; that Rivka's troubles were largely of her own making, a consequence of poor judgement and her relationship with Lizowski. And now, the situation had become compounded by the strike leaders insistence to push the authorities to the limit. No good would come of this strategy.

"Go see her, Alfred and tell her that I'm here. Tell her not to worry."

"Leave it in my hands," said Powers. "I'll see if I can get her out of here."

"I doubt that. If she is charged with sedition, there won't be any bail for her. They'll keep her locked up until the trial," said McCreary.

"This is what it's come to," said Powers, "we're living in a bloody dictatorship. And they're worried about the Bolsheviks."

"Come on, Powers, this way," said McCreary, leading the lawyer toward the stairs.

Hannah Nash smiled sympathetically. "For what's it's worth, Sam, I think they're wrong about Rivka," she said. "It's the strike, that's all. McCreary is right about one thing. People around city hall really are frightened. You should hear some of the talk."

"Yeah, well I'm sick of the whole mess. I don't know who's right or wrong, and honestly I don't care any more. They can all go to hell, Russell, Ivens, and Graham Powers."

"Would you like to walk with me outside for a moment. You need some air."

Klein looked at Hannah for a moment. Even her drab dark uniform dress and blouse, she looked attractive to him. And despite everything that was going on, she somehow managed to make him feel at ease.

"Lead on," he said.

They left the station, walked past the group of half-dozen constables now posted on permanent guard outside the entrance, and headed toward the river. Klein gave Hannah a cigarette, took out one for himself, and lit both of them. For about five minutes they strolled in silence, comfortable in each other's company.

"I think we've found Gertie," Hannah finally said.

"Where?"

"She's been seen in Vancouver. I got a telegram late yesterday from a detective there, who's offered to assist us. Seems he owes McCreary a favour for helping him solve a case a few years back, something to do with a robbery case involving a guy named Harrison."

"Yeah, I remember that. He robbed a bunch of banks in Vancouver before heading east. McCreary caught him at a house in Point Douglas after he started a fight. So do they know where she is?"

"Not yet. But a constable reported that a woman matching Gertie's description fled a hotel without paying. Seems the woman said she was from Winnipeg. The name in the hotel register was Gertrude Jones."

"Not very clever is she?"

"If she doesn't have any money left, she won't get far. The Vancouver police have promised to check out other hotels, especially down by the waterfront. Give them a few days, they'll find her."

Klein smiled.

"What do you find so amusing, Sam?"

"You like your work, don't you?"

"I do actually. It wasn't that way when I started. There was too much animosity from the men. But now, even McCreary has accepted me, at least I think he has. And the Chief has let me leave the station house and given me other responsibilities besides chasing after stray children and wayward women. I understand now why McCreary says he'll have a hard time giving it up someday. Kind of gets into your blood."

"And how does Mr. Nash feel about all of this?"

Hannah frowned. "Ted passed on a few years ago."

"I'm sorry, Hannah. I had no idea."

"Think nothing of it. He was a good man. He had a lot of dreams. Then one day he became ill with consumption. Three months later, he was dead. It all seems like a bad dream."

"And so you joined the police?"

"I'd been working as a secretary for one of the grain companies at the Exchange and wasn't really happy doing that. Then I learned that the Chief was recruiting women police constables. I arranged to speak with him and a week later I received some training. Mostly, though, I've had to learn on the job."

"You're a strong woman, Hannah, you'll go far. And don't let McCreary or anyone else push you around."

"Why thank you, Sam. That's very nice of you to say. Now what about you? You're married, I know. Any children?"

"Yes, two daughters and…another kid on the way."

"That's lovely. What are their names?"

"Freda's the eldest, she's a bright girl just like her grandmother was. And Bernice is nearly two and a bit of a handful. It keeps us busy."

"And your wife? Sarah's her name?"

Klein nodded but didn't say anything. He suddenly felt awkward talking to Hannah about his wife and family.

"You're a lucky man, Sam. I hope you know that."

"I guess I do, at least most days."

They had reached the river. Hannah shivered as a breeze blew up from the water. "Please allow me," said Klein, draping his jacket around her shoulders.

"You're a gentleman, Sam," Hannah smiled. "Has anyone ever told you that before?"

"Not often."

"Well, I'll vouch for you if you ever need it," she grinned.

"We should be getting back, I'd like to hear from Alfred about Rivka."

"Of course."

As she turned, her shoe became caught in a wedge of mud and she stumbled. Klein reached out to grab her arm and in that instant his hand caught hers. He helped her to stand and for what seemed like a long moment he did not release his grip.

"Thanks very much," said Hannah. "I'm fine now." She blushed slightly and pulled her hand away from him. They turned and walked back up Rupert Avenue. Every so often their arms would brush against each other, although neither said anything to the other until they reached the station.

Jacob Bower could barely move. Looking around Manitoba Hall, he estimated that at least two thousand veterans had shown up for the meeting. The main room was not that large and could barely accommodate the men. Dozens were forced to stand in the passage leading to the street entrance. Even with the windows open the air inside was stale and smoky. Bower made his way to a corner near the back and found a bit of breathing space. He was hot, uncomfortable and tired. He was also weary of posing as a dedicated Red and definitely tired of listening to the daily griping of the strike leaders. From his perspective, their talk about unions and fair wages paled in comparison to their disregard for Canadian law and liberty.

That afternoon, as usual, he had two reasons for attending the meeting convened by the Great War Veterans' Association. First, as a labour representative, and second, in his real capacity as a secret operative for the RNWMP. Bob Russell had sent him there to ensure that a pro-strike resolution would be passed. John Franklin, on the other hand, wanted him to identify the true Loyalists among the men, veterans who would be prepared to join Jack Scott's group. His task was to quietly approach them and inform them about another gathering and anti-strike parade Scott had planned for the next day.

"It's time to take action gentlemen," declared Roger Bray, standing at the front of a raised dais. "Many of you, before the war took you away from the city, were loyal, decent and proud unionists. It is time to rejoin the struggle, to fight the barons on the Committee of 1000, and to make a stand. Don't forsake your fellow workers. We already have the attention of the rest of Canada. Make this strike count."

A rousing cheer from the men greeted Bray's remarks.

"I move that this association officially declare its full support for the action of the Trades and Labour Council..."

"Hold on a moment, Roger." A lean man, perhaps thirty years old, in a brown three-piece suit, approached Bray from the front of the hall. "I thought that this association had decided to remain neutral," said John Newton. "That's why I agreed to become president of this chapter to begin with. Not to fight side by side with the Reds, but to protect Canadian democracy."

Another round of cheers along with a few boos roared through the room.

"You can't sit on the fence forever," said Bray. "We can make a difference and I say let's put it to a vote."

"You should've stayed in Russia, Bray. Why'd you ever come home? You don't belong here," said a young man wearing a khaki uniform.

Half-dozen tall and scrappy-looking veterans also in khakis followed him as he pushed his way through the crowd.

"And who are you?" asked Bray.

"Name is Lewis, Tommy Lewis. Been back only a few months, but long enough to see what's going on here. I didn't watch my buddies die so the likes of you can take over this city."

"We don't want any trouble," said Newton, "why don't you boys take it easy."

"I'm not looking for trouble," said Lewis. "But get that Bolshevik off the stage."

Bray turned back to the audience. "I want a vote on my resolution…"

Before he could finish speaking, Lewis and his friends mounted the stage and advanced towards him. Behind them about ten or so of Bray's men ran up and charged the group.

"Order, order," shouted Newton.

"Let'em fight John. This ought to be good," someone yelled from the back of the room.

"There'll be no fighting here. Joe, Charlie," Newton called out. "Get some men up and here and clear all of these goons off the stage."

In a moment six burly men were on the stage standing between the Bray and Lewis groups. "Go on boys, take a seat." For a moment nobody moved until, finally, Lewis turned and ordered his men to follow him back on to the floor. The hall erupted in a mixture of catcalls and cheers.

"I say we vote on Roger's resolution," a voice from the audience cried out.

"We want a vote," other men shouted.

"Order, order," repeated Newton. "There won't be any vote."

"Why not? This is a democracy, right fellows?" asked Bray.

"Yes," came the reply.

"The resolution is that the GWVA hereby supports the current labour action and the policies of the Trades and Labour Council. All those in favour, signify by saying Aye."

"Aye," most of the men in the room yelled.

"All those opposed, say Nay," said Bray.

"Nay," the group standing around Tommy Lewis called out.

"The 'Ayes' have it. The motion is carried," said Bray.

Again the crowd roared its approval as Newton, clearly upset, adjourned the meeting.

As the men filed outside, Bower caught up with Tommy Lewis. He knew it was dangerous to be so visible, but the conversation would be short and he had no desire to track down Lewis later. Moreover, in his view, Russell, Armstrong and the others were so preoccupied with the mundane details of the strike, they likely wouldn't have noticed if the RNWMP Commissioner himself was present at their noisy meetings.

"Hey, can I speak with you for a moment?" Bower asked Lewis.

"Who the hell are you?"

"A friend. Let's move over here," he said motioning to an alleyway.

"Okay, 'friend,' what is it you want?"

"I was impressed by the way you stood up to Bray and the others."

"They're damn fools. They have no idea what they're doing."

"I couldn't agree more. Listen, there's more of us who think the same way you do. You and your boys be at Broadway Street tomorrow at one o'clock right outside the university. Jack Scott has a parade to the Legislature planned, one that will show our loyalty to the King and God. And trust me there won't be any talk of supporting Bolsheviks or Aliens."

"Yeah, I've heard of Scott. He's a good man. One o'clock tomorrow. We'll be there. Thanks for the advice."

Bower watched Lewis and the other veterans with him walk down the alleyway and out of sight. He lit a cigarette, fixed his bowler hat and buttoned his jacket. That had been easy, he thought. He had recruited another six or seven men to the Loyalist cause. Franklin and Scott would be pleased, especially since so many veterans seemed determined to march on behalf of the strikers. He pulled out his notebook and a pencil from inside his jacket pocket and began making notes of the meeting. He would be prepared when Franklin asked for a more detailed report of the gathering. No sense in making him angrier than he already was.

Bower was so engrossed in his work that he failed to notice a man move from behind a trash can in the alleyway toward the street. Peter

Mitchell, a bit pale, wiped the dirt off of his suit trousers. Bob Russell had been right, Peter thought. A few days ago, when Russell had asked him to discreetly keep an eye on Bower, he thought his friend had gone off the deep end, that the strike had made him overly suspicious and mistrustful. From what Mitchell knew of him, Bower had seemed a loyal and committed member of the cause. But now, he had heard Bower with his own ears. The man was a traitor and a spy. How he would have liked to deal with him then and there. It wouldn't take much to find a crowd on the street who would have enjoyed pummeling the likes of Jacob Bower for this deception. My God, he had had Bower over to his home for dinner! He had sat at meetings where Bower had extolled the rights of labour against the evils of capitalism. All of it had been a lie.

He picked up his pace and headed towards James Street. He couldn't wait to see the look on Bob's face when he told him that Bower had betrayed them, had betrayed them all.

16

"KLEIN HOPED THAT A stop at Arkady's Steam Bath for a *shvitz* might relax him. Located on the corner of Dufferin and McGregor, Arkady's was a popular North End gathering spot for Jews, Russians and Galicians—pretty well anyone whose first language was not English, and who was not a union man or a Bolshevik. You wouldn't find members of the Arbeiter Ring or the Ukrainian Temple here; they preferred to use a steam bath on Selkirk Avenue. At Arkady's the men could relax and soak in the steam room, play poker or pinochle, gossip about the old country, do a little business, or just *kibbitz* for an hour or two before they returned home to their wives and children.

Today, however, the place was more crowded than usual. The strike had forced many of the North End's shopkeepers, tailors, merchants, and restaurant operators to take an unwanted holiday. And there was no better way to waste an afternoon than having a *shvitz*. No matter what was happening in the city, the men could always count on Arkady's being open. As long as those who frequented the place could remember, the steam bath was closed only three days a year—on the two days of Rosh Hashana and on Yom Kippur. Arkady Kessler, the Russian-Jewish owner who had come to Canada more than two decades ago from a small town near Kiev, was too much of a capitalist to heed the warnings of the strike committee.

"I don't give a damn about those Reds," he'd grumble to anyone who'd listen. Few of his customers did, although there was nothing but talk about the strike in the steam room at the moment.

"I hear they're ready to fire the whole police force," said Manny Morroznik, a pharmacist who ran a small shop on Mountain Avenue near Salter Street. "Then what's going to happen to the city? I don't know about the rest of you, but this strike is killing me."

Several of the men, all wrapped in large white sheets, nodded in agreement.

"They should let the army deal with the whole lot of them," said Hymie Plotzer. He ran a small dry goods store on Selkirk Avenue. "I can tell you my business is down forty per cent. I don't know how much longer I can take it. I haven't told Hinda yet. Why worry her?"

"Exactly," said Manny. "I got enough problems without having my wife worrying about this as well. Too bad the mayor can't call in the Cossacks. This strike would be over tomorrow. I remember when I was twelve years old, how they tore through the town..."

"Manny, not now," pleaded a few of men. "No more stories about the pogroms, please."

Manny threw up his arms in disgust and his sheet fell to the floor. He stood there naked for a moment, but no one seemed to notice. "Hey *macher*, you know what's going on?" he called out.

Klein had just emerged from the steam room feeling slightly better, yet a hundred details were still running through his head. He was concerned about Rivka, of course, and anxious to speak with Gertie Viola. First thing tomorrow, he was going to start asking some questions about Bill Simon.

But sitting in the steam, his head covered with a towel, all Klein could really think about was Hannah. Nothing had happened, and nothing would happen, so how come he felt so guilty? He found a white sheet, lit a cigarette and sat down on an empty chair in the corner of the lounge area.

"Sam, you deaf?" asked Manny.

"I hear you, Manny," said Klein, looking up, "but I was trying to ignore you."

"You're too much of a big shot now to talk to the rest of us. I knew you when you still worked at that whorehouse."

"Okay, Manny, what is it you want to know?"

"You hear anything about what's going on at the police station?"

"Manny, I got plenty of problems to deal with at the moment. You probably heard they arrested Rivka."

"I did."

"So why are you asking me stupid questions? Do I look like the mayor?"

"Hey, easy Sam," said Hymie. "Manny was just making conversation. There's no need to get mad."

"I'm not mad," said Klein. "I came here for a *shvitz* and to be left alone. You got a problem with that?"

Nobody said a word. "Listen Manny," said Klein, "I really don't know what Gray is going to do. But if you ask me, there's bound to be some real trouble before this thing is over. It's the soldiers, they're unpredictable."

"So we agree," said Manny. "Like I said already. Now do you want to play some cribbage?"

Klein shrugged. "Oh, what the hell, why not?"

Two hours later, having beaten Manny five games in a row and with ten dollars in his pocket from his victory, Klein walked the few blocks back to his apartment. The stop at Arkady's had made him feel better, and he was anxious to see his family.

"Sarah, I'm home. Girls, where is everyone?"

Sarah came running in from the bedroom. "Shailek, where have you been? I was about to call the police." Sarah was breathing hard.

"The police? What are you talking about? I stopped at Arkady's. I told you I'd be home after five. Here sit down, you look terrible." He went to the kitchen and brought back a glass of water. "Drink this, and tell me what happened. Where are the girls?"

"They're downstairs at Shusters. They're fine. Rebecca told me she'd give them something to eat." Sarah sipped the water. "Today near the P&B, a man threatened us."

"What?"

"He threatened to hurt the girls if you didn't stop asking questions about the Lizowski case," she said, her voice strained.

"What did he look like?"

"He was a big man. He had a black moustache. Shailek, he scared the daylights out of me. Do you know who he is?"

"I've met him before, but I don't know who he is. The bastard, I'm going to kill him," said Klein in a cold voice.

"What are we going to do, Shailek? I'm telling you he was serious. What if he comes back? What if he tries to hurt the girls?" Tears were running down her cheeks.

"Sarah, no one's going to hurt the girls. Trust me. I want you to rest. I'm going to check on Freda and Bernice, and then I'm going out for a while."

Klein went into their bedroom, opened his closet and reached up to the top shelf. He pulled down a small wooden box, took out a key from his pocket and opened the box. Inside was an old Colt pistol that Klein had gotten as payment from a gun dealer he had worked for a few years ago.

Klein preferred using his fists, maybe a knife if absolutely necessary, and therefore rarely carried a gun with him. The stranger who had accosted him and his family, however, had changed the rules. No one threatened his children. When they met again, and Klein was certain they would very soon, he would be prepared. Whatever else Klein believed in, whatever other opinions he held about politics, unions, immigration, women's rights, and religion, one thing was constant in his life, and that was his family. A man, he thought, as he loaded his gun, had a right to protect his wife and children from danger, no matter what the consequences.

"You're certain, that's what he said?" asked Bob Russell. He sat facing Peter Mitchell at a small wooden desk in an office at the Labour Temple. The two men were alone and the windows in the room closed.

"I'm telling you Bob, honest to God, Bower was recruiting for the Loyalist march. Whoever he is, I can tell you one thing for sure, he's not one of us."

Russell stared at Mitchell for a minute. In fact, he was not all that surprised by his friend's discovery. For some reason, he had expected news like this. He couldn't quite put his finger on it, but Bower had seemed different than the other men he worked with on James Street.

He was a little too enthusiastic, always quoting Lenin or Trotsky, always asking questions about this person or that person. It was as if he was acting and from what Mitchell had told him, that now appeared to be the case.

"Have you told anyone else about this, Peter?"

"Not a soul. You told me to report only to you and that's what I did. You know me Bob, I can follow orders."

"I know you can. We're not going to say a word about this to anyone else, understand?" Mitchell nodded. "Not until I can figure out what Bower is up to. And who he's working for, though I think I already know."

"The feds?"

"Yeah, I'll bet you a silver dollar that he's a Mountie agent."

Mitchell took a deep breath. "Bastards."

"Who else would be spying on us and trying to make so many problems? It has to be. Listen, Peter, from now on you have one job: to keep an eye on Bower. Stay close to him. I want to know where he goes and who he talks to."

"I don't know, Bob, a Mountie…"

He stood up and grabbed Mitchell by the shoulder. "Peter, you can do this. It's important. I think we're close to having Norris and Gray accept our terms. They'll force that damn Committee of 1000 to listen to us. I don't want the Mounties ruining everything we've worked so hard for."

"Okay, Bob, if it'll help the cause, I'll do it."

"Good," said Russell, "I knew I could count on you."

By noon the next day, a crowd of hundreds of Loyalists had gathered on Broadway. Tommy Lewis and his men dressed in khakis were there along with other returned soldiers. But there were also lawyers, accountants, insurance agents and real estate clerks. They had come to march, and to voice their profound disapproval of the strike. The former soldiers in particular were loud, boisterous and in a feisty mood. Many of them carried wooden clubs, while others hoisted an assortment of banners above their heads.

"We Will Maintain Constituted Authority, Law & Order," one banner read. "To Hell With The Alien Enemy. God Save The King." At the front of the march was Jack Scott, along with several representatives from the Committee of 1000, including George Runciman, Hugh Lyall and Tom Deacon.

"Remember, Scott," said Deacon. "This has to be peaceful. We don't want any trouble. The police are edgy enough, and most of them are pro-strike."

"You worry too much, Deacon. I can keep my boys in line. But if there is trouble, we can handle it."

"That's exactly what I'm afraid of," said Deacon.

"Easy, Tommy," said George Runciman. "Let them have their moment. We'll show the rest of the country that the Reds don't have control of the city."

At that, Scott waved his arm and shouted to the men to fall in line. The massive group, banners at the front, slowly paraded down Broadway, across Osborne, and towards the front steps of the Manitoba Legislative Buildings.

The politicians were waiting for them. "We support your call for law and order," Premier Norris shouted from the top of the stairs. "We're doing everything we can to end this illegal strike."

The men roared their approval. Twenty minutes later, after drawing throngs of spectators on Main Street, they reached city hall. At one point, a shouting match erupted between Tommy Lewis and a pro-strike veteran standing on the sidewalk. But fortunately, cooler heads prevailed.

The reception at city hall was similar. Mayor Gray, with General Ketchen at his side, greeted the Loyalist marchers. The mayor stood before the crowd in a dark three-piece suit. The chain of his watch hung loosely out of one vest pocket and across to the other. His right hand was planted on his hip.

"Welcome, loyal gentlemen," said Gray, "it's a pleasure to see so many of you who stand for decency. The Bolshevik menace will not win here. Not today, not ever."

There was raucous applause.

"Gentlemen, I have something to tell you. As of five o'clock this afternoon, Chief MacPherson is no longer in charge of the city police force. Deputy-Chief Chris Newton has agreed to replace him. As many of you know, the men on the force were required to take an oath of allegiance to the city and to the department. Many have chosen not to do so and have been dismissed."

Another round of applause and cheering rang out in Market Square. Gray knew that he wasn't being quite truthful. After failing to comply with the Police Commission's request to administer the oaths of allegiance, MacPherson was asked to take a leave of absence, but he had refused. The members of the Commission then decided to fire him and ask Newton, who had supported their position, and accepted their conditions, to assume command. But they had not taken into account that many of the constables would walk off their jobs in support of MacPherson. In all, two hundred and fifty constables had been dismissed and as of that moment the entire city of Winnipeg had only twenty-two active constables.

"We need your help," declared General Ketchen. "We'll deal with all Aliens and Bolsheviks very soon. I think that when the time comes for all of the information to be given to you officially, you'll realize that I have told you only a part of it. Right now, it is our duty to support civic authority, and I would ask you to do your best in backing up the mayor in whatever he puts before you."

"We'll do our best," shouted one of the men.

"Tomorrow morning," added the mayor, "be at the Auditorium at nine o'clock. We'll be swearing in special constables to keep order during the remainder of the strike. I can offer you six dollars a day for your service."

Again the men roared their approval.

"I can guarantee you that when this thing is over the British flag will still be on city hall, and not the red flag."

"Let's give three cheers and a tiger," said Scott raising his right hand. General Ketchen stood beaming at the audience.

"Hurrah! Hurrah! Hurrah!" shouted the men, "And Hurrah!" they added for good measure.

As each cheer echoed from across the street into his tiny cell, Metro Lizowski grew more impatient. He paced back and forth.

"Hey Red, if you don't stop that you're going to make a hole in the floor," said Constable Harrison Barkley, who was sharing guard duties this week. Unlike the majority of his colleagues and friends in the department, Barkley had willingly signed an oath of allegiance. He had no desire to be a member of any union, believed strongly that Canada should remain a democracy, and most importantly, had three young children to feed.

"Yeah, Red, listen to what Barkley has to say. Might learn something," grumbled Alex Andrews from another cell. Andrews was a retired teacher with a bad drinking problem. Two days ago at a strikers' rally in Victoria Park, he had been arrested for possessing a bottle of home-made whisky.

"Andrews, keep your mouth shut," said Lizowski. "You're a disgrace, has anyone ever told you that?"

"Every day, as a matter of fact," said Andrews laughing.

Lizowski sat down on the edge of his wooden bunk and tried to think. After more than a week, he'd had enough of jail. He was hungry, needed a bath, and was tired of waiting for his day in court. Besides, he was certain that they were going to railroad him for Simon's murder no matter what he said. He had been foolish to store that Bolshevik material at his home. He saw that now. Look at the consequences. His chances of an acquittal on the murder charges were slim, and Rivka had been arrested.

He had not seen her since they had brought her in, but Barkley had confirmed to him that she was being held in a special detention area for women one floor up. He missed her terribly, and somehow he had to speak with her. His time in jail had also allowed him to focus on the issues at hand more clearly than he had ever done before. He had arrived at several key decisions. For one thing, he realized that he was prepared to leave his wife and spend the rest of his life with Rivka. But that was only part of it. When he left Winnipeg for good, he was going to leave his tormentors and enemies a message, something they'd never forget. It was more daring and dangerous than anything he had ever thought of.

Who knows for certain what drives men's passions? Lizowski did not stop to think about the consequences of what he was about to do—

how it would merely confirm his guilt in the eyes of the law, his friends and the public—he only knew that he had to act. Glancing at Barkley, he suddenly keeled over in apparent pain and dropped to the cement floor.

"What's going on?" demanded the constable.

"I need a doctor," groaned Lizowski. "You got to get me outta here."

Barkley approached the cell and peered in. "Hey, Lizowski, get up. You just got a bellyache, that's all."

At that Lizowski writhed in more pain.

"And here I thought this shift was going to be easy," grumbled Barkley as he opened the cell door. He bent down to pull Lizowski up. The prisoner was limp and it took Barkely a considerable effort to lift him to his feet. As soon as Lizowski was standing, he slammed Barkley's head into the iron bars of the cell door, a hard blow that cut open his forehead and dazed him. He looked up in astonishment as Lizowski smashed him again with a wooden stool. Barkely's legs buckled and he fell to the floor unconscious.

"Have you gone mad?" said Andrews from the other cell.

"Go to hell."

"Take me with you."

Lizowski ignored him. He snatched the ring of keys from Barkley's belt and moved down the hall toward the door. Due to the mass dismissal of constables, the corridors in the station house were largely deserted. The new chief had been able to assign only a skeleton staff. Any remaining constables still on duty were out keeping the streets safe—that is ensuring that the strikers were kept in check. As silently as he could, Lizowski scampered up the stairs. There was a row of half a dozen doors in front of him. He could hear voices from behind two of them. He looked to his right and then left, and chose the door at the far end of the hallway. It took a few more moments to figure out which key fit the lock. Finally, after what seemed like an eternity, the lock opened and he peered inside. There were three cells, similar to the ones on the floor below, except this room was unguarded.

Rivka sat by herself in the third cell reading a book. Hearing the door open she glanced up to see who had entered.

"Metro, my God, what are you doing here?"

He raised his finger to his lips as he unlocked her cell. "Later. I'll tell you everything later, but first we're both getting out of here." He unlocked her cell.

They embraced each other and kissed. "I can't…I can't do this, Metro. Don't you see…"

He stopped her. "You must come with me now."

She hesitated, and he extended his right hand toward her. "Rivka, I love you, come with me."

She placed her hand in his and grasped it tightly. Together they proceeded down the stairs to the back door of the station, where they ran directly into a constable. Before he could react, Lizowski pushed him hard and he stumbled backwards down the stairs. Lizowski and Rivka ran through the door and down the alleyway.

17

KLEIN HAD TOSSED AND TURNED the whole night. Where was Rivka? How could she have been so foolish? A jail break, for God's sake! One minute he was furious with her, the next as worried as their mother would have been. He also knew what Rivka would have said to him—that she loved Lizowski, and believed in him.

"I have a right to choose my own path in life," he could almost hear her declaring. Rivka never did anything halfway. Whether it was fighting for the rights of workers, or organizing children's entertainment for the Bund's annual *Chanukah* pageant, she put all her heart into it. While he may not have told her often, he admired her conviction and dedication, qualities he sometimes found lacking in himself.

The only thing that gave him momentary relief was that the police department was in as big a mess as it ever had been. Klein had heard that the new chief had put McCreary in charge of tracking down Lizowski and Rivka, but had assigned him only three constables. Everyone Klein spoke to agreed that a showdown between the strikers and authorities was looming. McCreary and his team were bound to be distracted for a few days at least. Maybe Klein could find Rivka and Lizowski before the police did. Who knew what would happen if Lizowski was confronted. Did he have a weapon with him? Would he be stupid enough to use it? Would he put Rivka's life in danger? Klein rolled over and, still half asleep, reached for his cigarette case.

"Shailek, come quick," said Sarah from the other room.

"What now?" he muttered getting out of bed. He threw on some pants, fastened his suspenders without a shirt and slipped on a pair of wool socks. Then he lit a cigarette.

"Shailek, where are you?" The call echoed through their apartment.

He found Sarah in the kitchen. Freda was eating her breakfast. He gave her a pat on the head.

"What happened, Sarah? Coffee not hot enough?"

"Don't be such an idiot, Shailek. Here, look at this," she said.

"Mama thinks Papa's an idiot," yelled Freda, scampering out of the kitchen. "Bernice!"

"Wonderful, Sarah. You think you're still at Melinda's. For Christ sakes…"

"I'll talk to her. Will you please read this." She handed him a single sheet of paper folded in half. "I found it slipped under the door this morning."

Klein unfolded the note. On it, printed in Hebrew letters, was a message in Yiddish: "I'm safe. Don't worry." It was signed with the Hebrew letter "Raish" for the letter "R."

"You found this under the door?"

"That's what I said. At least we know she's alright."

Klein threw the paper into the garbage. "She has no idea what kind of trouble she's in. At least they're still in the city. They've got to be hiding out with some of Lizowski's Bolshevik friends."

Sarah handed him a mug of coffee. "Or maybe they went…"

"Where?"

"If you'd let me finish. Not too long ago, I spoke with Rivka about those secret compartments in Melinda's house."

"For customers who want real privacy."

"I think she's using them for stashing liquor now."

"I hadn't thought of that. But, I can't believe Melinda wouldn't let me know."

Sarah looked at him. "The things you don't know, Shailek, I could write a book about. If there's anyone who'd help someone on the run, it would be Melinda. Talk to her. It couldn't hurt."

Klein drank his coffee and sat down on a chair by the kitchen table. He had much to contemplate. Sarah might be right. Although Melinda had no sympathy for Lizowski's politics, he knew that she would do anything to help Rivka—even put herself in danger. Over the years, Melinda had amassed so many contacts at city hall that she probably thought she was invincible. But she was wrong. The stand against the workers was about preserving power for the city's wealthy, and no Point Douglas Madam was going to get away with harbouring a Bolshevik fugitive.

"Daddy, daddy," said Bernice tugging on Klein's sleeve.

"Yes, yes, Neicee, what is it?"

"Daddy, you idiot."

As Sarah laughed, Klein rose from the table. He had a half-smile on his face as he waved to Sarah. "I've got work to do. Will you please deal with her?"

"Bernice, come here, we have to talk."

"You can't be serious," said Jimmy Sykes. "Bower's a spy?"

"You heard right," said Peter Mitchell. "He's a lying son-of-a bitch. Now pass me that bottle."

It was not even noon yet but the two men, along with Scott MacDonald and George Timmins, friends from the factory, had been drinking for more than an hour. Mitchell had promised Bob Russell that he would keep the truth about Jacob Bower a secret. But the more he drank, the angrier he became.

"So what do you want to do about it?" asked Sykes. He was six feet four and had a well-deserved reputation for being a brawler. More than once, he had been thrown out of Main Street bars, and had often spent a night in the police station sleeping off a bout of drinking.

"We can't just do nothing," said Scott MacDonald. "I'm not very good at keeping secrets."

"I don't know," Mitchell. "I think Russell was going to handle it."

"And who appointed him judge and jury?" asked Sykes. "Seems to me that a few of the strike leaders are no better than the bosses. Think they're all high and mighty. Look at the mess they've got us into. My wife's yelling at me day and night. We got no food for the kids. I'll tell you guys, she doesn't want to hear anything more about unions."

"It's the same story at my place," said Timmins. "I don't know what I'm going to do if this trouble ain't over soon and I'm back to work."

The four sat passing the bottle of whisky for a few moments in silence.

"We need to teach Bower a lesson," Sykes finally said.

"As long as we don't hurt him too bad," said Mitchell.

"He'll never know what hit him," said Sykes with a smile. "Timmins, MacDonald, you with us?"

The two nodded in agreement.

"So what are we waiting for? Let's find that piece of shit and deal with him the way we deal with any bug—we'll squash him into the dirt."

Klein had not walked more than four blocks down Main Street before he ran into a gang of newly commissioned "specials." Wearing their Sunday best, they had been sworn in as peace officers by Mayor Gray, given wagon spokes to use as clubs, and ordered to patrol the streets exercising 'good judgement and restraint'. Almost all of those who volunteered for duty were veterans and supporters of the Loyalists. But there was also a group of students from the University of Manitoba looking to make a few extra dollars. In all, close to two thousand men had come forward to take an oath to enforce the law.

"You looking for Lizowski?" one of the specials asked Klein.

"I'm out for a stroll, that's it."

"I'd watch my back if I were you, Klein. You never know who might be waiting for you."

"You talk pretty tough with a bat in your hand."

Klein was in no mood for a brawl, but he had little patience for loudmouths who threatened him. He moved toward the man, but his friends blocked Klein's path.

"Go on your way, Klein," another of the specials said. "We don't want any trouble, at least not right now. Just doing our job."

Klein pushed his way through the men and proceeded down the street. His destination was Melinda's house, but by the time he reached the corner of Main and Euclid, he could see a mass of people moving in the direction of Portage Avenue. Other small groups of specials, some on foot and some riding horses supplied by Eaton's, followed close behind.

There was going to be trouble for sure, Klein thought. He knew that it was best to avoid it—he had enough problems at the moment. And yet, Klein rarely could mind his own business. It was one of his flaws that he was prepared to acknowledge. Maybe, he reasoned, someone among the throng of people might be willing to talk about Lizowski. Who knows who he'd find there? In less than a minute, he had determined his course of action and joined the march for Portage Avenue.

By the time he arrived, fifteen minutes later, a large crowd had gathered, perhaps two thousand people. Traffic had come to a standstill as the largely pro-strike mob poured into the middle of the street. There was a lot of noise and shouting, "We want our jobs back," someone yelled. "Unions will lead us to victory," another person shouted. Still, the mood was fairly cheerful, until the specials arrived.

Holding their wooden truncheons in one hand, a row of specials that stretched from one side of Main Street to the other waded into the mass of strikers. Klein recognized a few of the men, including Jack Scott leading a pack towards him.

"Move along, no standing here," shouted one of Scott's men as he shoved Klein in the back with his club.

"You think that piece of wood makes you tough, Scott?" asked Klein.

"Just doing my duty, Klein, but you wouldn't know anything about that would you?" Some of the men beside Scott laughed.

Klein turned and pushed Scott backward so hard that he fell into his friends. Before the specials could retaliate, a group of workers whom Klein did not know, rushed forward so that they stood between him and the specials.

At that moment, specials on horseback arrived and all hell broke loose. Someone in the crowd threw a bottle at one of the riders, and then another. Stones, and whatever people could find on the ground flew through the air. One of the bottles hit a mounted special in the head and he fell off his horse. Two constables ran to help him.

Within minutes, the cheerful pro-strike outing had turned into an ugly riot. The specials started swinging their clubs and there were screams as men and women ran for cover. One elderly gentleman was nearly trampled to death before Hannah Nash helped him up. Chief Newton had ordered McCreary to take as many constables as he could find and keep the peace. McCreary initially refused Hannah's offer to join him, but her protests eventually wore him down.

"I guarantee you, Mrs. Nash," he had said, "this is no place for a woman. But if you want to get yourself killed, that's your business."

Hannah noticed Klein first. She started walking toward him, then saw a special on horseback begin his charge. Holding his club like a lance, the rider took aim at Klein's head.

"Sam, watch out, behind you," yelled Hannah.

Klein swung around and ducked his head just as the special passed him by.

"Thanks," he shouted back. "That would've hurt, I think." Klein looked at Hannah, and the rioters swirling about her and decided, for once, to do the smart thing. He grabbed the startled policewoman around the waist, and ducked into an alley away from the chaos of the street.

John Franklin always bragged that he took advantage of the opportunities presented to him. When Commissioner Perry approached him about doing undercover work, he jumped at the chance and never regretted it for a moment. In fact, it suited his style and temperament much better than a posting at a prairie outpost. It was the same with his relationship with Bill Simon. The money Simon offered him for his services was impossible to turn down, but it was Simon's philosophy on life that ultimately cemented their friendship. He had never met anyone quite like him before. Simon had vision, a rare quality in most men, in Franklin's opinion. He grasped the significance of modern life with all of its various pitfalls—the dangers posed by mass immigration, unions, women's rights, Jews and Orientals.

To his mind, Simon represented purity, order and virtue. His death was a tragedy from which the city would never recover. Whether Lizowski killed Simon or not was hardly the point, thought Franklin.

There was, as Simon used to say, a certain order of things. It was nature's way. That Lizowski had to pay for Simon's murder made perfect sense to Franklin.

From the second storey window above Joe's Confectionery half a block from Portage and Main, Franklin finally found his prey. One quick bullet to the head and another problem would be taken care of. Then, he would deal with Lizowski and his Hebrew whore in his own way. He had not counted on Lizowski's escape, but here was an opportunity not to be missed. He was already hot on their trail and was confident that he could find them before the police did. After that, he knew he had to fulfill the contract he had made with Simon. He owed him that much at least, and besides, the world would be better for it.

He removed a Ross rifle, standard army-issue, from its case and poked its barrel through the window. Klein was talking to the policewoman. He looked through his scope. He had a clear shot.

"Are you all right, Mrs. Nash?" Klein asked as he shielded her body from another spray of broken glass flying into the alley.

"I thought I told you to call me by my first name." Hannah was still panting from their run. "After all, you do seem to have your arms around me."

Klein stepped back. Before Hannah could say another word, a new contingent of specials arrived out on the street and the crowd slowly started to disperse.

Hannah took a deep breath. "Well, it looks like the worst is over. Next time, Gray is liable to send in the army."

Two longish curls from her hair hung down over her eyes so that she was forced to brush them away. Klein stared, wishing he could brush them away for her. If only—

Bang! The bullet smashed into the masonry two inches above his head. Klein froze, wondering if he had been hit. Or worse, maybe Hannah—

"Move, Sam, now!" Hannah grabbed Klein's arm and yanked him farther into the alley.

A second shot rang out. This time it hit the ground just behind them There was screaming from the street as people realized a sniper was firing.

A few moments later, Klein and Hannah huddled in the recessed doorway of a loading dock.

"You okay?" Hannah asked, her eyes wide.

"I guess. I'm still in one piece, thanks to you."

"I could order some constables to…"

"Don't bother. Whoever tried to kill me is gone by now."

Hannah bit her lower lip. "I'm so glad nothing happened to you, Sam."

"Me too."

She moved towards Klein, touched his shoulder and then slowly reached up and kissed him. Klein did not pull away. He closed his eyes and kissed her back. After a long moment, they stopped.

"I…I don't know what to say," said Hannah.

"Nothing to say."

"I don't know why I…"

"Hannah," Klein's voice was thick with emotion, "We both had to do it, but we can never do it again."

A sudden scream startled them. "Someone help. A man's been hurt," a woman yelled from the street.

After one last hug, Klein and Hannah rushed back onto Main Street. Several specials were huddled around a body in a doorway.

"What's going on?" demanded Hannah.

The specials parted, and there in a pool of blood, lay Jacob Bower. Klein reached down to feel his neck.

"Is he dead?" asked Hannah.

"No. Not yet."

"Quickly, you two," Hannah said to the specials. "Fetch me a wagon. We have to get this man to a hospital."

"We don't take orders from no woman."

"I'm a Winnipeg constable," said Hannah showing them her badge. "If you want to keep your job, you'd better listen to me. Does anyone know this man's name?"

"It's Bower, Jacob Bower," said a woman who was standing nearby. "He works with Russell."

"None of our men did this," said one of the specials.

From the looks of it, the man had received a severe beating. Klein, too, doubted whether any of the specials would have gotten that carried away. This went way beyond the bounds of keeping the peace. But if the specials didn't do this, Klein wondered, who did? And more importantly, why?

18

"WHAT A FIASCO. I've never seen such incompetence. They were ordered to keep the peace, not start a bloody riot," said Graham Powers. He was pacing back and forth in a meeting room on the second floor of the Board of Trade building.

"Easy Graham, you're going to make yourself ill," said Tom Deacon. "The specials will do a better job next time."

"Next time! Is that all you've got to say, Tom?"

Deacon shrugged. "In a war like this, there's bound to be a few casualties."

Around the table were the four members of the executive of the Committee of 1000, along with Mayor Gray, General Ketchen and Chief Newton. Only George Runciman was absent.

"How many were hurt?" asked Graham.

"Nothing too serious," said Ketchen. "Several of the strikers were treated for cuts and bruises. One of our men, Fred Coppins, was injured. Says he fell off his mount when he was hit in the face by a rock. He's been treated by a doctor. He's ready to go back to duty. I wouldn't expect anything less from a soldier who received the Victoria Cross."

"I hear he was beat up by a gang of Austrians, CPR workers," said Hiram Maxwells.

"Anyone else hurt?" Graham asked.

"Someone took a few shots at your friend Klein."

"Jesus Christ!"

"Either the shooter had a bad aim, or Klein is one lucky bastard."

"My men searched the building where we think the shots were fired from, but we found nothing," said Chief Newton.

"Figures," said Graham.

"What do you mean by that?" asked Newton.

"Forget it. I meant that whoever tried to kill Klein was smart enough to cover his tracks."

"There was one more casualty," said Ketchen.

"All I heard was it was one of the members of the Trade Council executive."

"That's only part of the story. It was Bower. He's in pretty rough shape. I haven't been able to speak with him yet. The doctor says it'll be a few more days before he can talk. A real bloody mess."

"None of the specials did this. I had each of the group leaders report directly to me," said Newton.

"Someone found out who he really was," said Graham.

"I think so. Although, even for Russell this is bad. I wouldn't have believed it of him," said Ketchen.

"He's a Bolshevik, what's to understand?" asked Deacon.

"Talk to him, Brigadier," said Graham. "But you'd better report this to Perry and tell him that one of his agents is out of work. Now, dare I ask about Lizowski?"

"We're doing the best we can. I got as many men as I can spare going door to door in the North End. I have McCreary working around the clock. He'll find him, if anyone can," said Newton.

"I don't want him or Rivka Klein hurt, Chief. Tell McCreary to bring him in and then we'll deal with him," said Graham.

"And if he pulls a gun?" asked Deacon.

"Then, I guess McCreary will have to use whatever means he feels is necessary," said Graham.

"Exactly. How much longer does this Red have to give us headaches? Bill would've known what to do."

"Why don't you enlighten us," said Graham.

"He would have said two things. First, that liberty is meaningless without order. And second, when there's a blight or menace, when we have reached a point where impurities threaten the human race, then some hard choices have to be made."

"Which means what exactly?" asked Graham.

"It means that we crush this strike and soon. Then we get rid of the bad apples. The General already has a plan," said Deacon.

All eyes turned to Ketchen. "It's simple. We round up as many of the Reds as we can and lock them away at Camp Kapuskasing in Northern Ontario. Nothing but forest and trees up there to keep them company. It's just like Siberia, I'd bet. We deport who we can, but we find some way to keep them there for as long as necessary. As for the leaders…"

"Leave them to me. I'm already working with Ottawa on charges of sedition and treason," said Graham.

"No more marches and parades either. If I have to, I'll enforce the Riot Act." Gray said.

Graham Powers liked what he was hearing. His father had taught him to respect liberal values and to cherish freedom. And that's just what he was doing. Sacrifice, as Bill Simon used to argue, was essential in order to preserve the institutions of life that really matter. How many times did his father quote from the writings of Edmund Burke? "Among a people generally corrupt, liberty cannot long exist." Those words were now ringing in his head. Cure the corruption, rid the body of the cancer, and liberty will be preserved. There was no other way.

Look what had happened in the United States. Like every other member of the Committee, Graham had been shocked when news of the unsettling events of June 2 finally reached Winnipeg. Anarchists and Bolsheviks had planted a series of bombs at the homes of many prominent Americans, including Attorney-General Mitchell Palmer and Navy Secretary Franklin Roosevelt. Only good fortune prevented any of the intended targets from being killed or seriously injured.

Graham looked around the table wondering if his associates truly understood the dangerous times. The General was a decent man. Graham was confident that he could get the job done. Gray, Deacon and the other leaders of the committee were hardly exceptional men, but capable enough. Circumstances borne out of the prairie urban experience had pushed otherwise ordinary individuals into positions of leadership, and they had taken up their responsibilities with diligence

and enthusiasm. No one could fault them for that. The strike would end soon, he believed, and then the city would return to the way it was.

As Graham saw it, there was only one problem he could not control, and that was Franklin. When he heard about Klein almost being killed, he knew it had to have been Franklin who did the shooting. No one else would have been so brazen. At that moment, Graham made up his mind that Franklin had to be stopped one way or the other, no matter what secrets he knew, or who he could expose. Franklin was as corrupt as the Bolsheviks he was trying to defeat. Graham had ignored the journalist's death, which was probably a mistake, but not this. Things were getting out of hand.

"They're not here, I swear it, Sam. And will you please stop yelling," said Melinda.

"I want to see the room for myself," demanded Klein.

"It's being...occupied at the moment. You'll have to wait."

"Melinda, right now."

Klein was in no mood to be toyed with, not even by Melinda. What the hell had he been thinking? Flirting with Hannah, and then kissing her. And yet, as he made his way back to Point Douglas, all he could think about was the taste of her lips. Had they been anywhere else but in an alleyway, he wasn't sure if he would have been able to stop himself. Hannah had wanted to accompany him to Melinda's, but he had refused her offer. If Rivka and Lizowski were found, it would complicate matters with a constable by his side. He wasn't even certain what he was going to say to them, or how he would convince them to turn themselves in. Rivka he could handle, but why should Lizowski trust him?

"I'm telling you Sam, you're making a fool of yourself."

"Yeah, well, it's not the first time."

For an early afternoon, the house was busier than usual. Clearly not all the strikers were protesting at Portage and Main. As Klein marched through the parlour, he interrupted a high stakes poker game.

"Sam, what you doing here?" asked Frankie Thomas.

"Can't talk now, Frankie."

"Heard about your sister. They find her yet?"

Thomas, who grew up in the North End, had known Klein for years. He owned a small hotel in St. Boniface and was a frequent visitor to Melinda's.

"Not yet."

"You're welcome to pull up a chair."

Thomas meant well, he was just a bit of a fool, always had been. Over the years, he must have lost hundreds. The unluckiest man Klein had ever seen play poker. He couldn't win if his life depended on it.

"I'd love to take more of your money Frankie, but I have some work to do," said Klein. The door to the secret room was behind a large turquoise and black coloured wall hanging of a naked woman surrounded by male angels. Melinda had imported the "art work," as she called it, from a shop in Paris.

Klein peeled back the hanging and opened the door. "Rivka, it's Sam. Are you in there?"

"Sam, don't," said Melinda, trying to grab his arm.

It was too late. Klein entered the dimly lit and windowless room.

"Sam, nice to see you again," said Darlene, one of Melinda's most lovely girls. She was naked, on her knees, her body arched forward. Her eyes were glassy, probably from the laudanum that some of the girls used to make their lives more bearable. Standing in front of her, with his pants around his ankles, both his hands cupping her breasts, was George Runciman.

At first, Klein did not recognize him. Runciman stopped immediately, pulled up his trousers and buttoned them. "Melinda, what's going on here?" His face was red with anger and exertion. "I pay for privacy. What kind of sick…"

"Sam, you and George know each other?" said Darlene calmly, rising to her feet.

Klein shrugged. "Yeah. Runciman, right? You work at Simon's factory."

"Darlene, put a robe on now," said Melinda. "George, I'm sorry."

"Don't be mad at Melinda, Runciman. It's my doing," said Klein. "I thought someone I know was hiding in here. I should've known that Melinda was telling the truth."

"I'd say so."

"Listen, George. Come back another time. On the house. What do you say?" asked Melinda.

"As long as Darlene will be here."

"I'm all yours, honey, and we can finish what you started," she said running her fingers through Runciman's hair. It only took a wave of Melinda's hand and she left the room.

"Klein, I trust you can be discreet about this. I have a family, a reputation in the community," said Runciman.

"It's none of my business what a man does in his spare time."

"I come here because…"

Klein laughed. "Runciman, you don't owe me an explanation. But seeing how we ran into each other, I wouldn't mind having a word with you about Simon."

Runciman was silent for a moment. "All right, but not here. Come to my house tomorrow night and we can talk. I don't think anyone will be home then. I'm at 198 Spence, two houses from Broadway. It's a big house, you can't miss it."

"I'll find it. Seven o'clock?"

"Fine. Now if you'll excuse me."

A few minutes later, Klein and Melinda sat down in her parlour for a schnapps. "Feeling proud of yourself, Sam?" asked Melinda.

"Not especially. I'm worried about Rivka, that's all. She has no idea what she's got herself mixed up in. The city's like a powder keg, and those specials are as dangerous a lot as I've seen. More than one of them have spent time in jail."

"Yeah well, it's kept the cops out of my hair for a while. Thank God the girls don't want to organize a union."

Klein smiled. He pulled out two cigarettes, lit both and gave one to Melinda. She took it, inhaled deeply and patted Klein's cheek.

"Runciman come around here a lot?" asked Klein.

"Once every couple of weeks. Seen him a little more since the strike began, though. Nice enough fellow. And he always tips."

"So, Melinda, where is she?"

Melinda blushed, something Klein thought was physically impossible. "Oh to hell with it. They're at Hilda's, in the back room.

I promised Rivka I'd keep quiet." She shrugged. "Don't be rough with her, Sam."

Klein knew he needed to be calm. Anger and shouting were not going to get Rivka out of this mess, or save Lizowski from the gallows. He had to get them back to jail; Alfred Powers would have to do the rest.

Klein pushed opened the gate leading to Hilda's front door and stopped in his tracks.

"Thought we'd join the hunt," said McCreary, standing on the stoop. Hannah Nash was beside him. She looked at Klein and then turned away.

"One of the girls tell you?" asked Klein.

"Don't you know me by now, Klein? Some of these whores actually like me," said McCreary with a laugh. "I thought Mrs. Nash might be able to talk some sense into that stubborn sister of yours. Mind you, I had to twist her arm to come with me."

Klein joined them on the porch.

"I'm sorry Sam. I tried to respect your wishes about this," said Hannah.

"It doesn't matter," he said brushing her shoulder with his hand. "McCreary, let me go in first. I don't want any violence."

McCreary stared at Klein for a moment. "Get on with it. You've got five minutes," he said, pulling his revolver out of his holster.

"Is that necessary?" asked Hannah.

"We got a scared Bolshevik on the run for murder. Yeah, I'd say it's necessary."

Klein pushed the front door open. "Hilda, it's Sam Klein. I'm coming in."

Unlike Melinda's, the house was nearly empty. An elderly gentleman sat on a chair in the parlour puffing a fat cigar. Two young women, wearing little, knelt beside him on the floor. One of the girls had her hand in his pants.

"They're in the back," said the man, as the women giggled.

"My turn," said the other one who now put her hand inside the man's pants.

"Ten minutes and counting girls. I told you I could do it."

Klein moved silently through the long hallway into the kitchen. Hilda Meyers sat at a round pine table with Rivka and Lizowski.

"Sam, I was wondering when you'd be here. I told these kids they should leave, but no one listens to me. I have no *mazel*, you know that?"

"You okay?" Klein asked his sister.

"Shailek, we had to try. I told Metro you'd come after me."

"I can't believe…" Klein stopped himself.

"Listen, we want to surrender," said Rivka. "Both me and Metro. There's nowhere for us to go. Metro wants to speak with Alfred Powers."

McCreary marched in. "That right, Lizowski? You're going to come peacefully?" he demanded, his gun pointing at the two of them.

Lizowski nodded. He kissed Rivka, then held his hands out to McCreary. As the cop holstered his pistol to take out his handcuffs, Lizowski suddenly punched McCreary hard in the stomach, then pushed Klein so that he tumbled backward into Hannah.

"Metro, no," shouted Rivka, her hands over her mouth.

Lizowski slammed his shoulder into Hilda's back door and it flew off the hinges. He ran toward the fence.

McCreary scrambled to his feet. "Stop, Lizowski, or I'll shoot," he yelled.

"Don't. No," screamed Rivka. She ran at McCreary, pushing his arm upward as a shot rang out. The bullet hit the ceiling. By the time McCreary recovered, Lizowski was over the fence and gone.

"Goddamn it. I thought you said this was going to be easy, Klein. Nash, put the cuffs on her."

"McCreary, she's no trouble. Rivka's coming with me," said Klein.

"Get away from her," said McCreary. "I mean it." He pointed his gun at Klein. "So help me Klein, move."

Hannah slowly walked in front of McCreary. The pistol was now pointing at her chest. "Please Bill, put the gun down," she said quietly.

McCreary stared first at her, then at Klein. He shrugged and lowered the revolver.

"I'm sorry Shailek," Rivka said in Yiddish. "I really thought Metro was going to give himself up."

"What did she say?" demanded McCreary.

Klein ignored the question. "Tell them nothing, Rivka. Alfred will be at the station within the hour."

Hannah put her hand on McCreary's arm. "Go on, take her outside. I'll be at the car in a moment."

Hannah smiled ruefully at Klein. "I'll watch out for her, Sam. Don't worry."

"Thanks. I'd appreciate that. What a mess." Klein shook his head in exasperation. "Please go. I don't want Rivka alone with McCreary."

Hannah straightened her coat and dress. She squeezed Klein's hand for a moment, then left.

Klein collapsed on a chair in the kitchen.

"So who's paying for the hole in my roof?" asked Hilda. "Sam, I'm talking to you."

But Klein couldn't hear her. He was a million miles away, contemplating things he knew were better left alone.

19

KLEIN READ AND RE-READ the typed letter several times.

"The man you're looking for is named John Franklin. He was until recently an agent in the employ of the RNWMP. Look for him at the Stockyard Hotel in St. Boniface or at rooming house, 768 McMillan Ave. Be warned, he is armed and dangerous. But I'm sure I don't have to tell you that!"

"He's got a sense of humour. I'll say that much for him," said Klein.

"What's that, Shailek?" asked Sarah.

"Nothing. You're certain there was nothing else in the envelope but this piece of paper."

"You can check for yourself, if you don't trust me. There was no other writing, no return address, just the letter."

"Of course I trust you. Why are you starting an argument, Sarah?"

"I'm not. What's wrong with you? From the moment you came home, you've been as grumpy as an old bear. Snapping at the girls, yelling at me. I'm worried about Rivka, too."

"I know you are. Ignore me. It's been a long day, that's all." Klein had not told Sarah about being shot at, among other details he omitted about the last few hours.

"Have you heard from Alfred yet?"

"He sent a boy over with a message. Says he's coming by before nine."

"Well maybe he'll have some good news. Do you know this man, John Franklin?"

"Never heard of him, but I think we've met. I don't know who's decided to help me with this, but remind me to thank him one day."

"You missed Ladies Day at Victoria Park this afternoon. I guess everyone walked down after the terrible commotion on Portage Avenue had ended. It was much calmer at the Park. Helen Armstrong spoke about the strike, as did several other women. They even let them sit right up on the platform. Woodsworth is back in the city. Said he arrived by train from Prince Rupert only a day or two ago. He spoke about women being free to do as they choose. Taking control of their lives. Everyone began shouting 'we'll fight to the end.' It reminded me of Emily. Shailek, are you listening to me?"

"Emily, right."

"You haven't heard a word I've said, have you?"

"I told you I got lots to think about."

Klein took a bottle of whisky that he kept hidden inside a cupboard and filled up a glass. With Melinda's seemingly never-ending supply of booze, prohibition wasn't something that troubled Klein very much. He took a swig, lit a cigarette and sat in a chair by the window. The odd thing was, he did not feel guilty about what had happened with Hannah. It was, he kept reminding himself, just one kiss. Nothing else had happened. Nothing else could happen. And yet, his head was filled with images of her. She stood naked before him, holding out her hand...

"I think you need to see a doctor, Shailek. I'm putting the girls into their beds. You can do what you like."

Klein sat by himself for another few minutes, finished his whisky, poured himself another glass and lit another cigarette. He picked up the sheet of paper and examined it again. He would have to borrow one of Alfred's cars to drive all the way to the Stockyard Hotel on Archibald. He remembered from the last time he travelled into that part of St. Boniface that the stench was horrendous. But if he could find Franklin, see what he knew about Simon's murder and maybe exact a bit of revenge for that shooting, the week might end on a better note.

McCreary was another story, however. He understood that McCreary had lost his temper at Hilda's, that the strike had put him under tremendous pressure, and that he'd have a lot of explaining to do about Lizowski's escape. Nonetheless, Klein felt that he deserved better treatment from a friend. He had pointed a gun and threatened him and Rivka. No friend would, or should do that—at least that was how Klein saw the situation.

"Shailek answer the door, are you deaf?"

"Coming, coming," Klein muttered.

Klein undid the latch and swung open the door. There stood Alfred Powers and, looking a little tired, Rivka. She rushed forward to hug Klein.

"Rivka, I thought—"

"They let her go," smiled Alfred. "Took her in for a few questions. And then Graham and Newton told me that she was free to go, but she's not allowed to leave the city."

"They let her go? Why would Graham do that?"

"It doesn't matter, Shailek, does it? Where's Sarah, where are the girls?" Rivka ran to the back of the apartment to see them.

Klein rubbed the back of his neck. "They think Lizowski will come to her, don't they? Graham and Newton think they have it all figured out."

Powers nodded. "Yes, that's my view, though I didn't say anything to Rivka. Let her enjoy the moment."

"Your son, forgive me, is a real son-of-a-bitch, Alfred. Even for him this is low."

"I know it, Sam. I tried talking to him, but he's on some sort of crusade. He's trying to save the city and the world from the forces of evil, as he put it. I'm just trying to figure out where I went wrong."

"It's not your fault. Look at me. My mother used to say the same thing."

Powers grinned. "You got anymore of that whisky?"

Klein filled up a glass and handed it to his friend. "I'll speak with Rivka later tonight. If Lizowski does contact her, she'll have to tell me. There's no way, she's going to jail for that Red."

"What is it your people say? *L'Chaim.*" Powers gulped down the whisky.

"Yeah, to life. But what I need now is *mazel*, lots of luck. Rivka's more stubborn than I am."

It was well past nine o'clock before Hannah arrived home at her apartment on Stradbrook Avenue. She and her late husband Ted had moved there immediately after they were married. The décor was modest; inexpensive furniture from Meltzer's on Selkirk Avenue was about as much as they could afford at the time. They were saving their pennies, and one day, Ted had promised, they would buy a house.

Hannah loosened her blouse and took off her shoes. She put on the kettle for a cup of tea. How her life had changed since Ted had died. He never would have believed that she was capable of working for the police. As a young woman growing up in Brandon, and then Winnipeg, she was hardly assertive. "It isn't lady-like," her mother had told her whenever she had tried to state her opinion about this or that. Her father Andrew had been a fine man, a successful accountant, but in his eyes she was always his little girl. Just before the war, when Hannah began to speak to him about Nellie McClung and the other women fighting for their rights, her father would not listen to her. Nor did her mother for that matter. They were locked in another time and place and no amount of debating or arguing would change that.

Stubborn or not, she missed both of them. Her father had died first, from heart problems in late 1914 and her mother caught the flu around Christmas of 1915. She was gone by the end of April, about the time when the news stories about chlorine gas attacks at Ypres were in the papers. Ted was a big comfort to her then, but now he had left her too. She was the last person to feel sorry for herself, but she would've been lying if she'd said Ted's death had been easy on her. Without any brothers or sisters to lean on, she was truly alone. Yes, her friends had been supportive, and Ted's sister Norma was a kind person, but she and her family lived in Edmonton. Each night when she crawled into bed by herself, the sad reality of her life hit her. There was no denying that the other side of the bed was empty.

She knew she was in serious trouble with Sam. He was the first man she had kissed like that since Ted, and she desperately wanted him in her bed. She wanted to feel the warmth of his body next to hers. But, it wasn't going to happen, she told herself as she poured hot water on top of the tea leaves. Sam was devoted to his wife and family. He was not about to give up all that for her.

"Message for Mrs. Nash," a girl's voice cried out from the hallway. Since the strike had cut off telephone service in the city, the children of the members of the Committee of 1000, Winnipeg's young wealthy, as McCreary called them, had been employed to act as message runners for city council and the police department.

Hannah opened her door to find young Ellen Maxwells, the daughter of Hiram Maxwells standing in front of her. "Sorry to trouble you Ma'am, the Chief wanted to make sure you got this tonight," she said handed her a folded piece of paper.

"Thank you. Would you like to come in, have a cookie or something?"

"I'd love to Mrs. Nash, but I have two more messages to deliver tonight and then I have to get home. Maybe another time."

"You're a brave young woman."

Hannah shut the door and unfolded the message. Finally, some good news for a change. Gertie Viola had been found in Calgary. She was in the custody of the Mounties and was heading back to Winnipeg on a train the day after tomorrow. She'd arrive in the city at one in the morning late on Thursday.

"I have to tell Sam. He'll be so pleased," Hannah whispered. Then she shuddered. Whether she desired it or not, Klein was in her every thought.

"I don't know, Mr. Powers, it seems kind of risky to me," said Newton.

"That's why I'm in charge of this operation and you're not," said Graham, putting his feet up on Chief Newton's desk.

"Why would Lizowski go to his girlfriend? He must know that we'd be watching her."

"You really don't understand how the deviant mind works, do you Newton? First of all, Lizowski thinks he's smarter than the rest of us. He's already escaped twice. He figures he can't be caught. And second, and more importantly, he's a smitten man."

"Smitten?"

"You're married, Chief, right?"

"Yeah, what of it?"

"You ever wander, look at other women?"

"I've looked yeah, but that's it. Everyone does that."

"Well, Metro has done more than looked. He's marched into no man's land and he won't be able to stop himself, trust me. You keep your men on Rivka Klein and mark my words, we'll have Lizowski back behind bars before the end of the week."

"You heard about another shooting at Higgins near Main late today?"

"Anyone hurt?"

"No, but somebody took a shot at a group of Hebrew strikers. They were marching down towards Victoria Park for the labour meeting when suddenly shots rang out. They had women and children with them. Someone fired at Klein, now this."

"Who knows, maybe it was an accident."

"An accident? I doubt that."

Graham doubted it too, but he wasn't prepared to share his views with Newton on the subject of John Franklin. The second shooting, like the one on Klein, must have been his doing. The man had lost all sense of responsibility. Bolshevism had to be defeated, but in Graham's view that did not mean committing murder. There was a line and Franklin had crossed it long ago. He was relieved that he had reported Franklin's activities to the RWNMP Commissioner. Now the man would be stopped, although that was probably easier said than done.

"Chief, Mr. Powers, you have to come downstairs," said a breathless young constable.

"What's the noise about?" asked Newton.

"It's Bob Russell and George Armstrong, they're at the desk with four other men."

Graham trailed behind Newton to the front of the station. Most of the strike leadership was standing there.

"Russell, Armstrong." Chief Newton put his hands on his hips. "You've got some nerve. Don't you have some bombs to build?"

"We're here to show you that the strikers are not above the law. This is Peter Mitchell," Russell said, pointing out one of the four men sitting on a bench with their heads downs. "The others are Jimmy Sykes, Scott MacDonald and George Timmins."

"Why do I care?" asked Newton.

"Mitchell, you want to tell the Chief?"

Peter Mitchell, his hair tussled, his white shirt untucked, and his pants spotted with dirt, slumped forward. "We're here...we're here to tell you about Bower."

"Is that so?" said Graham. "What do you know about it?"

"We did it. The four of us. We had too much to drink and got a bit carried away. We didn't mean to hurt him that bad."

"Why would you Reds worry about that?"

Russell stepped forward. "Because, Powers, despite what you and your rich friends think, that's not what this strike is about. Forget what Dafoe and the others say. We don't want to take over the city. We don't want to start a revolution."

"What is it you want then?" asked Powers.

"Simple. We want justice. We wanted to be treated fairly. But as I said we're not above the law. So here, arrest these men. We'll take our chances with British justice."

Russell tipped his hat and he and Armstrong left the station.

"Well, go on Williams, book these men. They're charged with attempted murder," said Newton.

"Make it assault," said Powers.

"Assault? Have you seen Bower?" asked the Chief.

"He was spying on them. They were provoked. Let's go for assault. It's been a long day."

Metro Lizowski tried to make himself as comfortable as possible under a large heap of straw. Once he had eluded the police, he had stolen a horse and made his way out to a farm past St. James. The place belonged to an Irish cattle buyer named O'Leary. Lizowski had met him years ago through a mutual friend. He was no supporter of the strike, but he hated the authorities more. Any authorities. They had taken his only son, Stephen, from him. Stephen maintained that he had had nothing to do with the robbery of a church and O'Leary believed him. What good did that do? His boy was now rotting away in Stony Mountain.

"You can stay as long as you want, Lizowski," O'Leary had told his guest.

Lizowski figured he was safe for a few days at least. He had to somehow get word to his wife, tell her what was happening so she would be prepared. She would never understand, but it was the only way. Rivka, his beautiful Rivka, had anticipated everything. She knew her nosy brother would find them; she knew the police would be with him. His escape had been dangerous, though carried out with a certain degree of poise and skill. Now came the waiting, while Rivka put the rest of their plan into action. He had not told her everything. In the unlikely event that he should fail, he did not want her to pay for his actions. He knew where he could obtain the right supplies and his intensive studying would finally pay off. He only wished that fool Simon had lived to see his greatest exploit.

The moment was at hand. They would pay for their immoral lives, for their greed and treachery. He would have his revenge after all. And when he was finished, it would make what had happened a few weeks ago in New York, Washington, Pittsburgh and Boston seem insignificant. As he dozed off, he felt content for the first time in a long time. He and Rivka would be together soon. They would have the life they deserved far from the corruption of this tainted city.

20

KLEIN LEFT THE HOUSE before Sarah and the girls were up. Normally he did not carry a revolver with him. Today was different, however; today he was hunting for John Franklin and that was like hunting for a wounded animal: dangerous and unpredictable.

He stopped by Dolly's for breakfast, black coffee and toast with her homemade strawberry jam. The gossip in the café was that most of the iron factory bosses had agreed in principle to collective bargaining. After much cajoling from Graham Powers and Senator Robertson, the ironmasters had told Ottawa that they would listen to their men's demands, though they still refused to negotiate with the union executive of the Metal Trades Council. Nearly every one of Dolly's patrons that morning predicted that Russell, Ivens and Armstrong and the other leaders would never accept such a lame concession. A few voiced the opinion that a lot of the workers had had enough of the strike and were looking for any reason or excuse to go back to the factories.

After listening to the discussion, Klein felt that the strike committee still had a lot of influence. He, too, doubted that they would go for this latest offer. No, the strike was not over yet.

He borrowed one of Alfred Powers's more run-down jalopies for the day, a red 1915 McLaughlin truck. Alfred's servants used it for hauling goods and furniture. It was better than walking, but it made an awful racket. Klein was not about to surprise anyone driving up in that. Seeing the amused expressions of pedestrians as he chugged down Portage Avenue, he wished that the streetcars would start running again.

It was only a twenty minute journey down Osborne Street to Corydon and then over to the corner of McMillan and Lilac. Klein parked the truck in front of 768 McMillan. Before he got out, he checked his gun one more time. It was secure in a holster he wore around his left shoulder—a present from Melinda for his last birthday. She said she sent for it all the way from New York City. "All the detectives are wearing them," she had joked. He opened the gate, glancing in every direction. It was still fairly early, and in this middle-class neighbourhood the men should have been leaving for work, while their dutiful wives got the children off to school. But, as everyone kept saying, these were not normal times. As the strike dragged on, many businesses downtown opened only a few hours each day. Some were closed altogether.

Klein had used his trusty Henderson's Directory to determine that the rooming house was owned and operated by Mrs. Wanda Owens, a widow. The house had six rooms available, although there was rarely more than one or two vacancies. Most of the boarders were fairly permanent residents. Before Klein could knock on the door, Mrs. Owens opened it.

"Looking for a room, sir?" she asked. Her accent was London Cockney. She peered at Klein over her thick round glasses

"Me? No, I'm here to visit one of your guests," replied Klein.

"And who might that be? I can't be letting just anyone in here. What's your name? You're not one of them strikers, are you? Talk about bad for business. Whole city shut down…"

"My name is Klein, Sam Klein."

"The detective? Why, I've heard all about you. You have quite a reputation."

"Thank you, Mrs. Owens."

"And you know my name. You are as talented as they say. Come in out of the morning air, Mr. Klein. Maybe I could make you a cup of tea. Not every day I have someone as famous as you in the house. Mind you, about five years ago, before Herbert passed on, Lucy Maud

Montgomery stayed here during her tour of Manitoba. It was very exciting."

Klein smiled patiently. "I'm looking for a man named Franklin, John Franklin. Is he staying here?"

"Never heard of him."

"This man is very large, has a black moustache, a thick neck."

"Why, that sounds like Mr. Allen. As nice a man as there is. He's visiting the city from Vancouver. A businessman of some sort, I think. Why do you want to see him? He's not in any trouble, is he?"

"No, not at all. Is he still staying here?"

"As a matter of fact, he left this morning. Said he might be back in about a week. Paid me what he owed me, and left in a nice black automobile. There was another man in the car with him. I recognized him too. Seen his picture in the paper. Now what's his name?"

"It would be very useful if you could remember."

"Powers," said Mrs. Owens. "Mercy alive, how could I forget a name like that?"

"Pardon me, Ma'am," said Klein.

"The nice man who came for Mr. Allen was Mr. Powers, the lawyer. He's working for Ottawa. I hear he's trying to break the strike."

"You mean Graham Powers?"

"Yes, that's his name. Do you know him too? My, you travel in quite a circle, Mr. Klein. What an exciting life you lead."

"Yeah, I guess so, Mrs. Owens. And I suspect it's going to get more exciting very shortly. Thank you for your time."

The truck sputtered and spewed as Klein shifted gears and drove back toward Corydon. Graham and Franklin working together? It boggled the mind. Even for Graham this was low. Did he know that Franklin had likely murdered Maloney, tried to shoot Klein himself, and that he was probably mixed up in Bill Simon's murder as well? Klein pushed down on the gas and sped up to 15 miles an hour. Of course Graham Powers knew, he was the man in charge.

Franklin lit another cigarette and shifted uncomfortably in the seat of the car. He had been parked outside of the Lady Angela Apartment

Block on Burrows Avenue for more than an hour. There was no sign of Klein, nor of any one moving about in the second floor apartment. Had he stopped to think about it, he would have conceded that he hadn't really thought his plan through. He was tired of the game, and angry with himself for missing an easy shot the other day. He was on his own now; the telegram from Regina had been terse. Perry had ordered him back to Saskatchewan pending a review of his conduct in Winnipeg. They could all go to hell, he thought.

All around him was danger and anarchy. Didn't those fools know that? He had believed that Powers could be trusted, that he shared the same view of the world he did. That Bill Simon had. But he was mistaken. Powers was weak. He too would have to be dealt with, just as Klein and Lizowski would be. He found the bottle of whisky and took a swig. He had not given much thought to the woman and children. They might have to be sacrificed. At the very least, he could use them as leverage. He threw the cigarette out of the car, and noticed a small face peering out of the second floor window. He drained the rest of the whisky and got out of the car.

Where was he? That's what Klein wanted to know. What hole was Franklin hiding in? His trip to the Stockyard Hotel had been another wild goose chase. The drive there and back had taken more than an hour and all he had for his trouble was a whiff of the stench emanating from the slaughterhouse; the strike had shut it down and the animals and rotting carcasses were left unattended. At the hotel, his questions were met with blank stares and shrugs. No one knew anything. The desk manager had never heard of Franklin or a 'Mr. Allen.' He couldn't even get the hotel maid to give him a straight answer.

By the time he reached Main Street and headed north again, he could see that the patrols of specials were back on duty. After yesterday's protest, however, Main Street was fairly empty. If the strikers were planning another march, and Klein was certain they were, then it was only a matter of time before there was another explosion of violence.

Klein suddenly felt thankful for his wife and daughters, and was relieved that his sister was safe and sound. He realized how important all of them were in his life. Did he want to jeopardize all that because of a schoolboy infatuation? Because of lust? Klein remembered that it had been such desires that had got Alfred in trouble with Emily so many years ago. At first those desires had turned his life upside down, and then nearly ruined it. There were lessons to be learned in Alfred and Emily's tragic tale Klein thought. He had better not forget that.

He parked the truck on Burrows Avenue. He had promised Sarah that he would take the girls out this morning for a ride, and lunch at Dolly's. She deserved a break once in a while, especially now that her pregnancy was so advanced. Maybe his guilt was turning him into a model husband? Either way, he always looked forward to spending a few hours alone with his girls. He loved them almost too much, and they nourished his soul like no one else.

Klein reached for the door of the block when he heard the sound of glass breaking from above. He glanced up just as glass from his living room window rained down on him. "What the hell…"

He raced up the stairs. Their apartment front door was unlatched and open. Instinctively, Klein grabbed his gun out of the holster. "Sarah, girls, are you there?" he called, easing through the doorway. Clothes and toys were cast about, nothing unusual, Klein thought.

"We're in here, Sam, in the kitchen. Watch your step." It was Sarah, but she did not sound like herself. Her voice was strained. She had used the words, "watch your step." Long ago, as a precaution, Klein had set that phrase as a code word between them. It meant danger. Sarah had laughed when he had come up with the idea, telling him that he was *mishigna*, crazy. Well, at that moment he was glad he was. He gripped his revolver and moved slowly into the kitchen.

"Easy Klein, I wouldn't want to make a mess in here."

Franklin was holding a gun to Sarah's head, while Freda and Bernice sat quietly shivering in a corner of the room.

"Daddy," Freda whimpered.

"It's okay, honey," said Klein, "just stay there. Hold on to your sister."

Freda put her arms around Bernice and held her tightly.

"Tell me what you want, Franklin. Nobody has to get hurt."

"You know my name. I'm impressed. What I want is for you to throw that gun over here, nice and easy."

"Let my wife go, first, then I'll throw the gun."

Franklin turned his revolver away from Sarah and pointed it at the girls. "Klein, you know I'm capable of anything, so don't try to bullshit me. Throw the damn gun here, now." A bead of sweat trickled down Franklin's face.

"Take it easy, Franklin. Here…here's the gun." Klein dropped his weapon to the floor and with his right boot kicked it toward Franklin.

"You, girl," he said motioning to Freda. "Pick it up and bring it to me."

"Shailek," cried Sarah.

"Go on Freda, give him the gun."

Freda let go of Bernice, stood up and walked across the floor. She reached down, picked up the revolver and gave it to Franklin.

"You're a lovely young girl, has anyone ever told you that?"

Freda ran back to her sister and huddled again in the corner.

"Now what?" Klein edged a little closer to Franklin. "What the hell do you want?"

"Simple," said Franklin standing up. "I want you to come with me into the other room. You've caused me no end of aggravation, Klein. Making such a fuss over a Red like Lizowski, and then sticking your big Hebrew nose where it doesn't belong. To be honest, it'll be a pleasure doing this. All at once, not only will my problems be solved, I'll be doing the human race a favour. Move, Klein, now." He pointed the gun at Klein's face.

"Shailek," repeated Sarah.

"Be still. Nothing's going to happen to me."

Franklin laughed as he pushed Klein into the other room.

"How about letting me have a smoke first?" asked Klein.

"No time for that."

Klein glanced out the window. Where was a cop when you needed one? "Tell me, why did you kill Bill Simon? I know Lizowski is a Bolshevik and all, but he didn't do it."

"You're a fool, do you know that?"

"Here's another question then. How did someone like you, an agent of the RNWMP trained to protect the public, turn into such an asshole?"

"I think, Klein, that's your last question."

"Daddy, Daddy," shouted Bernice.

The cry from the kitchen made Franklin hesitate and turn his head. As he did so, Klein lunged at him, taking hold of his arm. As they struggled, Franklin's gun went off.

Half a block away, Hannah heard the shot. On the pretext of wanting to deliver the news personally about Gertie Viola she had, against her better judgement, decided to pay a visit to the Klein apartment. In actual fact, she was curious. She wanted to see Klein and meet his wife, see how she stood up to someone as beautiful as Sarah Klein. It was foolish, she knew, but she could not stop herself.

She ran up the stairs of the apartment block, when she heard another blast and then the scream of a young girl. She had no weapon with her—MacPherson and Newton had refused to permit the few women in the department to carry a gun. She had cajoled McCreary into showing her how to use one, and she was not a bad shot. But no matter how much she argued with her superiors, they would not agree to her wishes.

The door to the apartment was open. She had been taught to proceed cautiously in such situations. "A detective does not run blindly into an unknown situation," MacPherson had told her. But she disregarded that bit of wisdom and rushed in to the apartment.

Klein was on top of Franklin and he was pummelling him in the face. "Threaten my kids, you bastard," he said as he punched him again.

"Sam, stop," said Hannah. She grabbed his arm. "It's over, Sam, it's over."

"Leave me alone," said Klein, wiping blood from his mouth.

"What on earth happened?" asked Hannah. Before she could ask any more questions, Sarah and the girls rushed into the room as well.

"Sarah, keep them back," said Klein. He turned to Hannah. "We fought. I grabbed the gun and it went off. I think the bullet must have hit him in the head. He dropped like a dog."

Hannah leaned over Franklin.

"He's still breathing. I've got to get some help. There's a call box on McGregor. I'll put these cuffs on him and be back in a few minutes."

Klein did not reply.

"Daddy, Daddy." Freda and Bernice ran forward to hug him.

"I'm proud of you both. You were very brave, especially you Freda," he said as he picked both of them up.

"That's a bad man," said Bernice.

"You can say that again."

Klein took a deep breath. "Sarah, why don't you take the girls out of the apartment until they come for him. I think they've had enough excitement for the day."

Sarah took hold of her daughters' hands. "We'll go visit Doris and Fred upstairs. You sure you're okay?"

"Go on. The police will be here in a few minutes."

He glared at Franklin. The rage inside him was subsiding. He lit a cigarette and tried to calm down. He knew that he had lost control of himself. If Hannah had not shown up, he wasn't sure what would have happened, but nobody threatened his wife and children. Was there anything more important in his life?

21

I DON'T THINK HE knows anything more, Sam. You got to admit, he's as tough as an ox. I thought you were going to kill him," said Hannah. She was standing with Klein outside the Rupert Avenue Station.

"I was wrong, then. I guess it happens."

She smiled. How she wanted to hold him, comfort him. But she had seen him with his family. His pregnant wife and his beautiful daughters. This was a man who had too much to lose. She would not have that on her conscience.

"Here's his story so far," said Hannah. "Franklin was sent to the city by Perry to spy on the Trade Council. 'Agent 12' is what he calls himself. Bower, who's now recuperating at the hospital, was working for Franklin. Apparently the late Bill Simon had helped both of them. He's refused to say anything else. He says he doesn't know anything about Maloney's death. And he insists that Lizowski killed Simon. But he finally admitted that he didn't see him do it."

"So why was he trying to kill me, then?"

"To stop you from doing anything that would help Lizowski. He's convinced Lizowski is evil, his word, and that you were working with the devil."

"The devil?"

"That's what he said. Something about the Anglo-Saxon race being under attack. The aliens and anarchists who struck in the States last week are making their way to Canada."

"He sounds as if he should be sent to the Lunatic Asylum in Selkirk."

"I don't know, Sam. I've read the reports from Washington and New York. It's only a miracle no one was killed. There's more I'm sure, but he's not talking. Says he wants to be sent back to Regina. Maybe once Gertie Viola gets back here, she'll be able to tell us more."

"When's that?"

"Not until Saturday evening. The trains are moving slow because of the strike."

"If it were up to me, I'd keep Franklin here at least until then. He might talk eventually."

"That's what Graham Powers said."

"Is that so? You should ask Franklin about Powers. Seems like they knew each other."

"Mr. Powers has already explained that. Commissioner Perry had requested that Franklin report to him while he was here. The Commissioner and Mr. Powers are old friends."

"And did Powers know that that bastard was trying to kill me?"

"As a matter of fact, I didn't," said Graham. He walked up to where Hannah and Klein were standing. McCreary lingered behind him.

"So you didn't have anything to do with me and my family nearly being killed?"

"Sam, I'm surprised at you. Do you think I would do anything to harm your family? I know you don't agree with my politics, but..."

"You've put thugs on the streets with baseball bats, chains and pipes. You've had people arrested for no reason. Their homes have been broken into. You've spied on the Trade Council. Should I go on?"

"I had no choice in the matter. You were born in Russia. You should know what could happen. Have you any idea of the havoc that's going on there? A Soviet regime that is arresting and executing judges, bankers, businessmen. Is that what you want here?"

"Your father thinks you've gone too far."

"He's an old man. He doesn't see the danger. We can't allow this city, this country, to be taken over by socialists. There will be no end to it until a full-scale revolution breaks out."

"You're as mad as Franklin."

"Maybe I am, but trust me, one day you'll thank me."

"I doubt it."

"Well, at least you could thank me for passing you that message."

"You? Why?"

"Franklin was out of control. He had disobeyed Perry's direct orders. I figured you needed a bit of help. And believe it or not Sam, I didn't want to make that wife of yours a widow."

"Thanks. I'll tell her that."

Graham shrugged. "Now, Klein, Mrs. Nash, if you'll excuse me, I have a strike to break. They turned us down, did you hear, Klein? We were willing to recognize collective bargaining. But they turned us down. Said we had to accept their socialist council as their representative."

"So what about all your grand plans?"

"Oh, don't worry, I have another surprise for them. Wait until tomorrow, say noon. The strike'll be over by then."

"You're sure about that?"

"I am. And after that we'll deal properly with your friend Lizowski. He can't elude us forever. We'll find him. Right, McCreary?"

McCreary puffed quietly on a cigar.

"You're awful quiet, McCreary," said Powers.

"Don't have anything to say."

Klein glared at him.

"Mrs. Nash, I was wondering if I could have a word with you?" asked Powers.

Hannah followed Powers back inside the station.

McCreary threw his cigar to the ground. "Klein, I was only doing my job."

"You pointed a gun at me, you son-of-a-bitch."

"I lost my temper. Lizowski got away."

"So you take it out on Rivka. You know she's got nothing to do with this."

"Yeah, I know," he said. "Listen, Klein, this isn't easy for me."

"Go to hell, McCreary."

Klein had heard enough. In truth, he wasn't all that angry with McCreary. He didn't really expect that much from him. Still, he wasn't about to forgive him for what he had done, at least not yet. Let him think about it, he thought as he walked towards Main Street. You don't pull a gun on a friend. It was as simple as that.

Klein spent the rest of the day talking to sources throughout the city. Up and down Portage Avenue, past Eaton's, all the way to Colony, and then back to Main Street, stopping at a few bars, through Point Douglas, and finally home. He spent a couple of hours at Victoria Park talking with strikers and their families. Many of them were anxious to return to work. They were tired of doing nothing all day. They understood why Russell and the other leaders had refused the latest offer, but they were not especially happy about it. Graham Powers ought to have been with him, Klein thought. He should listen to what these people were saying, then he'd realize how wrong he was. These workers were no revolutionaries, all they wanted was a decent wage.

No one he spoke to cared much about Metro Lizowski or his plans for a Canadian Utopia. Most hoped that he'd left Winnipeg and would never return.

"Don't need his kind, here," Klein was told several times. "A troublemaker. Gives the rest of us a bad name. If he wants to change the world, let him do it somewhere else."

Lizowski had vanished. There was no sign of him at Melinda's or Hilda's and Rikva assured him she had no idea where he was. He decided to believe her. She seemed sincere in her desire to get on with life, put Lizowski behind her. She had spent the day helping Helen Armstrong feed the growing lineups of hungry workers. Naturally, Mrs. Armstrong was delighted to have her back and the rest of the women greeted her as they would a long-lost sister.

The anti-foreign sentiment was still very much alive in the city. Tolerance and equality were only words social gospellers like Woodsworth and Ivens spoke about. Such acceptance, Klein and every other Jew in Winnipeg knew, was often cheap talk. Neighbourhoods, clubs and summer resorts were still restricted. And yet, in the chaos and turmoil of the strike, something had changed. People seemed more inclined to work together. It was difficult to put a finger on it, but it was present nonetheless.

Klein had grabbed a quick bite of food with Sarah and the girls before heading out to meet with George Runciman. Alfred Powers had told him to keep the truck for as long as he needed it, so it was simple enough to get to Runciman's house on Spence Street. There was nothing quite like a drive down Broadway, with its elegant homes, tall trees and wide boulevard. Like every evening, there were people strolling, though the dark June sky appeared ominous. Manitoba was famous for its severe thunder and lightning storms. On a humid summer day like this, the clouds could suddenly explode with bolts of lightning, followed by booming thunder.

Klein turned left off of Broadway, and pulled up in front of Runciman's home. It was like every other house in the neighbourhood, a large two-storey with a screened porch, Runciman was waiting for Klein on his front steps. The wind had picked up in the last few minutes.

"It's going to be a bad one," said Runciman. "Look at those clouds. Why don't we sit out here on the porch until the rain comes. There's something about watching Mother Nature at work."

Klein followed him into the porch. There were three wicker chairs with green and white pillows.

"Care for a cigar, Klein? Katie and the children are visiting her mother in Toronto this week. Thought it was for the best until this trouble's over. Katie hates when I smoke these things, but since she's not here…"

"Yeah, I've seen what you do when you're wife's not around."

Runciman smiled thinly, though he did not appear to be all that amused. "I'm sorry you had to witness that Klein. What can I say? You've seen Darlene. But I've vowed to stay away for the next few months. I hope that this will remain between us. No need to involve the women in such matters."

"As I said, Runciman what you do in your leisure time is your own business. I just wanted to ask you a few questions about your late boss."

"What is it you want to know?"

"You were there when he saw Lizowksi that day?"

"I saw them together. There was an argument and Lizowksi left. That's all I know."

"You met Franklin?"

"Yeah, we were introduced. Not someone I'd put on my Christmas list. I hear he's in jail, and he's in rough shape. That your doing?"

"I thought Newton was keeping it quiet."

"I'm on the Committee, Klein. We know everything. Hasn't a clever man like you figured that out yet?" Runciman glanced at his pocket watch. "Should be starting in about an hour."

"What's that?"

"The one thing that should end this strike quickly."

"You enjoy talking in circles, Runciman?"

"Not especially. Powers warned me to be careful with you."

"I see. Well, Graham ought to know. These days he'd put his own father in jail if he thought it would end the strike."

"There's lots to be afraid of, Klein. That's one thing Bill Simon did understand. Before anyone else, he saw the threat from Anarchy and Communism. He just got a little carried away. Trying to buy off a criminal alien like Lizowski was futile."

"You really believe everything he said?"

"Not everything, no. But here, see for yourself." Runciman searched through a pile of books and magazines on top of a mahogany table. "Must be in the other room. Be right back."

Klein puffed his cigar and looked up at the blackening sky. He could see lightning, and hear the thunder. The storm was imminent. His gaze wandered over to a collection of framed photos on a side table. There was Runciman, his wife and their children. His wife, Katie, was a good-looking woman, happy with a bright smile. If she only knew about her husband's penchant for younger women she might not be smiling so much, Klein thought. And then there were the two children, a boy, perhaps about twelve and a younger girl, maybe ten years old. They seemed content enough, although there was something about the girl. Before he could determine what it was, Runciman re-appeared with a small green book in his hands.

"Just admiring your family," said Klein.

"That photo was taken on trip to Alberta last summer. That's Katie with Paul and Suzie. You ever been to the Banff Springs Hotel? You feel like you're in a French castle. And the hot springs were remarkable, especially for Suzie. Made her feel wonderful. Now, why don't you borrow this, a present from Bill last Christmas. If you really want to understand how he viewed the world, read it carefully. That's why he gave it to me, so I would understand."

"Did you?"

"A little. But see for yourself. It's called 'Race Improvement' by an American woman, La Reine Helen Baker. Don't know much about her, but this was published about seven years ago, I believe. Here, if you have a minute, listen to this," he said, opening the book. "Bottom of page seven and top of page eight, this is what she writes: 'It has been suggested that Eugenists are anarchists, tearing up the roots of government, blindly striking at civilized institutions, putting a bomb to the foundations of Church, State and Family. Let it be said here and now in such clear phrase as may be that Eugenics is the antithesis of anarchy. It means order. Eugenics opposes chaos in the interests of race. It is the most profoundly patriotic proposition ever laid before the people of these United States. Its conception is for the national good.' That, Klein, was what Bill Simon believed in."

"I don't know much about Eugenics, but it sounds like they want to breed children the way we do dogs and horses."

Runciman laughed. "Klein, read the book first, then come back and we'll talk some more. Now, unless you want to get soaked, I'd suggest you had better be on your way. That rain will be here in a few minutes."

Hannah would rather have been home curled up with a good book than spending all day following Rivka Klein. But orders were orders, and Graham Powers had insisted that she take this assignment. "Less conspicuous that way," he had said to her. "You can blend into the crowd a little better than McCreary or some other burly constable." So she did as she was told. Powers and Chief Newton were convinced that Rivka knew where Lizowski was hiding. Sooner or later, she would go to him. While Hannah agreed with their assessment of the situation, for some reason she had pangs of guilt. She wanted to tell Klein about what she was doing, but understood that she could not.

It was nearly eight o'clock, it was about to rain, and she was stuck on Selkirk Avenue without a streetcar to take her home. Rivka had been downtown nearly all day at the Oxford Hotel serving food to hungry strikers. Dressed as inconspicuously as she could in a light blouse, grey dress, and hat, Hannah had brazenly gone right into the Oxford to see the women's operation for herself.

It was impressive. There were rows upon rows of tables and chairs with men, women and children eating their meals. Rivka stood for hours serving soup and bread. Hannah may not have agreed with her politics, but Rivka was as dedicated a woman as she had ever seen. One look at her, and you could tell instantly that she truly believed in the cause that she was fighting for. Maybe some of that had rubbed off on her brother, thought Hannah. Beyond his good looks and natural charm, he did exude a certain degree of confidence and integrity. She suspected that it was this combination that made him so attractive to her.

Hannah felt the first drop of rain as she stood on the other side of the street watching Rivka enter a tailor shop near the corner of McGregor and Selkirk. Ten minutes later, she emerged with a large package wrapped in brown paper and string. The way she was struggling with it, whatever was inside must have been heavy. She stood on the sidewalk for a moment looking up and down the street. For a brief moment, Hannah was sure she had been spotted, so she ducked into an alley. As she turned, she heard a car lurch to a stop. She ran back to Selkirk, but it was too late. Rivka was gone.

22

IT WAS SIX IN the morning when Rivka started banging on Klein's apartment door. As it turned out, her brother was already up. He couldn't sleep, again. First the fierce thunderstorm had kept him awake, and then more thoughts about Hannah. By the time Rivka interrupted him, he was finishing his third cup of coffee, and attempting with limited success to make sense of the book George Runciman had given him.

"Rivka, is that you? What's going on at this hour? Stop the banging, you'll wake everyone up," said Klein.

As he opened the door, Rivka stormed in. "They've arrested all of them, those bastards." Rivka rarely swore so when she did the situation had to be grim.

"What are you talking about?" asked Klein.

"You haven't heard? You're the detective," she said shaking her head. "Early this morning, just after the storm was over, they barged into George Armstrong's home. They arrested George, Bob Russell, Roger Bray, William Ivens, even Abe Heaps, all of them. The strike's finished now. We won't win without them. The fools also picked up Moses Almazoff, Michael Charitonoff, Oscar Schappellrei and guy named Mike Verenchuk who was living at Bill Devyatkin's apartment. Other than Verenchuk who just got back from Europe, the others had nothing to do with the strike as far as I know. They're Jews and Ukrainians. I guess that's against the law now. "

Klein shook his head. "It had to be Graham. No one else could've done it. I should've known he'd find a way. Where were you?"

"What do you mean where was I? I was at my apartment. About one-thirty, Helen came over. She was hysterical. Said that just after midnight, the damn Mounties were at her door with their guns out. They put George in handcuffs, then tore the place apart. They threw George in a car. Helen actually ran behind the car to the station and telephoned Newton. He told her they had a warrant for George's arrest and the other members of the Trade Council. They're charged with sedition and conspiracy. They also seized what ever they could— pamphlets, books, and newspapers from the Labour Temple, the Ukrainian Church and the Liberty Temple. Wrecked the places, smashed tables and filing cabinets. They were like animals. Helen doesn't know for sure, but she thinks they've taken the ten of them to the penitentiary at Stony Mountain."

"What's all the shouting about?" asked Sarah. "The two of you are going to wake up the dead, never mind Freda and Bernice."

"I'm sorry," said Rivka, giving Sarah a hug. "The strike'll be over soon. They've arrested everyone who counts. I was so certain that we were going to win, Metro had…"

"What about Metro?" asked Klein. "Have you seen him? You know where he is?"

"No, I haven't seen him. Of course not. What I meant to say was that before, when we were hiding at Hilda's, he nearly had me convinced that the workers would win and rise up against the owners."

"Keep talking like that Rivka and they'll throw you in jail with the rest of them," said Klein.

"You're probably happy about it, Sam. Admit it, you are, aren't you?"

"I won't lie to you Rivka. I am glad the city might get back to normal. That we'll have bread and milk delivery again. But whatever you think about me, I'm no bloody capitalist like Graham Powers. Believe me, after reading this book on Eugenics, it makes Russell and Armstrong seem like kids. People like Bill Simon want to tell us who we can marry and when we can have kids. Keep things pure that way."

"I have no idea what you're talking about, Sam. Sarah, you know what he's saying?" asked Rivka.

"It's been like that since last night when he came home with that book. By the way, I was out for a walk late last evening, and stopped by for some tea. I thought you said you'd be home."

"I had an errand to run. I…I was back at about eleven, I think."

Klein stared at his sister for a moment. "I hope that's all, Rivka. Because if you're protecting Lizowski…"

"Don't be silly. Let me have a cup of coffee. Then I have to go see Helen. She'll know what to do next. We can't give up, not like this."

Graham threw the newspaper down on to the floor. "What kind of trash is this? Dafoe's betrayed us. How can he write that we've gone too far?"

Chief Newton shrugged. "Sorry, but that's what he thinks. Called it the government's strong arm policy. Thinks we're going to make martyrs of them. And here I thought he was on our side."

"Yeah, they'll gladly take our money for advertising. We just spent hundreds on those ads last week."

"You mean the ones calling for undesirable aliens to be deported. That got a lot of attention."

"Exactly. So why does the *Free Press* turn on us now? Here's another lesson to be learned from this whole blasted experience. Never trust an editor of a Liberal Party organ to do your bidding for you. They get all weak at the knees when you have to take some serious action."

"Did you read this cable from Tom Moore? Up to now, I'd say that the Labour Congress had been against the strike, but now he's threatening us. 'Organized labour will not tolerate strong arm methods for the suppression of legitimate labour demonstrations, and if the proof is not sufficient to show that the Winnipeg labour leaders were plotting against the state, the government will be held strictly accountable.'"

"'Strictly accountable.' Give me that," said Powers grabbing the telegram from Newton's hands. He tore it in half and threw it to the floor beside the crumpled newspaper. "It'll be snowing in June before I start taking orders from the likes of Tom Moore and his labour friends in Toronto."

"What do we do with Russell and his comrades now?"

"Put him on trial as quickly as we can, that's what I'm going to advise Meighen and Robertson."

"What about bail? They'll surely have lawyers."

"Questions, questions, Chief. Everything will turn out, as it should. I've already sent a cable to Meighen asking for further instructions. I'm certain he'll reply soon. And I doubt if Ketchen and his men will be happy if we let the Reds out on bail. That's something to think about."

"Maybe. But have you thought about all of the soldiers loyal to Bray? This is bound to make them crankier than usual. I've already doubled the number of specials on the streets, and the Brigadier is working overtime amassing more volunteers to help with patrols. As I understand it, he's got a force of nearly six thousand men ready and waiting to serve. Deacon, and others, are letting him use their steam whistles at the factories to signal them when to come in. It's quite ingenious."

"Good. I don't need another goddamn riot."

"Gray will read the Riot Act. There won't be any parades."

"Chief, I'm surprised at you. Do you really think that Gray's piece of paper is going to stop anyone from protesting? Most of the troublemakers are soldiers. They've got nothing to lose. They've been places, seen things you and I can only imagine in our worst nightmares. Mind you, and I would only admit this to you, this strike has gotten Winnipeg mentioned in every newspaper in North America. I've been getting telegrams from everywhere, from New York to San Francisco. I just hope that now they write about how we defeated the forces of Bolshevism and revolution."

The Chief shrugged. "We still don't know where Pritchard is. We hear he might be on a train for Vancouver, so we've alerted police in Regina and Calgary."

"I'm sure he'll turn up somewhere, unless he decides to take a boat to Russia."

"Not likely."

There was a knock on the door. Bill McCreary and a tired-looking Hannah Nash walked in.

"I read your report, Mrs. Nash, what the hell happened?" asked Newton

"Don't trust a woman to do a man's job," said McCreary with a sour smile.

Hannah frowned. "I must apologize, Mr. Powers. As I've already explained to the Chief, it was an accident. I thought she had seen me, and I didn't anticipate a car driving by to pick her up."

"A good detective always anticipates..." said McCreary.

"Will you shut up, McCreary. Let her talk."

"There's no point hashing it over," said Graham. "Where's Rivka Klein now?"

Hannah sighed. "She's at her brother's. I've had Constable Shillingday watching the apartment. He's called in twice in the past hour. I'm to relieve him shortly, or he's to follow her if she leaves, and then call the station."

"Excellent. I don't have to tell both of you that Lizowksi is the last piece of this puzzle. We've removed the strike leaders. But I can't go back to the citizens of Winnipeg with a murderer on the loose."

A quiet cough interrupted them. "And what is it you think you've accomplished, Graham?" Alfred Powers was standing in the entrance to Newton's office. "Arresting people without cause, taking away their civil liberties."

"Ah, Father, what are you doing here? Come to lecture me again?"

"You're past that point, I'm afraid. No, I've come to inform you that I've been in contact with Ottawa..."

"What?"

"Do you think that you're the only man in this city who has contacts in the government? I was dealing with John A. while you were still in diapers."

"Your point?"

"After you and your henchmen arrested the leaders of the strike, one of their lawyers, Moses Isaacson, came to see me. I've agreed to work with him on this."

"First, you're defending Lizowksi, now this. Father, why can't you just retire?"

"Circumstances have forced me to change my plans. That, and..."

"And what?"

"My fear that you, the Chief here, Brigadier Ketchen and the rest of your friends are about to turn this country into an autocratic regime. No different than the Soviets, I'd say."

"That's hardly true, or fair, Father. We're protecting liberty, not burying it."

"From where I'm standing Graham, there doesn't seem to be any difference. By the way, I've spoken to Meighen and Robertson, and they're not going to fight our bail applications. "

"I have to say—" A loud knock at the office interrupted him.

"Constable Smith, what is it now?" asked Newton.

"I…I'm not certain what happened, Chief."

"Out with it Smith, we don't have all day."

"It's Franklin, sir."

"What about Franklin?"

"He's gone."

"What do you mean, he's gone?"

"After the doctor treated him, I brought him to the cellblock, like you said. Gave him to Charlie. And…"

"And what?"

"Charlie swears he locked him in the cell, last one on the left. I don't know what happened. Charlie went to get a cup of coffee. He was gone maybe ten minutes. When he came back Franklin was gone."

"You're telling me that a man we're going to charge with murder just waltzed out of the station?" asked Graham.

"That's about it, sir," said Smith.

"Someone better get word to Klein," said Alfred Powers. "He's already tried to kill Klein twice that I know of. My God, maybe the strikers should be running the city."

"Newton, send another telegram to Regina. You tell Perry to send some men to help with Franklin. And let the Commissioner know that the police regard Franklin as armed and dangerous. I'll get word to Ketchen. He and his men should be able to assist. Can anything else go wrong today? There are two murderers on the loose…"

"Who said Lizowksi was a murderer?" Alfred said.

"And," continued Graham, "the city is liable to erupt any moment into a riot."

"I think, son, you've got trouble in your Kingdom."

"Everyone here? Where's Harry?" asked Lizowski.

"I'm over here, Metro. O'Leary was showing me all the damage done by the storm. Nearly tore the roof right off the barn," said Harry Griffins.

Sometimes Griffins drove Lizowski crazy. He was unreliable, and could be lost in his own world for days. But no one Lizowski knew was as good with dynamite as Harry. As a miner in British Columbia, he had been taught by the best explosives expert in the business, a German by the name of Prugger. It was there, too, while toiling underground for copper and coal in Nanaimo, among other locales, that Griffins had been introduced to the writings of Luigi Galleani.

Lizowski never doubted Griffins's dedication to the cause. Thanks to his mother, Maria, Harry learned to read and write Italian as a child. As he became more active in the labour movement, and then followed Lizowski down the path of radicalism, he embraced Galleani's philosophy, as many of them did. Except Harry was unique. He could recite long passages of Galleani's tracts that he had diligently translated into English. He would read every copy of *La Questione Sociale*, Galleani's newspaper that he had published for a period from his home in New Jersey. He also collected *Cronaca Sovversiva*, the periodical Galleani founded in 1903. It was Galleani's powerful oratory that appealed to an army of workers across North America—tailors in New York, cigar cutters in Philadelphia, bricklayers in Toronto, pressmen in Chicago, miners in British Columbia and machinists in Winnipeg.

"'When we talk about property, state, masters, government, laws, courts and police, we say only that we don't want any of them'," Griffins would repeat. Or, "'Continue the good war, the war that knows neither fear nor scruples, neither pity nor truce'."

He grew a Van Dyke beard like Galleani's and collected pamphlets and propaganda sheets by the master anarchist including *La Salute è in voi,* a manual on making a bomb using nitroglycerine.

So Lizowksi tolerated his various eccentricities. At this point, what choice did he have? Recent news that U.S. government officials had arrested Galleani following the attacks of June 2, however, had made Harry more anxious than usual. That did concern Lizowski.

The third member of Lizowksi's group was Aaron Mikeljohn, half Hebrew and half Ukrainian, the perfect combination for any revolutionary, Lizowski liked to joke. A tall and lean man, who sported a beard but no moustache—"I'm no Cossack," he'd tell anyone who would listen—Mikeljohn had arrived in Canada via Boston just before the war broke out. He had drifted from city to city until he landed in Winnipeg and a job at Vulcan Ironworks. He and Harry had become fast friends, and the two had met Lizowski one evening at the Brunswick Hotel.

"Enough of this jawing," said Lizowski. "Aaron, spread out the map again. I want to work through this one more time. O'Leary, maybe you better leave. This isn't your fight. I don't want you involved."

"I'm already involved, Metro. I'm keeping you here, aren't I?"

Lizowski gripped him on the shoulder. "Have it your way. We could always use an extra hand."

"You worry as much as my mother did," said Griffins.

"Be prepared for anything, Harry, remember that, or you'll wind up dead like that Italian in New York. The nitro leaked, and he wound up as fertilizer on Palmer's gardens."

"Okay, I get your point."

Mikeljohn unfolded a large map of Winnipeg and laid it on the table in front of them.

Lizowski studied it for a moment. "The potential targets are these three buildings: the Board of Trade, the Grain Exchange and City Hall. I ask you, comrades, which would shock the capitalists the most?"

After some excited discussion, Mikeljohn held up his hand. "Each of these targets has merit. But surely it is the City Hall that has the most symbolic value. These Winnipeg bourgoisie love its overblown design. For them, it sums up how this corrupt city will become the new colossus of the North."

The others nodded their heads. Lizowski smiled and turned to Griffins. "The detonation has to be just right, Harry. Was everything in the package?"

"Everything was there, the dynamite, fuses, detonation device, and a small vial of nitro. Just as you ordered. Rivka delivered it right on schedule. She has no idea, does she?"

"Rivka is not your concern," said Lizowksi. "You worry about getting it all ready for Saturday, and leave everything else to me."

"There's talk of a parade to protest the arrests," said Mikeljohn. "Maybe we should postpone it. There could be a lot of..."

"No! No more delays. I told the two of you long ago that in the war against greed and capitalism there will be sacrifices. Innocents may die."

"Like the way Bill Simon died," said Griffins.

"But in their death," continued Lizowksi, ignoring Griffins's comment, "they'll be furthering our cause. It's necessary, that's all there is to it. The world will notice, I guarantee it."

23

"DID THEY REALLY think their cell could hold me?" Franklin muttered to himself. It had taken him less than five minutes to pick the lock, and escaping from the station was hardly the most difficult thing he had ever done—even if he was bandaged and bruised.

He had some unfinished business with Klein, and then he would deal with Lizowski. Franklin was sure that he could find him a lot sooner than the buffoons working for Newton. Then, before he left the city altogether and headed down to Mexico, he would fulfill his last promise to Bill Simon. The world would be better off, and he would sleep a lot more soundly knowing that he had helped the cause. As Simon used to say, "Rome wasn't built in a day." Simon did his part, now Franklin would do his.

He slipped into the apartment block without being seen, and easily opened the latch of the door at Apartment "C".

"Hey, is there someone there?" Jack Scott emerged from his bedroom with his City of Winnipeg "special" club.

"Scott, you're not going to hit me with that are you? I've had a hell of a day," said Franklin.

"What are you doing here? I heard you were in jail. You look like shit."

"They let me out for good behaviour. "

"Why do I find that hard to believe?"

"You can believe what the hell you want. I'm going to be your guest for a couple of days. Here's a down payment," he said, tossing Scott a small bottle of morphine. "I picked this up special for you before I came here."

"I don't want this, you bastard. What I want is for you to get out of my place."

"Or what?" asked Franklin quietly.

Scott glanced at Franklin's eyes. "Or nothing, I guess."

"You guess?" Deftly, Franklin grabbed the club out of Scott's hands and jammed it into his stomach. Scott fell backwards on to the floor. Franklin stood over him and placed the butt end of the club against his throat.

"You know, Scott, one jab and you wouldn't need any more of those little bottles."

"Go ahead, you asshole. Do it."

Franklin shrugged. "Not today, Scott. You got anything to eat? I'm starved."

Rivka finished her coffee, hugged Freda and Bernice, and told Sarah she would see her in a day or two. It was a lie, yet another one, but there was no point in getting every one upset. She would be back, although not for a while, not until Metro's problems were resolved.

She was about to depart through the main door of the block, when she saw Constable Shillingday, a big bear of a man, trying to appear inconspicuous on the other side of Burrows Avenue. She had met him at the station house and would have recognized his bushy goatee anywhere.

Metro had warned her to take special care. It was best she followed his advice. She immediately turned around and followed the narrow hallway to the rear of the building. There was a back door. She pushed it open and ran out into the lane toward McGregor Street.

Methodically, she walked the twelve or so blocks down alleys and side streets. The house she was looking for was at 411 Cathedral Avenue, a white two-storey. A few children were playing outside. Other than that it was unusually quiet, although Rivka knew that people in this North End neighbourhood would have been gathering at Victoria Park for a rally to protest the arrest of the strike leaders. She had planned to be there, of course, but then she had received another message from Metro. He had one more errand for her.

She knocked on the door. A grey-haired woman with glasses and an apron answered.

"Good morning, my name is Rivka, I think there's a package here for me?"

"Yes, yes my dear. Come in. Here, would you like a poppy seed cookie? Just took them out of the oven."

"No, but thank you any way. I'll just take the package, please."

"You'll want Alex for that. I'll go fetch him for you. I think he's in the basement."

She opened the door at the end of the hallway and shouted for her son. Moments later, a scruffy young man appeared. He was carrying a small box wrapped in brown paper, not unlike the one she had picked up last night.

"You're Rivka?"

"That's right."

"Here," he said giving her the package. "Try not to shake this, and whatever you do, don't drop it."

"Why, what's in it?"

"Just do what I tell you. It's fragile, that's all."

Rivka knew better than to ask too many questions. All Metro had told her was that he was doing something to ensure "their future together," as he put it the other day. He had asked her to trust him! He was only helping some of his comrades finish the work he had started with them. He told her no one will ever forget the strike of 1919. She believed him, and was content to leave it at that, even if in her less clouded moments she began to imagine all sorts of scenarios.

In those moments of doubt, she asked herself what Emma would do. The answer was obvious. She would do what had to be done for the new social order. 'Anarchism is the great liberator of man form the phantoms that have held him captive.' Those words rang in her head as she made her way down Magnus to McGregor Street.

She was about to do something else that greatly troubled her, and time was of the essence. The streetcars were running again. A fair contingent of workers had accepted the Electric Railway Company's offer to return to their jobs. Scabs, in Rivka's view, who were protected by the specials to undermine the strike. She had no choice, however. She was on her own. She had little money, certainly not enough to hire a car, and she had to be all the way across the city to Osborne Street in less than an hour.

Gently pushing her way past a 'special' supervising the stop, she boarded a streetcar heading downtown. Much to her chagrin, it was full. Apparently lots of other Winnipeggers had no qualms about life returning to normal. With the leaders in jail, and specials and soldiers in the streets, was the strike really over? Had everything been lost?

Rivka took a seat at the back, holding her package tightly. She had to admit most of the passengers appeared to be happy. Who could blame them? They were only trying to put food on their table and live from one day to the next. They were not interested in changing the world or turning it upside down. They wanted to go to work in the morning, return each evening, and spend their leisure time with their families. Who, Rivka wondered, were the naïve and ignorant? Them? Or, Metro and his idealistic friends? She shook her head to clear these thoughts away.

Metro was waiting for her as he promised he would. The small house on the corner of Osborne and Wardlaw belonged to Metro's "wealthy" relatives, as he liked to call them. In fact, his first cousin Mike Lizowski, owned a used furniture shop a few blocks away. He made a decent living, yet in Metro's eyes he was a capitalist. When the strike was in its third week, Mike had taken his family to visit his sister-in-law in Montreal. Long ago, he had given Metro a set of keys.

Rivka ran to embrace him.

"First, the package that Alex gave you," said Lizowski.

She gingerly pulled it from her purse and handed it to him. "What is it?"

"Nothing you have to worry about."

"Metro, I've done what you've asked. You know the police are following me…"

"Not here?"

"No, I lost them back at Sam's."

Lizowski sighed. "I had to wear this to get here," he said holding up a straw hat and blue overalls. "I'm one of O'Leary's farmhands now.

This isn't funny. Why can't we just leave right now? The two of us. You've told Sylvia?"

"Yeah, I sent her a message. I told her I'd let her know where I am, but later. And that she should tell Frederick that I've gone out of town and won't be back for a while."

"So why can't we go? O'Leary can get us to the border in his wagon."

"I have some unfinished business, Rivka. It has to be done."

Rivka frowned. "Give me that package." She grabbed it from him and tore open the brown paper. Inside were two small bundles wrapped in rags.

"Be careful with those!"

She carefully removed the cloth and took out two bottles. They were filled with a clear liquid. She started opening the cap on one when Lizowski took them from her.

"Acid. I don't want you to burn yourself."

"What are you doing with this, Metro? Is it some kind of bomb? Are you going to blow something up?"

Lizowski smiled, then just as quickly it vanished. "They must pay," he said re-wrapping the bottles and placing them in a leather pouch.

"Who has to pay?"

"Those who have committed the wrongs, the injustice, the pain. How does Emma put it? 'Resistance to tyranny is man's highest ideal.' That's what I'm trying to accomplish. I thought you agreed with me."

Rivka bit her lip. "I don't care what Emma says. How many people will be killed so that you can make your point?"

"Sometimes the end justifies the means."

"That's all you have to say? I thought…" She paused, then picked up her coat.

"Rivka, please, don't leave. Not like this."

She swung around and glared at him for a moment. "This isn't the way," she whispered. She opened the door and was gone before Lizowski could say another word.

Klein spent most of Friday morning at Dolly's, drinking coffee, smoking cigarettes and wading his way through the book Runciman had given him. He had a weird feeling that the book related somehow to his case. He found La Reine Helen Baker's arguments in support of Eugenics compelling, even fascinating, but perverse. Reading *Race Improvement*, he felt as if he was listening to Graham Powers make his case in court before a jury who didn't quite believe what he was telling them. Eugenists, wrote Baker, 'aim at encouraging the best births and discouraging the worst, and all details of their propaganda must be subordinate to this great aspiration.' In other words, in the name of creating the perfect world with perfect human beings to live in it, any kind of regulation or sacrifice was justified.

Klein was no philosopher, but to his way of thinking this wasn't any different than what the Bolsheviks were shouting about. Both the revolutionaries and the Eugenists wanted to take away freedom of speech, freedom of choice, and the freedom of being an individual. The needs of the group came first. Why, Klein wondered? He didn't want to be told who he could marry, how he should raise his children, or how he should live his life. Nor did he accept Baker's view that the great evils of society—crime, poverty, and illness—were strictly the product of biological imperfections. There was no natural law that deemed the European immigrants who lived in the slums of the North End, who toiled in factories and experienced misery, were in that state because of biology and heredity. Pick out any of them, thought Klein, put them in a house on Wellington Crescent, give them all the opportunities and supports that someone like Graham Powers had, and then see what will be.

By the time the morning was over, Klein felt as if he understood Bill Simon much better, and also realized why so many people detested him. What he still was no closer to solving, however, was why Simon was murdered and by whom. It must have been Lizowski, thought Klein. It was simply a process of elimination. No one else had motive, reason or opportunity. He was anxious to hear what Gertie Viola had to say, but given how he felt about Lizowski, he very much doubted if she would change his mind.

By six o'clock he was at Market Square. Alfred Powers had shared two pieces of news with him, one more unsettling than the other. Franklin was on the loose again. No one had seen him, and the police had no idea where to look. Alfred had recommended that Klein be more cautious than usual, advice that in this instant Klein was willing to follow. He agreed with Alfred's assessment that Franklin was unpredictable, dangerous, and had nothing to lose.

More surprising was that Ottawa had ordered Graham to release the strike leaders on bail. The one condition was that they cease leading the strike. Alfred told Klein that Russell and the others had already decided to call the strike off and accept the offer made earlier by Deacon and the other metal trade owners. They were due to be released from prison the next morning.

"That's it? After everything that's happened, they're quitting?" Klein had asked.

"They don't see it that way," Alfred Powers had told him. "They're tired, their families have been through enough, and besides, they feel that they did win some concessions. As I said, they're not, and never have been, revolutionaries like Lizowski. The only thing I'm worried about is how the veterans are going to take this."

Standing among the crowd behind City Hall, Klein could understand Alfred's point. The mood among the hundreds of pro-strike soldiers milling about Market Square was tense. It wasn't helped much, Klein thought, by the large number of specials standing on the other side of Main Street watching and waiting. He surveyed the area, half-expecting to see Franklin among those in the crowd.

Mayor Gray stood on a small make-shift platform in front of the vegetable and fruit stalls trying to speak. But it was impossible to hear him.

"We want the streetcar service stopped," some of the men shouted at him.

"We want the leaders out of jail and we want to use the Board of Trade building," said another group.

Finally, after a few moments, one of the soldiers mounted the platform to announce that there would be a silent parade at two-thirty in the afternoon down Main Street starting at the Royal Alexandra Hotel. The mayor had what appeared to Klein a few unpleasant words with the veterans near him, and then left in the company of several armed police constables.

Someone touched Klein lightly on his arm. He swung around and had his gun half out of its holster.

"Sam, easy. It's just me," said Hannah.

"Sorry. I thought you were someone else."

"You mean Franklin? We're looking for him, Sam, but to be honest Lizowski is the main priority at the moment."

"Yeah, I'm not surprised."

"I was finally able to speak to Bower today at the hospital."

"And?"

"He's in rough shape. Says he doesn't remember anything, or he's not saying. Perry will be here in a day or two. Then we'll see."

"That lunatic Franklin murdered Maloney and I'm going to make sure he pays for that."

"Leave him alone, Sam. I…I don't want anything to happen to…" She turned away from him.

Klein's first instinct was to comfort her. He had even gone so far as to draw up a mental chart comparing his life with Sarah and the girls to one with Hannah. That's when he realized there wasn't much to discuss or deliberate over.

"So what do you make of all this?" he asked.

"I'm worried Sam, there's bound to be trouble tomorrow. Gray's already notified Brigadier Ketchen. They're getting the Lewis guns ready."

"The strike's over. These poor saps just don't know it yet. They're isn't anything else to fight about."

"Look at those specials across the street. I'm not sure who frightens me more, them, or this mob."

Klein took out his cigarette case and offered one to Hannah.

"No thanks. Not a good idea out here in public. Too many busybodies."

"I thought you didn't care what people think?"

"I don't, but life's easier sometimes without drawing attention to yourself, although I doubt you'd understand that."

Klein hesitated. "We need to finish our conversation from the other day, Hannah."

"Not here, Sam," she said squeezing his hand ever so slightly. "Later, after Lizowski and Franklin are caught and things are back to normal."

"That may be a while," he said, cupping his hands to light his cigarette.

"I have to get back to the station. The Chief wanted a report on this meeting before I went home tonight."

"You planning to be here tomorrow?"

Hannah nodded. "McCreary has been assigned to supervise the specials. I might go along to keep an eye on him."

"Good luck, you're both going to need it."

"Sam, there's one more thing. I probably shouldn't be saying this, but…please tell your sister to be careful. We're watching her."

"You think she knows where Lizowski is?"

"Does she?"

Klein shrugged. "I don't know. I haven't seen her all day. But to be honest, it's occurred to me too. Rivka can be stubborn."

"Family trait?"

"Beautiful and funny. That's a dangerous combination."

24

RIVKA SAT ON THE STOOP of her apartment block sipping a mug of coffee. It was a Saturday morning and the streets were quiet. If the police were following her, as Metro suspected, they were nowhere in sight. Maybe, she thought, they had other more important things to do. She turned her face upward and let the June sun warm her. For a moment, she nearly forgot that she had some very difficult decisions to make. She glanced at her pocket watch. It was eight o'clock and she was still not certain what she should do. The message Metro had sent her had been clear: she was to stay away from today's march down Main Street, and meet him at O'Leary's farm at seven o'clock with as much of her belongings as she could stuff into one travelling case.

Late last night, she had decided to abide by his wishes. Then Helen Armstrong had come to see her. George, Bob Russell, Roger Bray and the British and Canadian-born were to be released early this morning. But not the four "foreigners." Word on the street was that the government was keeping Almazoff, Charitonoff, Schappellrei and Verenchuk locked away.

"The absurdity of it is that not one of them ever attended a strike committee meeting," said Helen. "So much for British justice."

Before Helen had left, she had urged Rivka to participate in Saturday's parade. "George and Bob can't be there. But they didn't say anything about us, did they? We owe them that much."

As she finished her coffee, she heard Helen's words in her head. She did owe the strike leaders something. Who cared what Metro said? To hell with his plans. What could he do? She stood up and ran back into her apartment. She was going downtown.

From the vacant apartment across the street, Hannah pulled out her notebook and recorded a few observations. Her eyes were squarely on the main doors of Rivka's block. She had assured Newton that she would not let Rivka out of her sight today and that was one promise she aimed to keep.

Carefully and methodically, Harry Griffins and Aaron Mikeljohn inspected their handiwork with all the pride of master craftsmen. The dynamite was tied together securely and the detonator was in place. They gently placed the bomb into a leather satchel. Then they put the satchel in O'Leary's wagon and covered it with hay, and a sufficient amount of manure to keep any nosy constables away.

A heated argument with Griffins had convinced Lizowski to forget about using the nitrogylcerine, or the acid-based explosive that Galleani had concocted. It was too unstable, Griffins had explained. That's what had happened outside Palmer's house in Washington. The bomb had gone off prematurely and had killed the Italian. "Trust me," Harry had told Lizowski, "and no one will ever forget June twenty-first."

Lizowski emerged from O'Leary's house dressed in a new suit, brown fedora, polished black boots and his stolen special's club.

"You look good, Metro," said Griffins. "I like the hat."

"You'll fool them all," added Mikeljohn.

"Is everything packed?" asked Lizowski.

"It's all here."

"And everyone knows where they're supposed to be?"

"Metro, we know what we're doing. Take it easy," said Mikeljohn.

"I want those bastards to pay. This is the start of a new era."

"If you guys are finished jawing, we can get going. These horses can only go so fast," said O'Leary.

"One minute," said Lizowski. He pulled a small book out of his coat pocket, the English translation of *Revolutionary Catechism* by Sergei

Nechaev. Harry and Aaron gathered around him for a ritual they had done many times before. Other than the snorting and shuffling of the two horses, the air was still as Lizowski began to read out loud.

'The revolutionary is a dedicated man. He has no personal feelings, no private affairs, no emotions, no attachments, no property and no name. Everything in him is subordinated towards a single exclusive attachment, a single thought and a single passion—the revolution.'

Lizowski held up his fist, then urged his comrades to board the wagon. He had read those words many times before. With every ounce of his being, he believed them. No personal issues should ever impede the struggle. And yet, as he climbed up beside O'Leary, intense personal feelings confused his every thought. Why, he asked himself, was the only image in his head that of Rivka?

"You okay? Metro?" asked O'Leary.

"I'm fine. Let's go."

Klein was parked outside the Royal Alexandra Hotel. He had been there since eleven o'clock, and in the past thirty minutes the crowd of veterans had swelled. As he looked across the street at the railway station, there must have been five hundred people standing around waiting.

Inside, in a third-floor suite, the veterans' leaders were meeting with Mayor Gray, Senator Gideon Robertson, Graham Powers, and RWNMP Commissioner Perry, who had arrived in the city on Friday night.

"What the hell are they doing in there?" Klein muttered to himself.

"Trying to convince Gray to let them march, I figure," said a familiar voice.

Klein turned and faced a sheepish-looking Bill McCreary.

"I'm an old fool, Klein."

"Yeah, you are. But I never thought I'd ever hear you admit that."

"Never thought I'd ever say it. You want a cigar?"

"Not those cheap Roxboroughs."

"It's all I can afford on my salary."

"You're an asshole, you know that?"

"I have a temper."

Klein grinned. "Yeah. So where's Hannah?"

"What's with the two of you anyway?"

"As I said, you're an interfering asshole."

McCreary grinned back. "She'll be here soon, I'm sure."

"You hear anything more on Lizowski?"

"Nothing. I couldn't spare any men this morning. Chief says everyone has to be down here. He's expecting lots of trouble. He wants to call in the Mounties. Between those horsemen and the specials..."

"Why not just let them have their parade? What the hell's wrong with Gray?"

"He won't do it. They want to take over the Board of Trade Building, they want the streetcars off the roads. They're bloody Reds. Why should anyone listen to them?"

At noon, the mayor, looking weary, finally emerged from the hotel. "We have not reached an agreement. And I stand by what I said yesterday. There will be no parade today..."

Loud yelling and booing emanated from the crowd. Several of the veterans rushed towards Gray. McCreary instantly moved in front of the mayor and pushed them back. A wall of specials suddenly appeared. Armed with their wooden clubs, they encircled the shaken mayor and amidst the shouting they escorted him back into the hotel.

O'Leary pulled up his wagon near the foot of the Provencher Bridge. The time was 1:30 p.m. It had taken him a little longer than he had anticipated to drive his horses through the people who now lined Main Street from Portage Avenue all the way to Higgins Avenue. But as Lizowski had reassured them, they had an hour to put their plan into action. During the journey from St. James, he had gone over everyone's assignments several times until Harry and Aaron could repeat the plan backwards.

The bridge had a few stragglers on it, but otherwise it was quiet. If people had left their homes, they were on Main Street by now. Griffins uncovered the satchel and handed it to Lizowski.

"Listen, comrades," Lizowski said. "The plan is simple. You infiltrate the crowd and agitate. I'll go to City Hall and plant the bomb. If we do our jobs right, soon the streets will run with reactionary blood."

The men shook hands, then went their separate ways. Lizowski pushed through the crowd on Main Street, guarding his package with his arms, and walked briskly toward City Hall. He crossed at Bannatyne and turned right. City Hall, in all its Victorian glory, was one of Winnipeg's great landmarks. Ever since it had been erected back in 1886, it dominated both Main Street and the Market. Lizowski stared up at the clock tower as it struck 2:10 p.m. He pulled his fedora down low over his eyes.

"Hey scab, you think you're pretty tough? Put down that package and come here," a young man in a flat cap shouted.

Lizowski kept moving. He thought he had planned for every contingency. The special's outfit was supposed to permit him to get inside the building with a minimum of problems. What he had not counted on was the animosity from the pro-strike crowd. A group of four men were walking swiftly behind him. They were gaining on him. He crossed the street and six specials appeared. They were on patrol and had been ordered to report to City Hall.

"Good to see you guys," said Lizowski. "I got some trouble."

"We can see that," said one of the specials. "Leave it to us."

"I appreciate it. I've got to get this to the City Hall. The mayor himself asked me to deliver a package."

"Stan will help you with that," said the special.

The other specials left as Lizowski followed Stan across the street.

"Haven't seen you around much."

"No? That's funny. Been here since the beginning," said Lizowski. "Bloody Reds, they should be shot for the all the trouble they've caused."

"You can say that again," said Stan.

They reached the front doors of City Hall only to find another small group of specials guarding it.

"Let him through. He has a delivery," said Stan. "Mayor's orders."

The men parted and Lizowski tipped his hat as he entered the building. "Thanks fellas."

"Don't mention it."

Lizowski was sweating. He found the office he was looking for on the second floor. It belonged to the Commissioner of Parks. Harry had calculated that an explosion at the front of the building on the second floor might just take down the whole structure. Lizowski's bomb was potent—eight sticks of dynamite. That was the reason why it was decided to give Lizowski the timing detonation device they had managed to acquire. He placed the satchel by the window and checked his stopwatch. It was precisely 2:45 p.m. He set the timer as Harry had showed him, and left the way he had entered. The specials who had been guarding the building were gone. Lizowski looked towards Portage Avenue and saw the first group of armed riders advancing on horseback.

25

ANOTHER TWO THOUSAND people, maybe more, had arrived on Main Street within the past hour. In spots, the crowd was twenty people deep. By 2:30 p.m. most of the street was overrun with veterans, strikers, and a lot of spectators caught up in the excitement of the moment.

"McCreary," called Klein. "What's going on? Where's Gray?"

"Gray's gone. He went out the back of the hotel about half an hour ago. He's on his way to the barracks to ask Perry to get some men here. He doesn't think the specials can deal with this crowd. He'll be back to read the Riot Act."

Their conversation was interrupted by the sound of windows being broken. Then, a block away, the crowd let out a loud roar of triumph.

"What the hell's going on?" said McCreary.

"The streetcar, over there," said Klein. "Look, there's smoke."

They ran up to Logan Avenue, pushing through the excited crowd. Amidst the running bodies and smoke, Klein could see his sister. He put his arm around her and pulled her onto the sidewalk.

"Rivka, what are you doing here? What happened?"

"The driver wouldn't stop so they stopped it for him," said Rivka. "He's just a kid, probably a Committee volunteer. Everybody is out of control. I'm afraid they're going to tear him apart."

Klein and McCreary surveyed the chaos. The mob had pulled the car's trolley off its wires, smashed nearly every one of its windows, turned it on its edge, and then set a few seats on fire. Black smoke billowed out of the wreck. McCreary shook his head, pulled out his revolver and fired three times in the air. People ran in every direction.

"Are you crazy," shouted Rivka. "You're going to kill someone."

"It cleared them away, didn't it?"

"Everything is going wrong. I have to get out of here," cried Rivka. "Sam, be careful."

"Wait, Rivka." It was too late; she had disappeared into the throng of yelling protestors.

"Klein, help me with the driver," said McCreary.

The streetcar driver had agreed to operate the car that day as a sign that the strike was over. He was bleeding from his forehead and a bit dazed. As McCreary and Klein worked to patch the man's cut, more shouts came from the street.

"Here they come," said McCreary.

Fifty-four policemen on horseback, some dressed in their scarlet uniforms, others in khaki, reached the corner of Portage and Main. Nearly all of them were holding wooden bats or yokes. Behind them was a convoy of trucks with another forty men ready to do battle. As the police rode past the Union Bank, the crowd moved closer to them, almost surrounding them. The horses became increasingly anxious. The officer in charge yelled out an order and suddenly the Mounties charged into the people on the sidewalks. A few of the officers had also drawn their revolvers and Klein could hear shots being fired as terrified people ran in every direction. One man dropped to the ground. He had been hit.

"Things are getting nasty, McCreary," said Klein. He pointed to another line of horsemen advancing towards them.

"Yeah, time to go," agreed McCreary.

Both men climbed out one of the broken windows of the streetcar and leaped to the ground. Another group of strikers had returned and surrounded the car again, shouting and jeering at McCreary. He drew his gun, and as he backed up, with Klein at his side, nearly ran over a photographer who was taking a picture. McCreary knocked over the man's tripod, but not before he had snapped the photo.

When the Mounties on horseback passed City Hall, they turned and began another charge. At this point people picked up whatever they could find, sticks, stones and bricks and began to throw them at the riders. Several were hit and fell to the ground.

"Jesus, they've done it this time," Lizowski whispered. "This is what it must have looked like in St. Petersburg in 1905."

From the roof of the magnificent Bank of Montreal Building with its soaring Roman columns, Lizowski watched in angry disbelief as the Mounties began their third charge, this time with their revolvers drawn. As people ran for cover, they started firing blindly. Behind the horses, a long row of Mounties and specials, with guns and clubs at the ready, marched in precision. Stretching across Main Street, four or five deep, they looked like an advancing army.

Lizowski checked his watch. It was just after three o'clock. Why hadn't the bomb exploded? He waited another minute, then realized with horror that something must have malfunctioned with the timer. Shit. That meant he would have to go back and light the fuse himself. He knew it would be dangerous, even suicidal. Then he smiled to himself. With the mayor on the steps of City Hall, surrounded by his reactionary minions, what better sacrifice could he make for the socialist cause?

Rivka saw Sam and McCreary at the corner of Main and Market. Her brother's face was covered in soot from the burning street car. Mayor Gray, surrounded by police, now stood on the steps of City Hall reading the Riot Act.

"Sam," Rivka gasped, as she ran up to them. "I think I've done something terrible."

Klein frowned. "Rivka, what are you still doing here? You should be somewhere safe."

"Listen to me. I think Metro may have planted a bomb."

"What! Where?"

She grabbed him by the arm. "I saw him go into City Hall. You have to hurry."

Klein turned to McCreary. "Get her out of here. I don't think I've got a lot of time."

Klein raced up the back steps of City Hall. Two burly specials, armed with clubs, stepped in front of the door. Klein considered his options: he could attempt to reason with them, or he could use a more expedient method. He realized he didn't have time for pleasantries. With one swift movement, he pulled out his revolver and pointed it at the nearest special.

"Sorry, boys, I got to get inside right now. Lizowski has planted a bomb."

The two specials backed away. The bigger one snarled at Klein. "You've finally gone too far, Klein. If you're helping that Red, you're going to swing."

"Maybe," Klein shrugged. "Anybody else gone in here in the last few minutes?"

"Just one of our men, he forgot part of a package for the mayor."

"Hmm, I wonder who's going to swing when the chief finds out you've let a terrorist into the heart of City Hall. Now get out of my way."

Klein ran into the foyer. A secretary, her face streaked with tears, was coming down the stairs.

"Quick, woman. Have you seen a big man in a fedora anywhere in the building?"

The secretary stared at Klein. "What's going on? There's shooting outside and people screaming…"

"A man, a man with a package?"

"One of the specials is up on the second floor. He said he had a delivery for—"

Klein was already taking the stairs two at a time. He ran down the hallway, opening doors and calling Lizowski's name. At the end of the hall, he saw a door ajar. Taking a deep breath, Klein edged into the room. A man was huddled over a package lying against one of the supporting columns in the corner. Klein pointed his gun.

"Hello, Metro. Decided to prove to everyone that you really are a murderer?"

Lizowski whirled around. He had a match in one hand and a packet of dynamite in the other. He smiled thinly. "I'm just having a little trouble with this fuse. I don't suppose you know anything about bombs?"

"Sorry."

Lizowski nodded. "Under these circumstances, it may seem a little unlikely, but I really didn't have anything to do with Simon's murder. Not that it matters."

Klein cocked his pistol. "Just put the dynamite down. We can sort out everything else later. It's not too late."

Lizowski's eyes gleamed. "You're right. It's not too late."

With that, he flicked his thumb on the wooden match head. As it burst into flame, he held it next to the fuse. Klein hesitated for a second, thinking of his sister, then fired a single shot. He aimed for Lizowski's shoulder but the terrorist had begun moving towards the window. The bullet hit him in the chest. As he slumped to the floor, the bomb fell to one side as the match fizzled and dropped to the other.

Klein slowly holstered his revolver. Outside, he could hear the ominous rattle of machine gun fire, as the army moved in to clear the last of the rioters. It was obvious that the General Strike of 1919 would soon be over.

26

"WHAT'S THE SITUATION, CHIEF?" asked Graham Powers.

It was late Saturday night. They were seated around the boardroom table in Newton's office—Mayor Gray, Commissioner Perry, Brigadier Ketchen, McCreary, Hannah, and off to the side, Sam Klein. He was gazing out the window smoking a cigarette. Against Newton's wishes, Powers had asked Klein to be present to answer some questions about his sister.

"I'm not even sure where to start," said Newton, his voice quiet. "Main Street is blocked at Broadway on one end, and the C.P.R. Station at the other. General Ketchen has men out with machine guns, and they plan to be on duty well past midnight. We have more than ninety people in custody. Most were arrested in altercations with special constables near Market and James Streets. We ran out of room at the station, so General Ketchen took a dozen or so to the brig at the barracks. Two people were killed. Not including Lizowski. And I recommend we keep him out of the papers."

There was a general murmur of agreement. "Quite the day," said Powers, shaking his head. "History will never let us forget it. Have you seen the striker's newspaper yet?" he asked holding up a single sheet of newsprint. "They're calling it "Bloody Saturday." I want Woodsworth and Dixon arrested first thing tomorrow morning. They're responsible for this. Charge them with seditious libel. Take them to Stony Mountain. I'll inform Meighen."

"It's too bad about the men killed," observed the mayor.

"It was unavoidable," objected Ketchen. "My men acted properly."

"Shooting into the crowd against unarmed people. That's proper?" asked Klein.

"My men only fired when they were fired upon," said Ketchen.

The room was silent for a moment.

"Now, what about Lizowski's accomplice, Rivka Klein?" asked Graham.

"Well," said Newton, glancing at Klein. "We know she helped Lizowski get the dynamite." All eyes in room turned to Klein, but he said nothing. "But I have to say that Mrs. Nash has questioned her thoroughly. We do not believe she knew what the materials were that she was delivering."

Graham Powers frowned. "All right. What else?"

"We come now to Franklin." Commissioner Perry said, getting to his feet. "I want to say at the outset that I take full responsibility for this. I believed he could be trusted, and could deal with the situation properly. After speaking to agent Bower, I now understand that I was in error."

"Yeah, you might say that." Klein interjected. "He tried to kill my family."

"As I was saying, according to Bower, Franklin is indeed responsible for the death of the reporter Maloney. It seems that Maloney found out that Franklin was an agent, and in a struggle, killed him. I make no excuses for this. Bower also says that Franklin was working with Bill Simon, although he is adamant that Franklin had nothing to do with Simon's death."

"So why was he trying to kill me?" asked Klein.

"Bower doesn't know for certain. He believes that Franklin hated Lizowski so much that he was determined that he be found guilty of the murder and that you, Mr. Klein were simply in the way. That's all I can tell you."

"Thank you Commissioner," said Powers. "Does anyone else have anything they'd like to add?"

Hannah raised her hand.

"Mrs. Nash, by all means."

"I know that the Chief believes, like most of you, that Lizowski was responsible for Bill Simon's murder. And that now that Lizowski himself is dead, the file can be closed." The policewoman hesitated. "I don't think that would be wise under the circumstances."

"And why's that exactly?" asked the chief.

"We still haven't questioned Mr. Simon's secretary Miss Viola."

"Well, where is she?"

"Her train has been delayed yet again as a result of the riots. The C.P.R. stopped all of its trains for five hours this afternoon. She won't be arriving until Monday morning."

"And you believe she has something important to say?" asked Powers.

"I'm telling you it's a waste of time and energy," said McCreary.

"Jesus, McCreary," said Klein. "What does it matter? Let Hannah talk to the woman. I'd also like to hear what she has to say. Or are you afraid she's going to say something that will upset you? You're all so sure that justice has been served today. My friend is dead because of those high and mighty principles you want to preserve."

"Franklin doesn't represent us," said Gray.

Klein looked around the room at the assembled authority figures of post-strike Winnipeg. "Maybe so, Mayor. Maybe you really do believe in democracy and fairness. But just remember, you created Franklin, all of you. Now you have to live with it."

"It was nice of you to walk me home, Sam," said Hannah.

"It's the least I can do. You saved Rivka's life," said Klein.

It was close to midnight, and Ketchen's soldiers were still on patrol. Hannah wore her badge on her coat, as per Newton's instructions. Once or twice the soldiers, with their guns out, approached them, but merely tipped their hats when they saw that Hannah was a policewoman.

Hannah nodded. "She was pretty shaken up. My God, what might've happened? It's unbelievable. I know it happened in New York, but here?"

"I'm not defending Lizowski. But I don't think he felt like he had a choice. He may have tried to set off the bomb, but Powers, Perry, Gray, they all helped."

"You sound like a university professor, Sam."

"Yeah. I've been listening to Rivka for too many years."

"What did Perry tell you?"

"Says I can see her in the morning. I think that Graham is going to let her go. He's got enough trials to worry about. Why waste his time with Rivka? They have no case against her."

"That's good, Sam. Listen, do you want to be in the room tomorrow morning when McCreary and I speak with Miss Viola?"

"Newton will never go for that."

"McCreary already talked him into it. Something about owing you."

Klein grinned. "I'll be there then."

"You think she knows something?"

"I do. She must have been spooked to have gone all the way to Vancouver."

They reached the foot of the Main Street Bridge and started walking across. Underneath them the Assiniboine River was still and dark. Hannah touched Klein's arm. He pulled her close and they kissed. He ran his fingers through her hair.

"Hannah, I...I..."

"Don't say it, I know Sam. I know."

They walked down River Avenue in silence. In minutes, they reached the front door of her apartment block.

"I'd ask you to come in," said Hannah.

"I want to, I do," said Klein. "It's just..."

"Complicated?"

"Something like that," he said with a sad smile.

She kissed his cheek and went inside.

He lingered for a while, smoking a cigarette, thinking of what might have been.

The CPR Station on Higgins Avenue was almost empty. Its mammoth hall, usually buzzing with hordes of travellers was quiet. There was a

Metis family milling about, and a few businessmen, no doubt returning home after a weekend they would not be able to tell their grand-
children about. And perhaps a dozen or so people waited for the train
to arrive.

It was only ten on Monday morning, but Hannah guessed that after
Saturday people were staying home. The city was still in a state of
shock. Some businesses were open on Main Street, and Portage
Avenue, but many remained closed. On Sunday the churches were
filled, somewhat odd for June, when most Winnipeggers would rather
be playing at the parks than praying to God. But after June 21, nothing
was the same. The downtown streets remained deserted except for
soldiers and police.

There was a rumour circulating that the strike would officially be
called off late on Monday, although Newton did not believe it. Already,
Perry's men had found J.S. Woodsworth at the McLaren Hotel and
arrested him. Fred Dixon had thus far escaped their net, but Perry and
Newton were confident he would also be taken into custody shortly.
The strikers' newspaper, *The Strike Bulletin*, which Woodsworth and
Dixon had been producing ever since its editor William Ivens had been
arrested, was shut down and the presses seized. Yet Dixon was
ingenious. By nine, there were boys on the street with more of the story
of "Bloody Saturday."

"What shall the sacrifice profit Canada if she who has helped destroy
Kaiserism in Germany shall allow Kaiserism to be established at
home?" asked Dixon. "Whoever ordered the shooting last Saturday is
a Kaiser of the deepest dye." It was a good question, thought Hannah,
when she read it. Whatever General Ketchen and Mayor Gray had said
the other night, it seemed the indiscriminate shooting was an over-
reaction at best.

Three burly constables accompanied Hannah. She was to escort
Gertie Viola directly to the station where the interrogation was to take
place. Newton was still unhappy that McCreary had told Klein he
could be present, yet the Chief had decided to permit it nonetheless.

Finally, the ten o'clock train from Regina pulled in. Hannah waited
patiently for the other passengers to disembark. There were hugs and
handshakes as people greeted family and friends. Then two Calgary
plainclothes detectives emerged. They helped Gertie Viola down the

stairs each taking an arm. Hannah approached them. Between the two policemen, Gertie looked tiny. Her hair was a mess and her dress creased. She almost appeared relieved to see Hannah.

"Miss Viola, at last. I'm sure you're glad to be home," said Hannah.

"Can I please go to my apartment? Then, I'll answer your questions. But I really need a hot bath."

"I understand, but I can't. The bath will have to wait. You'll have to answer the questions first."

27

"LET'S START WITH this, Gertie: Why did you run away?" asked Hannah.

She was pacing. Chief Newton was seated at a chair to the right of her, and McCreary was beside him. Klein stood against the wall, watching and marvelling at Hannah's composure, as well as waiting for something, anything, that Gertie might say that would shed some light on Bill Simon's murder.

Gertie took a sip of the coffee Hannah had brought her. "It was that terrible man, he was going to kill me. I just knew it."

"What man, Gertie? Who were you afraid of?"

"Franklin. He had been at Mr. Simon's office that day."

"Why didn't you just tell us?"

"I don't know," she cried. "I was frightened. I just wanted to get as far away from him as possible."

"Did Franklin kill Mr. Simon?" asked Newton.

Gertie shook her head. "I don't think so. No, he didn't. He couldn't have."

"Go on, Gertie, please," said Hannah.

"Can I have a cigarette please?"

Klein took one out of his case and gave it her. She inhaled deeply. "That day, I helped carry some papers to Mr. Simon's car. He was talking with Franklin when I got there. Then…then Lizowski arrived. He said something or other to Simon, and they started arguing.

Franklin grabbed Lizowski and sent him on his way. A few minutes later, Franklin also left. That's the last I saw of him until he showed up at my apartment."

"Gertie, when we first questioned you, do you remember what you told us?"

She buried her head in her hands. "Yes, yes. That I had seen Lizowski with Mr. Simon by the car. It wasn't quite the whole truth."

"No it wasn't. Why did you lie to us?"

"Mr. Simon."

"Mr. Simon what?"

"Before I left the car, Mr. Simon told me that I was to never mention Franklin to anyone. That it was very important to him. I was scared. I had heard of Lizowski and all the trouble he caused. Mr. Simon said he was an agitator, a revolutionary who threatened everything good in this country. I was upset by Mr. Simon's death. I was sure that Lizowski had done it."

"You were sure?" said McCreary. "Jesus."

"Please, Gertie continue," said Hannah.

"He planted a bomb, didn't he? Was I wrong? He was as evil as Mr. Simon had said. Isn't that so? I have to say, I'm not sorry he's dead. There's nothing more Franklin can do to me. As you said, Mrs. Nash, he's probably long gone from here now."

Everyone in the office was silent for a moment.

"I have a few questions," said Klein.

Newton nodded his head. "Go on, Klein, but make it quick."

"When Mr. Simon and Franklin were talking by the car, did you hear what they said to each other?"

Gertie nodded. "Yeah, some of it. It had something to do with Nessie, Mrs. Simon's daughter."

"I didn't know Simon had a daughter. Doesn't he only have two sons? What are their names?"

"You mean James and Arthur? Yes, Nessie died, a few years ago. She...she wasn't well."

"What happened to her?"

"I don't know anything else. Why don't you ask Caddie Simon? She can tell you everything you want to know."

"Caddie? Isn't Mrs. Simon's first name Carolyn?" asked Hannah.

"For detectives, you sure don't know very much do you? Yes, her name is Carolyn, but everyone calls her Caddie. It's been her nickname since she was a child. Now, if there's nothing else, I really would love to take a bath."

The first thing Klein noticed was the specials patrolling Wellington Crescent. Teams of young men holding clubs and pistols walked and drove up and down the street. And why not, he thought. If Anarchists were going to strike again, bombing one of the mansions on the Crescent made perfect sense. From the point of view of the grain barons and wealthy businessmen who lived in this elite neighbour-hood, the past few weeks must have seemed like their world really was turning upside down. It appeared now that the Citizens Committee of 1000 had won, yet no one could yet predict the future consequences of this victory. Klein had heard that there was to be an official announcement from the strike committee tomorrow. He suspected that Russell and the other leaders would announce that the strike was over. It would be interesting to see the reaction of the business com-munity. Would they show the compassion and understanding preached by the Social gospellers, or would they take retribution against the perpetrators, much like the victors were doing with Germany at the peace talks in Europe?

Klein found Hannah waiting for him in front of the Simons' home. With the sun beaming down on her, he had to admit that she looked beautiful. He had resolved the matter of Hannah in his own mind, and yet each time he saw her the submerged desire re-surfaced.

"Quite the house, isn't it Sam?" asked Hannah.

"The question is, does money buy happiness?"

"In this case, I suppose not. Still, it would be nice."

"Where's McCreary?"

"Says this is a waste of time. I don't care what he thinks."

Klein laughed. McCreary never had a chance with her.

The house was at the corner of Brock Street, some distance from the majority of homes that were located up to Harrow Street. This far down the road, it was like living in the country. The Simons' house was set back far from the road, close to the river. Through the large gates with a giant "S" carved in the middle, there was a circular stone driveway. There were gas lamps to light the way at night. The house itself was as grand as any Klein had seen. With its brick edifice and peaks, it reminded him of the drawings of French castles he had seen in books at the library. With Hannah at his side, he knocked on the dark oak door. Immediately it was opened by an elderly gentleman attired in a black suit.

"We have an appointment to see Mrs. Simon," said Klein.

"Yes, She's expecting you. Come with me please."

He led Klein and Hannah into a magnificent parlour with a wall of books on one side, a grand piano, and the finest furniture money could buy.

"Mrs. Simon is in the garden." He opened two French glass doors that led outside. There was a brick patio, a finely manicured lawn and an array of flowers and greenery, not much different than Alfred Powers's place. A pathway led to the river bank where there was a dock, and a fine wooden Peterborough cruiser.

Carolyn, "Caddie" Simon was on her knees trimming her plants, and pulling out weeds. "I'll be with you in a moment," she said. "How about some lemonade, Gilbert?"

"Right away, Ma'am," said the butler and returned to the house.

Mrs. Simon was a striking woman. She had large dark eyes, and a genuinely warm smile. Her brown hair was cut short and she wore a light sun dress that covered her ankles.

"You must be Mr. Klein, and Mrs. Nash. It's very nice to meet you. Please take a seat. I just love this time of year, everything in bloom."

There were several wooden patio chairs on the lawn and the three of them sat down. Gilbert arrived with the lemonade.

"That's all for now, Gilbert. Please no disturbances while I chat with my visitors."

"Thank you for seeing us, especially under the circumstances," said Hannah.

"Think nothing of it Mrs. Nash. After the dreadful week this city has had, I'm more than happy to answer any questions you have."

"That's very kind of you. We wanted to ask you about your late husband, if we may."

"Go ahead. If you must know, Bill was a loyal man, but he wasn't all that nice a person. Frankly I doubt we would have lasted together. In fact, we weren't even talking before he died."

Klein raised an eyebrow. "And why was that?"

"Well, the truth is, and I'm sure I'm not telling you anything you don't already know, Bill was an opinionated man. But that was only part of it. Did Gilbert walk you past our library in the parlour?"

"Yes, he did," said Klein.

"Then you saw them."

"Ma'am, I'm not sure what you mean."

"The books, Mr. Klein. The books. Six or seven years ago, Bill became interested in the Eugenics movement. Are you familiar with that?"

"A little. I've been reading a book by a woman named Baker."

"*Race Improvement.* Yes, that was one of Bill's favourites. He became obsessed with the subject. He began reading, studying and writing letters. I could show you a box full of replies from all over the United States and Europe. Bill insisted that unless the population in North America and western Europe was properly controlled, the human race had no future. It was as simple as that. He gave hundreds, probably thousands of dollars to the Eugenics societies. Bill helped finance sterilization campaigns everywhere from Oregon to Virginia. The feeble-minded, the insane, prostitutes, all of them, in Bill's opinion, had to be sterilized. Otherwise, the human race was doomed. A world of Kallikaks, he used to say."

"I'm sorry Mrs. Simon, who are the Kallikaks?" asked Hannah.

"I'll show you the book by Goddard later. The Kallikak family, although I don't think that was their real name, were uneducated paupers who lived in the backwoods of New Jersey. Goddard found them and studied their genes. He traced the family's problems right back to the American Revolution when their ancestor, whom he called Martin Kallikak, made a young, feeble-minded barmaid pregnant. That was the beginning of the family's 'degeneration.' No matter how much I tried to explain to Bill that there were a dozen other facts to take into account, that poverty was not an illness and that sometimes crimes were committed out of desperation, he refused to listen. For him, it was purely a matter of heredity. That was why…oh dear."

"That was why what?" asked Klein.

Mrs. Simon's eyes welled up with tears. "That was why he had such a difficult time with Nessie, our daughter. Our beautiful Nessie."

She stopped herself.

"Could we get you anything?" asked Hannah.

"No. I'll be fine in a moment. Nessie was our middle child. She was born on April 28th, 1906. She had big blue eyes. Around her third birthday, we noticed that she wasn't quite right. She couldn't speak properly, and she was very slow to learn almost anything, certainly not like James. We took her to doctors, but no one could give us any reason. Then one day, Nessie would've been about eight, Bill decided it was my fault, or rather the fault of my family. That it was my genes which had led to his daughter being a moron. That's what he called her, a moron. We had terrible fights. Finally, he agreed to send her to an asylum in Michigan where they were using the most modern techniques. There was a doctor named Singleton. Very progressive, and she started to improve. I moved down to Pontiac for a short time. Her speech was better, and then...then on June 4th of 1916, I will never forget that date so long as I live, Nessie...passed away."

"Here, take this," said Klein, handing Mrs. Simon his handkerchief.

"The doctors told me she just died in her sleep. That it happens. What did I know?"

"What do you mean, Mrs. Simon?" asked Hannah.

"It's too terrible to even say."

"Please, tell us."

"About a month ago, there was this dreadful man who came to see us. He had a walrus moustache. There was something about him that gave me the willies. I didn't trust him for a moment."

"His name was Franklin?" asked Klein.

"Yes," Mrs. Simon stared at Klein. "Anyway, Bill was yelling about this and that when he mentioned Nessie. I didn't think anything of it, but it nagged at me the rest of the day. I asked him later that evening what he was talking about, and then he just blurted it out. Like it was nothing." She noticed the look of astonishment on Hannah's face. "That's right Mrs. Nash. Bill, my husband Bill, killed her. He suffocated her. To stop her from ever having children. Sterlization wasn't good enough. He had to end her life so that the 'gene infection' would stop."

"He killed his own daughter," said Klein. "How could someone have done that?"

"For the good of the race, Mr. Klein, for the good of the race."

"You're awfully quiet tonight, Shailek," said Sarah.

Klein had not told his wife about what he had learned, and he did not know what to say about it. Hannah, too, had been dumbfounded by Mrs. Simon's story, and neither of them knew what to do with the information, or what part it may have played in Simon's death. They agreed to meet the next day after Hannah reported her findings to Newton. Mrs. Simon had given Klein a box of her husband's letters in the hope of finding some clue. He had started examining the correspondence, but was so troubled he put the box on a shelf in the closet. He'd get to the letters later.

Klein's first reaction was that Simon was insane. But then he began re-reading parts of Baker's *Race Improvement*. He stopped on page 32. The words almost leaped right off the page.

'Race improvement requires, under modern conditions of life, eternal vigilance and deliberate aim…The degenerate child is neither beautiful, robust, nor mentally sound…Almost every prison in the civilized world bears record to the direct injury inflicted on the community by the degenerate class…Eugenics is capable of revolutionizing these terrible conditions…'

Did this make sense? How could it? Where would such thinking lead in the future?

"Daddy, Daddy read us a story," said Freda. She climbed up on his lap.

"Come on Neicee, you too." He picked up his younger daughter, and placed her on the other side. "What should I read?" asked Klein, as if he didn't know. Freda handed him a beat-up copy of *Mother Goose's Rhymes For Children*, a present from Rivka on Freda's third birthday.

"Pussycat," yelped Bernice. "Pussycat."

Klein opened the book. "The three little kittens. They lost their mittens. And they began to cry…" As his daughters looked at the pictures, Klein wondered how any father could do what Bill Simon did.

"For Christ sakes," said Klein. "It was staring me in the face the whole bloody time Son of a bitch."

"Shailek! Not in front of the girls," said Sarah from the kitchen.

But Klein wasn't listening. He lifted the girls off his lap. "That's it," he muttered. "That has to be it. Sarah, I'm going out."

"Where are you going at this hour?" she asked.

"General Hospital."

"The hospital? Whatever for? Is someone ill?"

The door slammed. He was already down the stairs and out in the street.

28

D̲R̲. HENRY KLUNDER was a friend of Klein's from the North End. They had been chums for years, and promised each other that some day they'd travel the world together. While most Jewish boys were lucky to finish grade school, Henry had persevered and refused to work in a garment factory, or haul garbage for the rest of his life. He worked nights as a musician playing at the Walker Theatre—he was a hell of a trumpet player—and eventually put himself through medical college.

"Henry, how are you?" The two men shook hands. "I was searching the halls for you. Nurses said you were with a woman who was having a baby."

"It was a boy. Now listen, I got your earlier message and I looked up the file. But Sam, I'm breaking every rule there is around here. You're going to get me fired."

"Listen Henry, you know I wouldn't be asking you this if it wasn't important. I have to know. Someone's life might be in danger."

"Hold on a minute, I'll get the chart."

"Shailek, did you hear the news?" Sarah was bubbling with excitement. "Early this morning, they announced it. The strike is over as of tomorrow morning. Thank God. Things can get back to normal. Have you heard from Rivka yet?"

Klein smiled. "Relax. Think about the baby. If you'll calm down, I'll tell you. Alfred telephoned a few minutes ago, while you were out.

Graham has agreed to drop all charges against Rivka. There's some paperwork to do, but she'll be out in an hour or so. He says that she's very upset. She hasn't been eating or talking."

"She'll be okay. Give her some time. She can stay here if she wants, the girls always make her happy."

"I knew Lizowski was nothing but bad news."

"That's what happens when married men cheat on their wives," said Sarah wrapping her arms around Klein.

"Yeah, I guess so," he said pushing her back.

"Shailek, is there something you're not telling me?" she asked playfully.

"Sarah, I'm waiting for a telephone call. Not now."

Alfred Powers had already filled in Klein on the all the events leading up to the end of the strike. Russell and his committee had visited Graham and Premier Norris early in the morning with the news. The strikers were giving up. Deacon and the other metal trade bosses had promised that they would reduce the weekly schedule by five lousy hours, from fifty-five to fifty hours. Nobody was getting a raise, however. It was the same with Manitoba Telephones; some, but not all of the girls could have their jobs back, but they had to re-apply, as if they were starting from scratch. Somebody was going to pay for the strike and it seemed to Klein that it was the workers.

Graham, Alfred said, was in a bit of hot water, since the authorities in Ottawa felt that releasing the strike leaders on bail was one of the reasons for the "Bloody Saturday" riots. Yet Graham had already publicly stated that Russell, Ivens, Bray and the others had done everything they could to prevent the violence. None of them, of course, had anything to do with Lizowski. At the moment, there was only one piece of unfinished business, and that was Franklin. Alfred said that Graham and Commissioner Perry believed he had fled the city. Klein wasn't so certain.

"Shailek, the phone," said Sarah.

"I've got it." He picked up the ear piece. "Millie, is that you?"

"Yeah, Sam. I'm back. I'm starting to wonder why I ever left. This strike—"

"The call, Millie."

"One moment. Say hello to Rivka for me. Tell her we're all thinking of her." The wires crackled, and then Klein heard the voice. "Sam, it's Henry. I double-checked the information. It's just as you thought."

Klein put on his jacket, checked his gun, and ran to catch the streetcar. His mind was racing. Henry confirmed that his hunch had been correct. That meant the danger still existed, even if the family thought the opposite. He got off the streetcar on Main and Broadway and caught a westbound car. It took another ten minutes until the streetcar reached Spence Street.

He jogged up to the house and knocked. A young girl about ten years old opened the door, but she just stared at Klein and smiled.

"Is your father here?" he asked gently.

"Suzie, get away from the door, dear, Daddy will speak to the man." George Runciman came around the corner and took his daughter by the hand. "Go play in your bedroom," he said deliberately. He waited until she had left before he turned to Klein.

"Katie's out with Paul. Went to buy some groceries. You know the strike's over."

"She's not all there, is she Runciman? Feeble-minded, I think is what the doctors call it?"

Runciman's face flushed. "Suzie's just fine. What is it you want?"

"She's still in danger you know. I don't care what Newton or Powers says, Franklin is still in the city."

"So what does that have to do with me?"

Klein glared at Runciman for a moment. "He was going to kill, Suzie, just like he did to his own daughter. Isn't that right?"

Runciman's shoulders sagged. "Things just got out of hand, you have to believe me."

"Tell me what happened."

"One day, after I started working for Simon, he told me about what he had done to Nessie. He was proud of it, for God sakes. He was actually proud of what he had done. At first, I didn't believe what I was hearing, but after listening to him spout all that Eugenics trash about curing the evils of the world, making it pure again, I came to the realization he was telling the truth. You read that book I gave you. It's all in there."

"I read it, yeah. Go on."

"He started telling me that I had to do the same to Suzie. It was an accident with her. When she was born, something happened. The cord was wrapped around Suzie's neck. Katie said it was only a minute, but the damage had been done. She was deprived of oxygen. We noticed something was wrong with her after her first birthday. She doesn't talk much. Her brain just doesn't work like everyone else's. I've taken her to doctors in Toronto, New York, all over. There's nothing any of them can do for her. That bastard Simon wanted me to kill her. Kill my own daughter! Then…then when I refused…"

"Franklin."

Runciman nodded. "He hired Franklin to do it. That's what I found out the day he was killed. He and Franklin were discussing the job after Lizowski had left. I ran after him and found him at his automobile. We had a terrible argument. He threatened to have me killed as well. I…I don't know what happened, Klein. I remember grabbing him. There was a rope in the back seat of his auto. I took it…oh my God, what could I do?"

Klein grimaced. "So you let them blame Lizowski."

"He was a Red. Look at the trouble he caused. What did it matter?"

"You don't really believe that, Runciman. Why didn't you tell someone? Talk to a lawyer. He was threatening your family."

The sound of a muffled cry stopped Klein.

"What was that?"

"It was from upstairs."

"Someone's in the house," said Klein.

"Franklin!" said Runciman. "It's Franklin. He's here for Suzie."

Klein jumped to his feet. "Runciman, listen to me. Go call the police now." He pulled out his revolver and moved to the bottom of the stairs. He heard some scuffling and then another cry. He started up the stairs when Franklin suddenly appeared on the landing. He was holding Suzie over his shoulder like a sack of potatoes.

"Klein, you take one more step and I'll snap her neck. You know I'll do it. Now drop that gun."

Klein shook his head. "There's no point to this. Simon's dead. You don't have to do this."

"See, that's where you're wrong. I made a promise to Simon. I have a duty to carry out. You do it one at a time, Simon used to tell me. And before too long, there won't be any of them left."

"You're not going to save the world by hurting her."

"I said drop that gun, Klein."

Klein didn't believe in giving up his gun, but the man was holding a little girl.

"Okay, take it easy." He threw his gun to the floor. "Now what are you going to do?"

"I'm taking the girl with me." Franklin inched his way down the stairs. "Move back."

Klein did as he was told. With Suzie crying louder, Franklin stepped towards the front door. He pushed it open.

Runciman came around the corner. "Klein, do something, he'll kill her."

On the front steps of the house, Hannah stood waiting. She had a pistol aimed at the back of Franklin's head. She concentrated as best as she could. Everything she had learned about shooting a gun flashed chaotically through her head.

"Franklin, turn around slowly and let the girl go," she ordered.

Franklin stopped. "Sure, pretty lady, I can do that." He lowered Suzie to the floor. As he stood up, a silver-plated revolver flashed in his hand.

Hannah fired without thinking. The bullet hit Franklin in the arm, spinning him around. She fired again, hitting him high in the chest. Without a sound, he dropped to the ground.

Hannah stood still for a long moment.

"You okay?" asked Klein, putting his hand on her shoulder.

"I think so." She took his hand and gripped it in hers for a moment.

Klein smiled at her. In another time and place, maybe it would've worked. But love, in all its forms, was a funny thing. He glanced over to where George Runciman was sitting. He was rocking back and forth, holding his daughter tightly in his arms.

29

"DID YOU READ today's paper, Shailek?" asked Sarah, her nose still red from the cold walk to the corner store.

Klein smiled at his wife. "Yes, I've seen it."

"So everything turned out okay. It's only one year, probably less. He'll make it."

A jury had found George Runciman guilty of manslaughter. It had taken several months for his case to come to trial. Alfred Powers had defended Runciman, and had done his usual superb job. He had, in effect, put Bill Simon on trial along with his own client. The story of Simon's murder of his own daughter, as testified to by Carolyn Simon, and then the threat on Runciman's daughter by Simon and Franklin did the trick. The jury also recommended leniency, and the judge agreed. Alfred was appealing the sentence, something about the judge's charge to the jury being incorrect, and Klein had no doubt that he might get Runciman out of jail altogether.

The *Free Press* that day had other stories as well that caught Klein's attention. There was a small item buried on page four: "Policewoman leaving city for Calgary." The Calgary police department had recruited Hannah to be its first female detective. Chief Newton had offered her the same job in Winnipeg, but she had turned him down. Klein had bumped into her at Eaton's perhaps three weeks ago and she had told him about the offer. She said she needed to start over, and the job offer in Calgary was promising. He told her that he'd be sure to look her up if he was ever in Alberta on business, but they both knew that he would not.

From New York, there was another article about more deportations. Since the June 2 bombing, US Attorney General Palmer had rounded up hundreds of aliens and Bolsheviks, sending them back to wherever they came from. Galleani was one of the first. They put him on a ship for Italy at the end of June, without his wife and five children. Emma Goldman, too, was facing the same fate. The story noted that Goldman was in a prison in Jefferson City, Missouri, and would likely be deported to Russia at the end of the month.

It was a slightly different story in Canada. A few of the foreigners involved in the strike were deported, as well as about ten men known to be associated with Lizowski, whether they were guilty or not. But since all of the strike leaders were British, with the exception of George Armstrong, the lone native-born Canadian, deportation was out of the question. Instead, Graham Powers put the strike leaders on trial for seditious conspiracy, and offered a taste of British justice.

That legal process had dragged on through the summer. In early September, Helen Armstrong, with Rivka by her side, had led a peaceful parade of men and women down Main Street to protest the trials. The Crown's main case, backed by the federal government, was that Russell, Ivens, Armstrong and the others had actually directed the strike as Lenin, Trotsky and Stalin had directed the revolution in Russia. But hard evidence was difficult to come by. That the leaders had acted in a "conspiracy" was even more impossible to substantiate. Yet, no matter how much Russell's lawyer Robert Cassidy argued, he got nowhere. Klein was in court a week ago to listen to Judge Thomas Metcalfe's charge to the jury. He more or less informed the jury that by his conduct during the strike—the permits for milk and bread delivery and the organization of the parades and protests—he was guilty. And the jury agreed. On December 23, they found Russell guilty on all charges. Metcalfe sentenced him to two years in Stony Mountain, but in a display of sympathy, had permitted Russell to spend Christmas with his family.

Out in the street, it was cold and windy, a typical late December afternoon. The specials were long gone; most of the men had returned to jobs in factories or had left the city in search of other work. Stores and shops were filled with post-Christmas shoppers, Jewish peddlers were back hawking rags and bottles, and the streetcars were ploughing their way through the snow. It was as if a terrible storm had passed over the city that June and had finally departed. People were cheerful, there was hope for the future.

As Klein walked to the grocery store on Selkirk Avenue, he knew that the happy holiday mood was merely a façade. The citizens of Winnipeg might not have understood it, but the strike had altered the city in several different ways. Labour had suffered a terrible setback. The workers had lost, there was no getting around that. There was no collective bargaining, and the union's struggle for recognition and real power was weakened. Some members of the labour community already announced their intention of running candidates in the next civic election, but Klein doubted if they would have much success.

After much contemplation, Klein finally grasped that Bill Simon's desire to control nature was merely a response, albeit an extreme one, to the threat of insurrection. Simon's version of the future was tainted with the notion that racial purity would save the world. Yet for Klein, it came down to this: any world in which a father could murder his own daughter so that the white Aryan race, as they had started referring to themselves, could achieve glory, was a world he wanted no part of.

"Shailek, the girls need porridge and the baby's crying, please come help," said Sarah from the other room.

Sarah had given birth to a boy on September 28. Sam Klein finally had a son. The boy had dark eyes and a full set of hair. Sarah insisted they call him Melvin. "It means 'friend', and that's what he'll be to the girls." Klein wasn't crazy about the name, but within a few days he was proudly displaying little "Mel" all over the city.

After kissing his wife on the cheek, Klein gave Freda and Bernice bowls of porridge. They stared at his offering as if he had pulled it from the garbage.

"Hans came by with something when you were with the baby," said Sarah. "I put it on the kitchen table."

A week earlier, Klein had finally taken down the box of letters Carolyn Simon had given him, and began examining the correspondence and papers. Inside, he found a bundle of newspaper clippings, mostly from the United States. There was a speech given by Herbert Spencer at the First National Conference on Race Betterment, in Battle Creek, Michigan from 1914, handbills supporting sterilization laws for the feeble-minded in at least a dozen states, and a personal invitation from Charles Davenport to join the newly established Galton Society in New York. The society wanted 'native Americans, who are anthropologically, socially, and physically sound, no Bolsheviki need apply.' In a hand-written letter, Davenport said the founding members, him included, had decided to make an exception for Simon "as a result of his loyal service."

Tucked at the bottom of the box was one letter that caught Klein's attention. It looked like it had a German military seal on the front of the envelope. The document was an official looking letter on fine white paper. It was April 5, 1919, and the postmark was from München, which Klein knew was Munich. From what Klein could initially determine from the English note accompanying it, the letter had been sent to Davenport from Max von Gruber, a professor of hygiene in Munich, who in turn had forwarded it to Simon.

The note read as follows: 'In view of our recent conversations, I thought you might like to read this. Sorry I did not send along the English translation, but I assume there are enough Germans in Winnipeg that it should not be a problem. Please let me know your thoughts. It may be wise to raise necessary funds. Professor von Gruber would like to recruit the young man, but he too has no money to help. Hope to see you soon. All my best, Charles.'

Klein immediately took the letter to Hans Rosenberg, an Austrian dressmaker who lived on Pritchard Avenue. He promised Klein that he would write an English translation for him in a few days. That had been five days ago, and Klein had almost forgotten about it. Hans had returned the original letter, along with an English version. Klein unfolded it and began to read.

Dear Professor von Gruber,

It was good of you to visit with me the other day. As you know, I am still unwell, the result of the mustard attack that nearly blinded me. I'm glad you concurred with my decision to seek a discharge. These have been terrible times. The turmoil caused in the city by the Bolsheviks and the Jews is truly troubling. We can only hope that this revolution will end soon and more intelligent men will be there to assume leadership. I am still committed to a career in politics. My friends tell me I have some natural ability as a speaker. I am not so certain.

I have read the articles and books you sent along and am most impressed. Had I more funds at my disposal, I would certainly contribute to your plans to promote mass sterilization of degenerates. This is as you said, 'the sacred duty of the state.' I would go further than this, in demanding the sterilization also of Bolsheviks, Jews and other troublemakers. What better way to build a strong fatherland?

I would be honoured to attend the conference you mentioned, but again, my finances are poor at the moment. Perhaps we could meet next week to discuss this further.

Yours,
A. Hitler, Corporal
7th Company of the 1st Reserve Battalion, 2nd Infantry, Munich

Klein read the letter again, crumpled it up and threw it into the fire. So Bill Simon was not alone. There were others like him in the United States, in Germany, and elsewhere, ready to inflict on the world their vision of racial purity. Klein lit a cigarette and glanced out the window. It was snowing. Simon was gone, but there were others, so many others to replace him. How far would they go before they achieved their goal, Klein wondered. How far would they go?